Them And Us

Purple Heather Productions

Special thanks to:

Susan Millar DuMars and Kevin Higgins.
Also to my Son and Daughter, Simon and Nicola and friends for their
support and encouragement.

Public Relations: Mike Daly

Printed by Standard Printers, Galway. Tel. 091 755373

Published by:
Purple Heather Productions, Turloughmore
Co Galway
www.purpleheatherproductions.com
Email: vmduffy403@yahoo.co.uk

ISBN 978-0-9555665-0-9

Introduction

Summary

A fictional story about a relationship between a young traveller man and a Garda Officers daughter. A visual story of love, hate, laughter and fun, suspense and prestige.

Set in rural Ireland in the sixties and seventies. A young traveller man loses his wife and children in a tragic blaze. Some years later he meets up with an old acquaintance from his teenage tears.

Contents

Chapter One   1
    Abby Cross, Co Tipperary

Chapter Two   28
    Mary meets Máirtín for the first time

Chapter Three   40
    Fourteen Years Later
    Ballinasloe Horse Fair

Chapter Four   56
    Mary Buckley's Flat

Chapter Five   73
    Christmas 1978

Chapter Six   85
    Máirtín in bed having a Nightmare

Chapter Seven   98
    Mary gives Halting site a visit

Chapter Eight   110
    Helen Conway goes to Dublin

Chapter Nine   126
    Helen breaks the News to Mary

Chapter Ten   151
        Knock Shrine, Co Mayo

Chapter Eleven   163
        Máirtín and Mary get Engaged

Chapter Twelve   172
        St Anita's Psychiatric Hospital Dublin

Chapter Thirteen   194
        St Patrick's Day Parade

Chapter Fourteen   211
        BMW found at Travellers Halting Site

Chapter Fifteen   218
        The Wedding

www.purpleheatherproductions.com

Chapter One

Abby Cross, Co Tipperary

It's 1964, the Ward family of eight children, with one on the way, their Uncle Martin, their mum Bridie, load up their Red Morris Minor van and trailer with all their belongings. They have lived in a camp site on the side of the road at Abby Cross, Co Tipperary for a number of years, accompanied by two greyhounds and a piebald pony. They move to Westport, Co Mayo. They have decided to move to Mayo after the death of Bridie's husband, who was killed one night by a drunken driver.

Bridie Ward who is in her early fifties, decided she was unable to live in Abby Cross much longer because of the memories she had living there with her husband. She decided to move lock stock and barrel to a little Village called Ballycrackn, outside Westport town, where she had visited some time before; and hoped that one day she would come back to Ballycrackn to live.

It's midnight, a night of a full moon. They head for Ballycrackn, arriving there at day-break, to set up camp.

Ballycrackn Village, Westport, Co Mayo

Early next morning, local Garda Timothy Buckley (or Tim as he preferred to be known) is getting ready to go on duty, he puts on his new Garda uniform to go to work. Tim is a devoted family man who loves his wife and two children Mary and Timmy.

"I'm off, I'll see you all later."

He gives his wife Sheila a kiss on the cheek.

"Now hurry up you two and don't be late for school again

today, I don't want your teacher getting on to me again," he says.

He goes out the back door of his house to go to work. On his way to the Garda station, he notices a tinkers camp, set up on the side of the road.

"What's this, when in the hell did they come here, by heck the local farmers will have to lock their chicken houses now sure they will with this gang around." he says to himself, slowing down his car to take a better look. He notices the Red Morris Minor van, and a piebald pony tied up to a car trailer, a few greyhounds and God knows how many people are asleep inside the camp.

"Ah well; it's a free country, the best of luck to them, as long as they don't bother with me, I don't mind, fair play to them, that's all I can say. I better give them a call later on today," he says to himself.

At the same time his wife Sheila, and two children are about to leave for school, when a knock comes to the front door. Young Timmy tells his mum that there is somebody outside, she tells him to go and open the door to see who is there.

"Do you want me to do everything around here, go on answer the door, and hurry up, you are late for school already."

Young Timmy opens the door. He gets the fright of his life when he sees an old tinker woman, dressed in black with a black shawl thrown over her shoulder, a black wrinkled face from camp fire smoke. Timmy gets a fright, the old woman scares the hell out of him by her appearance. He runs back into the kitchen to tell his Mum.

"Mammy," he screams; "There is a banshee woman or a witch or something scary at the door."

"How do you mean some witch, for God sake Timmy, I have no time for this fooling around, you are late for school as it is; who's at the door?"

"Ya, mum she looks like Grandma when she was dead in the coffin." Timmy yells, with a frightened look on his face.

"Which grandmother are you talking about Timmy, mine or your father's? I knew well I should not have taken you to your grandmothers funeral, I don't think you are right ever since, the shock of seeing a dead person must have gone to your head."

She goes to the front window to see who is there. She notices the tinker woman standing out with a milk churn in her hand.

"Now what did I tell you Mum."

She opens the door.

"Who the hell are you, what brings you around here this time of the morning," Sheila asks, as she is frightened of the tinker woman.

"I'm Bridie Ward. My husband died last year God rest his soul, and me and the children's Uncle Martin have just moved to Ballycrackn Village late last night," says the tinker woman, with a pitiful cry in her voice.

"And where do you live now," asks Sheila.

She stands at the front door, getting annoyed, knowing that her two children will be late for school again today.

"Ah, just up the road Mam in a camp site, please Mam 'tis not for me at all, 'tis for the children, all I want is a few auld bits and pieces you're not using yourself," she cries.

"Like what Mam, what do you want from me."

"A drop of milk for the children's breakfast, and any spare clothes for some of the younger ones that you're not using, it's only for the children. I'm all right myself, God be good to me, it's only the children you know, they feel the chill you know, oh God bless them but the Winter cold goes right through their bones; the poor creatures with no father to take care of them. 'Tis their Uncle Martin that's trying to look after us now, and God be good to him he's a good man, he does his best," cries Bridie.

"All right so I will see what I can do, I'm not promising you anything now you know."

Sheila goes back into the house and goes to the children's bedroom, to fetch some old clothes and takes them to Bridie. Timmy and Mary are staring at Bridie, standing at the door. Sheila gives her the clothes.

"Thank you kindly Miss and may God bless you and protect you and your children; you might have some spare food and maybe a small drop of milk for the children as well would ya, they're famished back at the auld camp, I won't get a chance to go to the shops today," says Bridie, with a poor mouth.

Mary and her younger brother Timmy are on their way to

school, they are dead late for class again today. They notice the tinkers' campsite on the side of the road. It's made up of canvas and sticks. There are a few greyhounds and a Red Morris Minor van. The greyhounds are barking at Timmy and Mary, as they are passing the camp site.

"Run Mary, run for your life!" says Timmy.

They both run as fast as they can past the camp site. They are terrified. When Timmy and Mary get to school they tell the teacher, Mrs Doherty, what they have seen; and why they are late for school.

"Timmy and Mary, you are twenty minutes late for class again today. I will have to talk to your parents about this, it can't go on, ye come in here as bold as brass, and interrupt the rest of the class and don't seem to care, well what is your excuse this time Timmy Buckley, not that I need an excuse from you, but you can give me one anyways. The rest of the class have a good laugh?"

"Sorry for being late Miss Doherty, but it's not our fault."

"Go on Timmy tell me, I'm listening." Teacher puts her eyes up to heaven.

Another pupil, Helen Conway starts to snigger.

"What are you sniggering at Helen Conway, stand over there in the corner please, I'll deal with you later."

Helen gets up off her seat and stands over in the corner of the classroom.

"Well Timmy; I'm listening."

"I'm sorry we are late for class Miss, but you have to believe us this time, we seen a witches house on the side of the road on our way to school Miss, and she has two mighty big dogs, as well, they were like two great big giants," cries Timmy.

His sister and the rest of the class burst into a fit of laughing.

Teacher tries to keep a straight face.

"Now Timmy and Mary Buckley, how do you expect me to believe that story, now none of your nonsense, that's the best excuse so far this year I have heard for being late for class, it's hard to believe your father is the local Garda and your Mum works in the bank, now take to your seats fast, come on hurry up, I have a good mind to send the both of you straight home again, and we'll see will Garda Timothy

Buckley like that. Well, did you ever here the likes of that," Teacher says.

Timmy and Mary hurry to their school desks and open their school bags, taking out their books. All the rest of the children in the class start to laugh.

Tinkers Campsite, Ballycrackn

Later on that day; Garda Timothy Buckley is driving through Ballycrackn Village in his squad car. It's a nice sunny Autumn afternoon, the village is quiet, there is only one farmer, Jim O'Sullivan, walking his cows to the river for a drink.

Timothy is on his way to give the campsite on the side of the road a visit. As he approaches the campsite he notices smoke bellowing from the top of the camp; pulling over the squad car he gets out and goes over by the camp.

"Hello, anybody there?" he calls out.

Martin Ward comes out of the camp, with rugged skin black from smoke, smoking a homemade cigarette; dressed in an old ragged pinstriped suit, with a brown neck tie holding up his trousers.

"Well Sir, what can we do for ya?" asks Martin.

About eight children come out from the camp; the children are black as soot from smoke inside with their hair uncombed, they are scruffy and dirty.

"Well Sir, I was just passing, I'd just said I'd stop over and say hello."

Tim has a good look around.

"What can I do for ya Sir," says Martin.

"Ah, by the way, I'm Garda Tim Buckley."

"Well, pleased to meet you Boss, I'm Martin, Martin Ward."

He shakes Garda Timothy's hands, squishing it tightly as he does so.

"We just moved here last night you know, ah ya, I suppose it was about midnight, when we left Abby Cross. I'd say we arrived here at about six o'clock in the morning, a great night it was too for travelling I tell ya, a full moon there was, do you know something Boss, it was like day light sure it was. Nothing like a full moon bright as day," says Martin.

"I'm sure it was, and how long are you planning on staying here Sir."

"As long as we are welcome Garda, now that's the way I'll put it to ya, as long as we are welcome, not everybody has a welcome for the tinkers you know Boss."

"Ah, well you're welcome to Ballycrackn Sir," says Garda Timothy.

"Thank you Sir, I'm these children's Uncle you know; their father was killed one night just outside his campsite in Abby Cross."

"Would that be in Tipperary Sir?" asks Garda Timothy.

"By feck you're on the ball there Boss, there's no flies on you, you know he didn't stand a chance, he was mauled down by a drunken driver, driving a great big Mercedes car he was."

Tim is busy taking notice of the pony and dogs.

"Sorry Sir, I lost you there, who was mauled down by a drunken driver?"

Tim looks a bit confused; taking note of all the children that's around Martin.

"Sorry about that Sir, maybe I didn't explain myself good enough, 'twas my older brother Johnny, a great singer he was too."

Timothy looks around at all the children, noticing how dirty their clothes are.

"Ya, he was as drunk as a skunk. I'm looking after my brothers wife and children now you know, I'm all they have got now, would you like a wee drop of something to start off your day Sir?"

"I will, I suppose," replies Timothy.

"Come inside Garda Timothy."

"Never mind your Garda Timothy, from now on you can call me Tim, and never mind Garda, I'd think we would get on better that way, don't you think?"

"Ah well, I suppose you're right there Tim."

They all go into the camp, Martin takes out an old tin cup and gets a bottle of Poítin from underneath the straw bed where he sleeps, and fills the tin cup with Poítin, getting a steaming kettle off the stove to add a drop of hot water, and two spoons of sugar to make a drop of punch, gives it to Tim.

"A drop of punch never killed no man," says Martin.

He takes a drink of punch from a fancy pint glass with a handle, tapping one of the young boys on the head.

"See this young man here Tim. He is just like his old man, he is a mighty man, he is called Máirtín after myself of course. Do you want to know something, he is as tough as nails God bless him. I tell ya something for nothing Tim, he is as strong as an Ox, isn't that right Máirtín?"

Young Máirtín is giving weird looks at Tim as he takes out the crucifix his father gave him before he died.

"I'm sure he is strong," replies Tim.

He drinks the hot punch from the tin cup.

"That's a great drop of punch, where did you get it Martin?"

"You wouldn't believe this now if I tell ya; and it's no word of a lie, I found it Sir."

The children start to snigger.

"See that now Tim, they think something is funny ha," Martin says, referring to the children and giving them the eye to quieten them.

"Anyway Martin I must be off, I have a few other calls to make. Sure I will call around again, I be off now, take care of yourselves."

Tim leaves the camp and goes into his squad car and drives off.

"Well he's not a bad Guard, now is he," Martin says to young Máirtín.

"Well now Uncle, I wouldn't trust that bollox at all, see the way he was watching everything around here," replies young Máirtín, who is about fourteen years of age.

Tim is driving along the road, he notices Bridie by the side of the road. She is searching the pockets of dark navy blue trousers that belonged to himself she got from Sheila, to see were there any coins or notes left in the pockets. Then she dumps Tim's old navy Guards trousers over a wall into the field. Tim takes notice of this.

"Well now that's interesting, that looks like my old uniform trousers ha, I wonder where did she get them from; well, is my old uniform not good enough for her or what," he says to himself, as he passes Bridie by the side of the road.

Mass On Sunday At Ballycrackn Church

A couple of days later it's Sunday morning, all the local people are on their way to Mass, some drive in old cars, some cycle and others walk. The tinkers come to Mass also, some of them walk and about four of them are up on the back of a piebald pony. It's a beautiful dry sunny morning and everybody is in great spirit.

All the tinkers make their way up to the top of the church.

Father O'Breen comes out on the altar with four altar boys, to say Mass. He gets a stifling smell in the church, he is sniffing like a blood hound. It's a smell of smoke and body odour, everyone in the church smells it. The altar boys can't help sniggering with Father O'Breen's reaction to the smell.

When Mass is over the priest goes outside the church, shaking hands with the people as they come out of the church and thanking them for coming to his service.

"Thank you for coming and it's very good to see you back on your feet again Molly, and how is your father keeping, I haven't seen him in the congregation now for a while, his contribution to the church is greatly missed sure it is, he was always very generous. Sure I suppose as long as he is living you could bring the contribution along to the church for him couldn't you Molly," as he shakes her hand.

Molly Walsh is on crutches with a bandage on her left leg.

"I'll tell him you said that Father," replies Molly.

The tinker family comes out of the church, Father O'Breen welcomes them.

"Well, you're all very welcome to my parish!"

He shakes Martin and Bridie's hands.

"I hope you will be very happy here, and don't mind them old hags over there," he says, referring to the couple of old women including Molly Walsh, that are gossiping about the tinkers.

"They cannot mind their own business around here you know, they cannot help it I suppose, they have to keep their auld tongues wagging all the time don't you know, they're afraid they might miss out on something," says Father O'Breen.

"That was a mighty fine sermon you gave there Father," says Martin.

"It certainly was Father," says Bridie.

"Well, thank you very much indeed tis great to hear that, the people around here never say too much to me at all you know, by the way I'm Father O'Breen, and what's your own name?"

"I'm Bridie, and this is my dead husband's brother Martin, my husband was killed on the side of the road one wet winter's night by a drunken driver."

"Oh my Lord, that must have being awful Bridie, you must have been in a terrible state after that I'd say, well I don't care about what anybody says about you tinker people, I think you have a hard life."

He looks at his watch.

"Oh, is that the time, I must be off now my lunch will be on the table in five minutes. Good bye now, hope to see ye again soon."

He gets up on his bike, and speeds off.

"Well, he is a funny Priest, wouldn't you think so Martin?"

"I think you're right there Bridie, he sounds like a bit of a queer to me."

They walk to the large oak tree where the piebald pony is tied and is eating the tops of the roses of the church flower bed. The women are still gossiping about the tinkers.

"They are living on the side of the road you know."

"That's right Molly, they don't even wash themselves, did you get the smell off them in the church when they came in, oh God love them the poor creatures, sure they cannot help themselves, they were in my shop the other day and God love them but wouldn't you think they would wash themselves at least," says Miss Waters, the local shopkeeper.

"Sure isn't that the way they want to live, sure it's not our fault that the tinkers want to live on the side of the road," says Nellie Conway, a local farmer's wife.

"Well God loves them that's all I can say. I remember when I was young, my mother often brought the young tinker kiddies into our house at home to warm them, sure why do you do that says my father, they will be worse with the cold now when they go outside, he'd often say," says Nellie Conway.

She gets up on her bike with beautiful prints of horses on her red pixie scarf. She cycles off on her bicycle home to get her husband Jack's lunch prepared.

Martin and Bridie join the children under the oak tree.

"Mum did ya see them old hags over there, they never stopped shitting talking about us all the time."

"I know Máirtín, never mind them and don't be using bad language like that outside God's house, you won't get into Heaven if you keep using language like that."

"Come on Mum, I'm hungry," says Katie, Bridie's oldest daughter.

"Lets head off so," says Uncle Martin.

They all head out the long avenue to go back to the camp site. One of the young tinker boys called Johnny the Singer starts to sing a rebel song as they walk along the avenue on their way home.

The Red Morris Minor Van

A few days later Martin, Bridie in the front, and the children, and the two greyhounds, are packed into the back of the Morris Minor van. They are on their way to visit the local farmers to see what they can get in the line of handouts like food and clothing.

"Well Máirtín, I couldn't help watching that young lass at Mass last Sunday the way she was watching at ya, I say she fancied ya, ha, what do ya think Johnny," says Martin, slaging young Máirtín.

"What's that Uncle Martin? I wasn't listening to ya, I am trying to take this dogs stinking arse out of my face," says Johnny the Singer.

Martin and the rest of the children have a good laugh at that.

"Ah shut to feck up you Uncle, 'twas you she was watching because you're so scary looking with your scary long nose and your black wrinkled face, anyway Mum, what was that row about with dad's friend Luke the bookie and Uncle Martin," remarked Máirtín.

"Leave that now will ya? I thought I told ye to forget that, 'tis nobody's business at all," she replies.

All the children have a laugh as Bridie gives a sour look at Martin.

"Why is he called Luke the bookie?" Johnny asks.

"Give us an auld song there Johnny will ya and never mind Luke, sure all he does is go around the country taking good money from poor unfortunates like ourselves."

He smells something stinking.

"Who farted, was that you again Willie?"

"'Twas not Uncle Martin, now piss off, it was probably yourself."

They all have a good laugh.

Johnny the Singer starts to sing a song, Katie, his sister, takes out a Tin Whistle and starts to play. Timmy plays the drums on the bottom of two buckets; they have a sing-song as they drive along the road. Bridie is sitting in the front seat with a quite contented look on her face, as she says the rosary. She is enjoying the fun and laughter. Uncle Martin is having crack with her children. After driving a couple of miles along the road, Martin notices a farm house on the left hand side. The house is in a bit from the road. It is a brand new two story farm house freshly painted in black and white.

"Well, we might go into this farm house to see what they have for us; you never know we might hit the jackpot in this house, it looks to be a fairly new house I'd say. Anyway this crowd could have money, I'd say ha, what do ya think yourself Bridie?" Martin says, as he admires the farm house and outhouses as he drives into the back yard.

Local farmer Jack Conway is painting his plough white and bright blue before he retires the plough in his back haggard for the winter. When Jack sees the Red Morris Minor driving into his yard he mutters to himself,

"By God who have we here now I wonder?" leaving down the paint brush carefully on the top of the paint can so the brush wouldn't fall on to the ground and put white paint on his newly tarred macadam back yard. Jack goes over to the Red Morris Minor van, leaving his two elbows on top of the van roof and starts to talk to Martin through the driver's window.

"Well lads, what can I do for ye?" asks Jack, looking at the Morris Minor.

"Well anyways I'm Martin Ward I tell ya one thing you have a fine place here Sir, sure you have."

"'Tis, 'tis indeed, that's a fine van you got there. It's not often you see a tinker with a Morris Minor. What age is she?" asks Jack.

"I'd say around fifty nine, I'd say," Martin says.

"By heck she is in good condition," Jack replies, inspecting the condition of the van.

"I tell you straight now what I'm after Sir, you wouldn't have any auld horse hair or any old batteries or scrap iron to give away would ya?"

"Be heck I might, by the way Jack is my name, come with me now one minute, till I see what I have in the barn, 'tis a great day isn't it Martin."

"'Tis indeed Jack."

"I haven't seen you around here before," he says, looking at the children coming out of the van, walking towards the barn after Martin.

"Is this all your clutch?" Referring to the children.

"Ah no Jack, they're my brothers children, he was killed last year on the side of the road by a drunken driver, drunk as a skunk he was. I'm come from Tipperary myself."

"Good man, I'm sorry to hear about your brother, and I suppose the drunken driver got off scott free," says Jack, opening the door of the barn, entering with Martin and the eight children.

"Do you know something Jack you never said a truer word."

He picked up a galvanised bucket to inspect it.

"Scott free is right," he says.

"And the thing that angers me Jack the most, when the Guards came on the scene of the motor accident, there was the driver of the car as drunk as a skunk and no notice at all taken."

He turns the bucket upside down on the floor and sits on it.

"Well, I suppose Martin, the day will come when this drunken driving will stop. Now lets see what I have here for you now, don't touch anything there now children let ye, my own little girl and her friends are always in here messing about, and do you know something Martin, I can never find anything after them, they throw everything all over the place."

Jack speaks to the children as they began to take some of the tools that we're spread out on the barn floor.

"When did ye arrive in Ballycrackn?"

"Ary, sure we only got here a few days ago, it's not a bad spot at all now is Ballycrackn. My brothers widow, she is sitting in the van outside, she was here some years ago, and do you know what? She wasn't happy till she came back here to settle, ha now isn't that a good one?"

Jack takes the horse hair down that is hanging up on the wall and puts it into a canvas bag that he uses to put the corn into. He gives the bag of horse hair to Martin.

They go out of the shed and walk down to the haggard where they pick up the scrap iron that Jack doesn't make use of anymore; they put the horse hair and scrap iron into the back of the van.

Martin looks around, the children can't be seen anywhere.

"Well where in the hell is them scutts gone now I wonder," he says to Jack.

"They couldn't have gone far, 'cause they were with us just a minute ago."

They hear a lot of commotion coming from the garden next to the house. When Jack and Martin go to the gate that leads into the garden they notice young Máirtín, Willie and Katie up on the back of Jack's jackass, that Jack uses to work on the farm.

"Now, could you be up to them lot," says Martin.

"Come down off that jackass, will ye for God sake before ye fall off and harm yourselves."

Jack is laughing, Bridie takes notice of the two men looking over the gate.

"What's up Martin?" she asks, winding down the van window that's on it's last legs.

"Ah faith, they're all right they're only having a bit of fun," says Jack taking out a packet of Woodbine and giving one to Martin.

"Thanking you, you're a decent man Jack, may God Bless ya."

"Never mind that talk, wait until I see has Nellie anything in the kitchen," Jack says.

He goes in the back door of the house, calling his wife Nellie as he enters.

"Jack what's up with ya. Is there something wrong?" asked Nellie.

"Look I have a tinker family in the yard; you wouldn't have anything for them the poor creatures. I'm sure they are famished with the hunger."

"Of course I might have," replies Nellie.

She fills a bottle of milk and gets a cake of bread and wraps it up in tinfoil. She wraps twelve free range eggs with newspaper and puts them into a cardboard box. She takes them herself out to Bridie in the van, with Jack following behind her. Martin has all the children gathered up and put into the back of the van. Nellie gives the food to Bridie. Bridie recognises her from Mass on Sunday gossiping with her friends, but doesn't say anything.

"Thank you Mam and may God bless you." Bridie says.

"Mum, that's the auld hag that was shit talking about us on Sunday."

"Have a bit of manners you will ya Jimmy, never mind him Mrs, he has no manners."

"You're all right, leave the poor creature alone," replies Nellie.

"Well, thank you for the beautiful food. May God be good to you wherever you go and save you and your family from all evil and harm. I didn't expect that at all Mam," says Bridie.

"Why don't ye all come inside, oh look at all the beautiful children. I couldn't help noticing ye all at Mass on Sunday," says Nellie, looking into the back of the van at the children.

"Are they all your own?"

"They are Mam, their father was killed last year, by a drunken driver man, he mauled him down on the side of the road, a great big Mercedes car it was too, right outside our campsite it was. Oh my God when I heard the screams, God bless his soul, I knew straight way it was my husband God be good to him, a great husband and father he was too Mam you know, a great singer he was too, he was very good to me and the children," says Bridie, as she cries and wipes the tears from her eyes and blows her nose with the sleeve of her cardigan.

"Ah ya poor creature, that must be terrible hard on you," says Nellie with pity for Bridie.

"'Tis Mam, 'tis very hard sometimes. A widow's life is not easy, it's not easy at all," says Bridie, still blowing her nose and wiping the tears from her eyes.

"And who's that fine handsome man talking to Jack."

The children have a good laugh at that statement Nellie made.

"That's my dear husband's brother Martin, the children's uncle, he takes care of the children, now he's all we have."

It starts to rain.

"Ah, you poor creature, you must be famished, come into my house for a hot cup of tea and a slice of treacle cake I just made this morning," says Nellie.

"Oh thank you Mam."

All the children hop out of the van again, and run into the house. When they get inside they are bewildered with what they see. A big black farmhouse range, a large kitchen table with a flowery table cloth, and chairs. They all fight to sit on the chairs.

"Be quiet now children," Bridie shouts.

"You make out you never seen a house before; what's wrong, Jimmy and Willie be quiet. Johnny, sit down now will ya."

Johnny the Singer sits down quietly on the black and white tiled floor.

"I'll make some tea, you might get a drop of punch for himself; will ya Jack," Nellie says, as Jack and Martin enter the house.

"Right to be, by feck I will," replies Jack, opening a cupboard and taking out a bottle of Poítin.

Nellie makes the tea. Jack pours out the Poítin into three glasses, pouring in hot water from the kettle that was boiling on the range, adding a spoon or two of sugar to sweeten the punch.

"Do you take a drink of punch at all yourself Mam?"

"No, not at all Bridie, I never touch the stuff," Nellie says.

She is taking out the freshly made treacle cake and cutting it into slices and laying it on the centre of the table.

"Sure, Jack wouldn't let me take a drink anyway, even if I wanted to."

They all sit around the great big kitchen table, drinking tea and eating treacle cake, and drinking punch.

"I tell ya now, that's a great drop of punch; did you make it yourself Jack?"

"Not at all Martin, there's a man in Connamara that sells it around here. He sells fish and brings a couple of bottles of Poítin in his van under the fish, now I wouldn't be telling the Gardaí about that sure I wouldn't."

"You're right there Jack, sure if the Guards take it off ya, they would be only keeping it for themselves anyways, sure they would. Ah, I gave the Garda man a drop the other day and he didn't take a bit of notice, he just drank it down and went on his way," says Martin.

"Well, he will be watching you now Martin from now on, to see where you are getting the stuff from, mark my words on that now Martin," replies Jack.

"What did I tell ya Uncle?" says Máirtín.

Helen, Jack and Nellie's daughter comes home from school.

"Ah here she is the woman of the house. This is Helen she is the only one we have God bless her," says Jack.

"Where did all those people come from Dad?" Helen asks. She takes notice of all the tinker children.

"They're our new neighbours love, they moved to Ballycrackn last week from Tipperary," replies Nellie.

"Oh ya, Mary Buckley was talking about them in school today, she said she fancied one of them."

All the young tinker children are sitting very quiet, until they hear Helen say that and they all slag Máirtín and have a good laugh.

"I'd say it's time we should be on our way, and we are much grateful for all you have done for us Jack, yourself and your good wife," says Martin.

The children get out from the table, and run out to the van, bringing a packet of biscuits and a few slices of treacle cake with them. Bridie thanks Jack and Nellie for everything. They go outside, get into the van and drive off.

Harry Lynch's Pub, Ballycrakn

It's Thursday afternoon on the 11th of October 1964; Dole day. Martin Ward has collected his dole that was transferred to Ballycrackn from Abby Cross, Co Tipperary. He is on his way to the local pub in the Village. It's an old country style thatched pub, with a great big open fire and some old style wooden pub stools, and wooden seating. Jack Conway and a few neighbours are at the counter, having a few pints. The pub owner Harry Lynch is serving behind a high old style mahogany counter.

"I see Jack you're very friendly with the tinker family, had them in for tea I believe," remarks Harry, looking at an old man called Bertie smoking his crooked stem pipe, sitting outside the counter beside Jack.

"I wouldn't trust them lads at all Jack, sure they would steal all your chickens and eggs you know, sure they would."

"Well, is that so now Bertie."

They all have a good laugh as Jack sits wondering and a bit bothered.

"Remember Harry last year when two of Brian O'Flaherty's cows weren't giving any milk, and the vet couldn't find anything wrong with the two cows, well apparently, wasn't the tinkers over in the neighbouring Village Limsvalley coming all the way over in the middle of the night and milking the cows dry," Laughs Bertie.

Martin Ward comes into the pub smoking a hand made cigarette, looking tired and still wearing a shabby old brown pin striped suit.

"Steady up yourselves now lads let ye, here is one of them coming in now, what can I do for you Sir?" asks Harry, looking at Martin with suspicion as Martin approaches the counter.

"Can I have a half one and a pint of Stout please Sir."

He is smoking a hand made cigarette.

"Oh how are ya Martin?"

"Good evening Jack, Men," says Martin.

He salutes the men at the counter by lifting his shabby old hat. Martin sits down at a table by the fire on his own. Harry takes the half one, and the pint of stout down to him where he is sitting. He puts the drinks on the table.

"Will you be staying around here for long, yourself I wonder?" asks Harry.

"You have nothing to be wondering about at all Boss, we're only passing through," replies Martin.

He spits chewed tobacco out of his mouth onto the sawdust floor.

Another man called Jim O'Sullivan is sitting at the bar.

"Well Sir, you wouldn't happen to have a few auld buckets for me would ya; the ones I have are full of holes you couldn't put nothing into them, they are only good now for bringing in the turf," says Jim.

"I'm sure I have, how many do you want?" he says, smoking his homemade cigarettes.

"Three or four I suppose," says Jim.

"I'll bring them around to you tomorrow afternoon, is that all right?" replies Martin, taking a sip out of his glass of whiskey and chasing it down with a drop of Stout.

"You don't know where I live," says Jim.

"Don't you worry about that Jim, he will find ya," replies Jack.

Martin sits on his own for a while. When he finishes his drinks he pays Harry the pub owner for the drinks and leaves.

Jim O'Sullivan's Farm

Next day Martin turns up at Jim O'Sullivan's farmhouse with the buckets. He takes four buckets out of the van and leaves them on the ground. Jim comes out of one of the barns and joins Martin to check out the buckets.

"By heck, it didn't take you long to get here," Jim says.

He picks up the buckets to inspect them.

"Well Jim, you won't find a better bucket this side of the River Shannon, sure you won't. Look at that will ya, ha," Martin says.

He shows off the bucket to Jim.

"I suppose I won't, how much? Now, don't be too hard on me now, times are hard these days you know," Jim says.

"Ara, I tell ya what I will do, gives us a half a crown I

suppose."

"That's fair enough all right I suppose, I tell ya one thing; I won't argue with that," replies Jim.

He puts his hand in his pocket and gives Martin the half crown and spitting on it as he does so for good luck.

"Any old batteries or scrap iron knocking about the place you're not using Jim?"

"Well do you know something Martin, 'tis Martin your name is isn't it."

"Aye," replies Martin.

"I'd say you might be lucky there, I might have a few old bits and pieces down the back yard."

They both walk towards a heap of scrap metal that was taken off old farm machinery,

"How much will you give me for the lot?" Jim says.

He spreads out the scrap iron on the ground to display it for Martin.

"Sure where would I get money to pay ya with? I tell you what I will do with ya now Jim, I'll give you another bucket, how's that, now I couldn't be much fairer than that now could I ha," Martin replies.

Martin squints one eye as he takes notice of the hen house at the back of the yard and about twenty of the finest hens he has ever seen, sitting up on their perch that Jim made out of logs of wood.

"Right to be so, it's a deal," replies Jim.

They both load the scrap iron into the Red Morris Minor van.

"You have a fine van there God bless ya," Jim says.

"Do you know how I came to have this motor. Ya will not believe this now Jim"

"Go on tell me," Jim says.

"When my brother died, God rest his soul," as he blesses himself. "He left two of the finest working horses behind him. Do ya know what I did Jim, I traded them in to a farmer in Abby Cross for this beautiful motor."

"You're a crafty auld devil Martin Ward. Come into the house for a drop of the strong stuff," Jim says.

Garda Tim Buckley's House

Later on that evening the Buckley family are having their supper. They sit around the table with a roasting hot fire on in the range and a homemade currant cake baking in the oven.

"Dad, everyone is talking about the tinker people that live on the side of the road. Why do they call them tinkers Daddy, what's tinkers?" asks Timmy, as he eats his supper.

"Well Timmy, tinkers are what they call themselves," says Tim, eating some meat and mash from his plate.

"And why's that Dad?"

"Because they make buckets and tin cans and pots that's why now Timmy."

"How do they make them Dad?"

"I don't know son. Someday I will take you to watch Martin Ward, the tin smith make a bucket. How about that Timmy?"

"I'm sure Martin Ward wouldn't be too pleased to have you hanging around his place," says Sheila, with a smile on her face.

"One young boy said today at school that those people that live in canvas tents steal things off other people. Dad is that true?"

"Now Timmy my son, don't believe all you hear."

Mary is sitting at the table, and is interested in the conversation that is taking place.

"Dad, can we go tomorrow, it's Saturday, we have no school."

"We will see tomorrow Timmy."

"Right Dad I can't wait to go."

Sheila is enjoying having her supper with her family.

"You know, I can't stop thinking about the poor children sleeping out at night in that camp, I passed that way today coming from Westport and do you know something, the camp looks awful, sure the rats and mice could get in there easily."

"Well I tell you one thing for sure Sheila, the rats won't be going next or near that camp with two greyhounds inside and that's for sure."

"I don't know Tim, wouldn't you think they would live in a house like the rest of us at least," says Sheila.

"I seen them at Mass, the older one is very handsome, I found out today Máirtín is his name, Mum is that an Irish name?"

"It is indeed Mary, it's Irish for Martin, how do you mean handsome? How could you tell, sure his face was covered in dirt, in fact they all were filthy, and the smell of them, pooh, wouldn't you think they would wash themselves?"

"I don't care Mum, I think he is gorgeous," replies Mary.

"Gorgeous, look lass I'll have no more of that kind of talk, keep your eyes off them tinkers, we don't mix with their kind at all, now have nothing to do with them."

"How do you mean Dad? Their kind, what's that supposed to mean Father?"

"They are gypsies, they travel from town to town, they never stay anywhere for long, they rob from the farmers, by heck you would want to keep your eyes on them lads now sure you would," says Tim.

He is getting annoyed with Mary for fancying one of the tinker boys.

"Sure that's what I was doing Dad, keeping my eye on him," Mary says, with a smile.

"I don't mean it like that now missy, you know perfectly well what I mean."

He is getting more annoyed with Mary.

"Look, stay away from that crowd that's all I'm saying."

"Dad do you not like the tinkers, or gypsies or whatever you call them."

"Listen to me now missy, forget it now," says Tim, getting more angry with Mary.

"Have you homework; or something else to do besides talking about fancying tinkers at your age!"

"Relax Tim, she is only just gone thirteen, what the hell is coming over you, look, just take Timmy to see the man make the buckets tomorrow, and let that be the end of it," says Sheila, getting annoyed at Tim because he has no time for the tinkers.

"Right I'm off out, I won't be long, I have to go to Westport on business," says Tim.

Standing up from the table, he washes his hands and face, and goes out the door in a huff without saying good bye.

"Hu, what's his problem?"

"Never mind him Mary; he probably is afraid you might end up marrying into the tinker family or something like that."

"I wouldn't mind that at all Mum." Is Mary joking with her Mum?

"Now Mary, that's the end of this conversation now and let me never hear you talking like that again, now come on the both of you, go do your homework."

Willie Ward Gets Shot

Midnight Saturday; and there is a new moon, the sky is bright, the stars are shining brightly, one of the tinker boys, Willie, is sent out to fetch some eggs from a local farm. He takes off across the fields at the back of Jim O'Sullivan's farm, he climbs over the wall, goes into the hen house to steals a half a dozen eggs. He puts them in his jumper; the hens make a lot of noise, wakening up Jim O'Sullivan.

"Shee; did you hear that Anne?" as he wakes up his wife Annie.

"Hear what, Jim, go back to sleep will ya you're dreaming again; 'tis that hard stuff your drinking, you're raving sure you are, go back to sleep," she cries.

"Do you hear that noise can ya? Shee, do ya hear that?"

He sits up on the bed.

"What?" asks Annie.

"That noise the hens are making, I bet there is a blasted fox in the hen house again."

"Go back to sleep will ya and never mind the hens, they will be all right, look I'm tired I want to get to sleep."

She turns over to go back to sleep.

"No I'll get him this time, it's definitely a fox in the hen house, I know it is, I'll blow his head off with the shot gun sure I will."

Jim gets out of bed, fetches the gun and loads it with a cartridge. He goes outside, and runs across the yard kicking one of the buckets that he got from Martin Ward, makes a noise as he makes his way across the back yard.

Willie hears the bucket making noise and makes a run for it. Jim sees something brown moving in the moon light. He thinks it's a fox. Willie jumps over the wall. Jim fires a shot, shooting Willie in the arse. Willie lets out a shout, Jim hears the shout. He thinks it's the fox and is very proud of himself for shooting the fox. He goes back to bed.

"Well, Jim did you shoot the fox or what?" asks Annie.

She wakes up again when Jim enters the bed room.

"I sure did, you would want to hear the screaming out of him, be-jesus it was like ringing a pig's nose, with the noise he was making, I tell ya something Annie, he won't be coming back here in a long time, and that's one thing for sure, if I was that fox I'd stay away from Jim O'Sullivan's hens if he knows what goods for him," brags Jim.

He leaves the gun at his bedside and goes back to bed.

The young tinker Willie is lying on the ground with half the eggs broken. The eggs are dripping down his brown Jumper, he rubs the back of his Pants with his hand and sees the blood.

"Oh feck it I'm shot, Oh for God sake," cries Willie to himself.

He goes home limping, barely making it across the fields, he goes into the camp, falls flat on his face on to the straw bed, tells Martin his Uncle, what has happened.

"What are you saying Willie, where in the hell are the eggs I sent ya for?"

"I'm sorry Uncle Martin, I-I-I broke the stinking eggs, I'm shot I tell ya, I'm shot in the hole, and there are the rest of your eggs," cries Willie, throwing the broken egg shells at Martin and the two eggs that survived.

"Mum look I'm covered in blood," he says as Bridie wakes up and so does young Máirtín. Bridie gets out of bed, takes down Willie's pants and sees six holes in his bum. Martin gets a pinchers from a wooden box where he stores his tools for when he works as a tin smith. He goes to pull out the pellets with the pinchers. Willie is screaming with pain, waking up the rest of the family.

"Stand still now Laddy, this will be sore boy," says Martin.

He pours Poítin on Willie's bum to kill any infection.

"Jes-us, Martin your hurting me, ah, ouch, oh golly gosh, Martin what are you at, you're killing me, ouch."

The rest of the family are having a good laugh, while Uncle

Martin is pulling the pellets out of Willie's bum.

"Stand still lad, I'll have them out in a minute, by feck it's the last time I'm sending you to fetch the eggs, from now on tis Máirtín that will fetch them instead," Martin says, as he pulls the pellets out.

Next day it's Sunday afternoon, all the farmers and their wives and families, including Jim O'Sullivan and his wife and a few locals all are in the local pub after Mass. The men are sitting at the counter having a pint, while the women are sitting down at a table enjoying their drinks. Harry Lynch is in full flight serving alcohol to thirsty customers. It's a regular occurrence on Sunday after Mass, that there be a family gathering at Ballycrackn pub. Harry Lynch is slagging the farmers about the announcement that Father O'Breen gave over the altar referring to the foxes that's attacking the local fowl.

"Well men, I hope you paid attention to that good advice that Father O'Breen gave ye, ha, I tell you one thing lads 'tis more than foxes that's at the hen's houses around here you know," Harry says, as he pulls a pint of Guinness for Jim O'Sullivan.

"By heck Harry, I tell ya one thing, I shot the bastard last night right on the arse! I got him I tell ya! One thing for sure, that fox won't be coming around my farm after my hens again for a long time," replies Jim O'Sullivan.

The tinkers family comes into the Pub; Martin, Bridie and the eight children.

"Well look men who's coming in now will ye, ha," says Harry.

All the men at the counter turn around to see who's Harry referring to. They notice the tinkers enter the pub. The men at the bar turn around to face the bar again to drink their pints.

"Well, did you kill him Jim," asks Tom, another man sitting at the bar.

The tinkers go to sit down, young Willie that was shot in the arse stays standing up.

"I tell ya something Tom, I don't know," says Jim, as he turns to watch the tinkers.

"Did you look in the fields to see if he's dead anywhere?" says old man Bertie, sitting at a table smoking his pipe with a pint left on the table in front of him, listening to the conversation going on between the men.

"Indeed I did Bertie, but there was no sign of that fox anywhere," replies Jim, drinking his pint of Guinness.

"You didn't kill him so didn't ya. Well, I tell you one thing Jim, if you didn't kill that fox last night, he will come back, and the next time, he won't leave a chicken or a feckin' egg ever to ya, and that's for sure, did you ever hear the saying as cute as a fox?" says old man Bertie.

"They're like those fellas behind us, they're as cute as any fox," says Tom, winking one eye at Harry, referring to the tinkers sitting behind them.

"I wouldn't mind, not one egg did the hens lay that night, I cannot understand that at all," says Jim, shaking his head.

"That's the fright from the fox now Jim, he frightens the hens so much they cannot lay eggs, and they mightn't lay an egg again for days you know," says Tom. He looks at Harry and smiles as he winds up Jim over the fox.

Martin Ward comes up to the counter, stands besides Jim smoking his woodbine, looking smartly dressed because it's the Sabbath.

"What will it be Sir?" asks Harry, taking note of all the children, sitting down at the table with their mother Bridie.

"I'll have a pint and a half one please, and a glass of brandy for herself please Harry if you wouldn't mind, 'tis her first time in a pub ya know, I'd say this is the only pub in the country that allow women and children into it I'd say," says Martin. He finishes his woodbine and stamps it out on the stone flag floor covered in sawdust.

"Is that right, well I never knew that, sure I thought women were allowed into pubs everywhere nowadays."

"Say no more. Harry, say no more," says old man Bertie.

"And what are the children having," asks Harry, looking at Bertie with a frown because Bertie doesn't like women in pubs.

"Ah well do you a have bottle of Mi Wadi?"

"I have indeed Martin, will I pour it into glasses for them or what."

"No, not at all, have you a jug of water," Martin says.

"Be-Gobbs I have," replies Harry.

The other men are looking at Martin and are amused at the way he is ordering the drinks for the children.

"Well give me the full bottle and a jug of water, that will do them," says Martin.

"By heck you are saving yourself a couple of quid by doing it that way," says Tom.

Harry leaves the jug of water and the bottle of Mi Wadi on the table where the tinker children are sitting down except young Willie, who was shot in the arse the night before and cannot sit down because his arse still hurts. Katie pours the Mi Wadi into the jug and they all drink out of the jug by passing it around. Martin pays Harry for the drinks, and goes to join his family at the table.

Tim Buckley, dressed in plain clothes, comes in, he looks around and sees all the tinkers drinking out of the jug, he gives them an unpleasant look, goes to the counter says hallo to everyone.

"Well Tim what can I get you?" Harry says. He takes note of the way Tim was looking at the tinkers.

"Half one please Harry, I've seen it all now," he says, referring to the young tinkers drinking the Mi Wadi.

"What's that Tim," asks Harry.

"Nothing, nothing at all," replies Tim as he pulls down a high stool and joins the men at the counter.

"I hope I didn't wake you up with the gun last night Tim."

"No Jim not at all, I was sound asleep, why, was it you that was shooting at the foxes."

"Why Tim, what did you hear?" winking one eye at Harry behind the counter.

Harry looks at Tom to drag him into the conversation.

"Ah well, somebody was telling me he heard a shot all right last night, and we were making out it was only someone after foxes, and didn't Father O'Breen announce it out over the altar this morning, I wonder who told him?"

"Twas foxes all right Tim, I shot him right in the arse sure I did, and to answer your question Tim, I think it was the wife that told Father O'Breen before Mass," says Jim.

"You might watch where you are shooting, it's not only foxes who are after your chickens around here now you know," Tim says, as he is looking at the tinkers.

Young Willie, who is still standing looking at Garda Tim, overheard what the men were talking about. He goes over to Martin and his Mum to tell them the conversation the men are having at the bar with the Guard.

"Don't mind them at all Willie, they will never find out it was you who stole the eggs," says Martin. Bridie sits quietly and sips her brandy.

"Well Tom, how's that new tractor going for ya. I heard it's very fast."

"By feck Tim it's a flyer, you can get at least eighteen miles an hour on the straight road, 'tis nearly faster than some of them old cars that's on the road these days."

"Mind yourself now Tom the Garda don't give you a ticket for speeding," says old man Bertie, still sitting on his own, drinking his pint.

"Ah, what are you saying Bertie, well I never heard the likes of that, how can you get a ticket for speeding with a tractor, ha, or can ya?" asks Tom

"Well, if I was you Tom I'd slow down, I might give you a speeding ticket," Tim says.

He slags Tom and smiles at Harry.

"Well lads, isn't that a good one now, a speeding ticket for a tractor, well could you beat that now," Tom says, scratching his head, in wonder.

"Anyway men, I'm off. I'm on duty later on," says Tim.

He puts his money on the counter, says good luck to the men, and leaves the pub.

"Well, he's in a hurry, he had only one drink," Jim says.

Harry notices young Willie standing up all the time.

"Excuse me Mam," he says to Bridie, "would you like a stool for the young man, he seems to be standing up all the time," says Harry.

"Ary, he's all right Sir, he likes to stand up, it makes the young lad look taller." she says.

All the young tinker children have a good laugh.

"Well, suit yourself Mam," he says, returning behind the counter.

Chapter Two

Máirtín Meets Mary For The First Time

On Monday after school, Mary Buckley and her school friend Helen Conway, are sitting on the wall outside the local shop. They are eating ice cream. The young tinker boy Máirtín Ward comes along on his piebald pony with a dirty face, dirty clothes, and smelling of smoke. Mary fancies him. Her friend Helen starts to tease her about Máirtín.

"Mary, here is your boyfriend coming to pick you up with his piebald donkey to take you out tonight," says Helen.

"Shut up you Helen, you're only jealous,"

Mary almost pushes Helen off the wall with a friendly blow.

"Hello tinker boy," Helen says.

"Hallo yourself, woh, woh, steady up Molly," says Máirtín, pulling back on the reins to stop the pony.

"What's your name tinker boy?" asks Mary.

"Máirtín, Máirtín Ward from Abby Cross, Co Tipperary miss, my Uncle took us here after my father was killed on the side of the road by a drunker fool," replies Máirtín.

"I am sorry about your father. What kind of name is that?" Mary asks.

"Why what's wrong with it," he rubs the Piebald's mane.

Helen starts to snigger, and is embarrassing Mary.

"Nothing, I think it's a lovely name," Mary replies, hitting Helen on the shoulder to stop her from sniggering.

"It's Irish for Martin, I got this name from my father's brother Martin, they say that there were too many Martin Ward's in the family, so they put that name on me. Why, what are you laughing at, do you think there is something funny about me?" he asks.

Helen is still sniggering at Máirtín.

"There's nothing funny at all," says Helen.

She gets red in the face with embarrassment.

"And why are you grinning across your face like an ass having a foal," asks Máirtín.

Helen gets into a fit of laughing. She laughs so much that she falls off the wall into a bunch of nettles.

"Well tis good enough for ya now. That will teach ya not to be laughing at tinkers like that," Máirtín says.

"Don't mind her, she is only a silly bitch," Mary says.

Helen gets up on her feet and goes home crying to her mother. She is all stung on her legs and hands from the nettles.

"Well that's good enough for ya," shouts Máirtín after Helen as she runs across the fields.

"Let her off, she will be all right. She can be such a child sometimes. How come Máirtín I don't see you at school?"

"School, I did go to school once, and I didn't like it, 'twas just like in prison locked up in a room all day. Ha, no that's not for me miss, anyway what's your name?"

"I'm Mary."

"That's a real country name all right the same as mine."

"How long did you go to school for?" asks Mary.

"Two or three days miss."

Mary has a laugh.

"Is that all, oh my God, how do you read or write?"

"I don't," he says.

"You mean you cannot read or write, oh my God that must be awful."

Mary finishes her ice cream and hops down off the wall.

"Sure none of the tinkers can read or write," Máirtín says.

A woman with a child in a pram is entering the shop and takes note of Mary talking to the tinker boy. When the woman goes into the shop she asks Miss Waters, who owns the shop, has she seen Garda Buckley's daughter talking to the tinker boy outside. The two women go to the window to peep out at Mary and Máirtín.

"My father told me why ye are called tinkers, because you make tin cans, is that true?"

"My Uncle Martin is a tin smith, he is teaching me how to make buckets out of tin and one day I will become a tin smith," he says.

"What's tin?" she asks.

"That's what we use to make buckets. It's like zinc or galvanise, we make buckets and other things from tin."

"Why is your face always dirty like that?" asks Mary.

"I do wash my face sometimes Mary, we don't have much water anyway, and we don't live in a house like you do either," he says, getting annoyed with Mary for being personal about him not washing himself.

"Are you poor?" she asks.

"Mind your own shittin business you, 'tis none of your bloody business whether we are poor or not! At least we don't have to borrow money for to put a roof over our heads like ye people do," replies Máirtín maddeningly.

"I'm sorry, I didn't mean to upset you. I don't care whether you are poor or not," cries Mary.

"Well, mind your own business then and never say things like that again about the tinkers."

He gets upset and goes to move off.

"Wait, I'm sorry, don't go yet," Mary says.

"Look now young woman, my family can't get proper jobs. We only buy and sell scrap iron and sometimes work for the farmers picking spuds and making hay, that's the only work the tinkers can get," he replies.

"I'm sorry I didn't mean to upset you," Mary says.

"Anyway, what do your parents work at?" asks Máirtín.

"My father is the local Garda and my Mum works in the bank, she is also president of the local I C A," she replies.

"What's that local I C A at all?"

"I don't know exactly, I think it's something to do with the local women. Something like that I suppose, sometimes they make things like stools and cakes and have nights out, things like that," says Mary.

"Mary, could my mother go to the I C A?"

"I don't know, I'll find out for ya. I think my father don't like your people, you know, tinkers like, he says that tinkers steal from the farmers, that's what he says, is that true Máirtín?"

"We do not steal anything miss. How does he know that?"

Máirtín is sussing out Mary for information.

"My father said that he knows everything that goes on around here, it's only a few weeks ago he caught the man that was stealing radios out of cars," Mary says.

"He's wrong there now, we wouldn't ever steal from anybody, my father before he died worked hard as a tin smith making buckets and selling them around the country for clothes, food and money, and you tell your feckin father that we would never steal from anybody, we are honest people and you can go to hell, good day to you Miss."

He rides away on his pony in anger.

"My father doesn't like tinkers because he says ye are smelly, dirty and ye rob chickens from the poor farmers," Mary shouts in a loud voice after Máirtín as he rides off annoyed and upset.

She is sorry for what she said. Miss Waters and the other woman are still listening at the shop window, with the shop door left open so they could hear the conversation between Mary and Máirtín. Mary is disappointed with herself for the things she said to Máirtín, she is sad and puts her head down and walks home.

Her father is on duty and is going out on Garda business in the squad car. Just as he is approaching the shop at Ballacrackn he discovers he's almost out of cigarettes. He pulls over and goes into the shop for his cigarettes.

"Well Tim, how are you, what can I get ya," says Miss Waters, just as Tim enters the store.

"Good afternoon Mam, I'll have twenty Major please."

Tim picks up a packet of Silver mints that is displayed on the counter.

"I see Tim your lass seems to be very good friends with that young tinker lad."

"What are you talking about Mrs, what tinker lad?"

Tim gets annoyed that the neighbours might be gossiping among themselves about his daughter Mary. The other woman with the child in the buggy is listening.

"The one with the dirty face, you know he rides a piebald

horse, or is it a donkey? Anyway, what ever it is, I tell ya something he fancies young Mary. You never know now Tim you might have the tinker lad for a son in law yet," says Miss Waters.

"Has anybody else around here seen our Mary with that tinker?" Tim Asks. He gets annoyed.

"Not that I know of Tim, I cannot say, why have I said something wrong?"

"Well, I'll put it this way Miss Waters, over my dead body will them tinkers have anything to do with my family," says Tim in a rage.

He pays for his cigarettes and storms out of the shop, getting into his car and speeding off.

"Well, what have I said wrong now I wonder," Miss Waters says to the other woman.

Garda Tim is fuming with rage as he drives past the tinkers' campsite on the side of the road, he is hesitating whether he should call into the tinkers' camp to warn young Máirtín to stay away from his daughter. He decides not to. Little does he know that inside the tinkers' camp, Máirtín's sisters Moll and Katie are slagging off Máirtín about courting the Garda's daughter. Some of the tinkers are having their supper, bread, eggs and water, while some of them are playing outside. Johnny the Singer is sitting on the dry limestone wall outside the camp singing a love song to annoy Máirtín.

"Mum, did you know that our Máirtín is courting the Garda man's daughter," says Moll with devilment in her eye.

"Mama, tell her to shut up, I wouldn't go around with any Garda's man daughter, you're full of shit Moll, you know nothing," Máirtín says. He throws a piece of egg across at Moll to shut her up. Bridie is astonished with what Moll just said. Katie has a good laugh.

"Do ya hear that Martin?"

"What's wrong with ya now Bridie," says Martin.

He repairs a tear on the canvas on the horse's saddle for a local farmer, and has his supper at the same time.

"Our Máirtín has a girlfriend, and do you know something, she's the Garda's daughter, my God, what do you think of that Martin," says Bridie.

"Will ye shut up the whole lot of ye. Moll and Kate ye are

nothing but shit stirrers," shouts Máirtín.

"Be-Jesus I heard it all now. Look young man. Stay away from that lot I tell you now, you're only bringing trouble on yourself, getting involved with that crowd, they will be watching us like hawks the Guards will, have no more to do with them and let that be the finish of it now," Uncle Martin says.

Máirtín bursts out of the camp to go outside to calm down, Johnny is still singing to annoy Máirtín.

Teacher Visits Tinkers Campsite

The teacher at Ballycrackn school is just pulling up outside in her brand new, bright blue Volkswagen. Máirtín goes off down the road for a walk. Some of the other children are playing outside while others are inside the camp with Bridie and Martin. The teacher notices Johnny singing.

"Hallo young man, I'm Miss Doherty, I teach at Ballycrackn school, what a good singer you are. You have such a beautiful voice, what is your name,"

"Johnny, Miss, and what brings you around here," he asks.

"I came to see your Mother, is she home?"

"She is inside, go in for yourself if you want to talk to her," Johnny says.

Looking annoyed because the teacher is calling to see his Mum, he starts to sing a verse of "Kevin Barry".

"Right so, young man, nice to meet you," she goes to enters the camp.

"Hello anybody there?" Teacher calls out.

"Who the feck is that? Look Katie, go see who is outside," says Martin.

Before Katie gets a chance to get on her feet, Miss Doherty comes into the camp, so does the few other children who were playing outside, they all sit on the ground on canvas cushions, around a handmade solid fuel stove that has a roasting fire on. It's very smoky and smelly, and Miss Doherty finds it hard to breathe.

"I'm Miss Doherty. I teach at Ballycrackn school." She starts to cough.

"What can we do for ya Miss?" asks Martin, hiding behind a black puff of smoke that covered the camp when Miss Doherty opened the canvas door.

"You might close that canvas behind ya, you are stopping the draw," says Martin.

"I was wondering if your children would like to go to school?" she asks, closing the canvas as she comes in. The smoke begins to draw up the hole in the top of the camp.

"Did ye hear that, do ye want to go to school or not," Martin asks the children.

"No," replies the children.

"Well Miss, ya heard them now for yourself, they don't want to go to school," he says.

"I think if they got a chance to learn to read and write they would be much better off," says teacher.

She is disappointed with the children's reaction to school.

"You heard what they said now Miss, and be off with you now," Martin says.

"Look Sir, it would be much better for the children if they had the chance to get an education with our world becoming more modernised as time goes by, they would be lost in society when they come of age," Teacher says.

"I think she is right Martin, it would be a chance for the children to learn to read and write," cries Bridie.

"My father and his father didn't need to go to school, and I didn't need to go to school. They don't need to go to school either. What do you want, that we become one of them, what's coming over you woman, we are tinkers and that's the way we are staying!" Martin says with a frown.

Miss Doherty looks very disappointed.

"I must be off. If you change your mind, your children are more than welcome at Ballycrackn School." She leaves that thought to Martin and Bridie. Miss Doherty drives off in her brand new Volkswagen.

Máirtín has calmed down and has come back from his walk. He goes inside the camp.

"Jesus it's cold outside lads, what did that woman want?" he asks his mum. He goes over to the stove to warm himself.

"That was the teacher in Ballycrackn school, and she was wondering if ye wanted to go to school to learn," says Bridie.

"You know something, I wouldn't mind going to school at all," says Máirtín, as he sits down beside the stove to warm himself.

"Sure why wouldn't ya, so you could be with the Garda's daughter all day then," Willie says, getting up and going outside.

"Go away you ya buffer before I kill ya!"

"Settle down now you Máirtín and don't be taking notice of them at all," says Bridie, as she gets up to make a pot of homemade rabbit soup.

"Who would like rabbit soup," she asks.

"I do!" they all say.

"Right, Jimmy will you fetch me the two rabbits you caught with the snare this morning."

Jimmy gets up and goes outside to fetch the rabbits while Bridie and Katie prepare the vegetables in a pot of water over the stove. Uncle Martin is finished repairing the horse's saddle, so he takes a well earned nap. He lies down on his straw bed, puts his hat over his face and falls asleep. When the soup is cooked they all sit around the stove and eat the soup out of tin mugs that Martin made.

Tinkers First Day At National School

It's early morning and Máirtín is outside his camp washing himself out of a bucket of cold water. He scrubs himself from head to toe, puts on some of the clothes that his mother got from Mrs Buckley. The clothes belong to Mary's brother Timmy. He doesn't realise this because his mother didn't tell him where she got the clothes. He is off to Ballicrackn National School.

He arrives at school looking very clean and smart, with all his sisters and brothers in tow looking very clean and smart also. The young boys' hair is Brylcreamed, their sisters' hair is tied up in a bun and others have pig tails. They all go into the classroom. Teacher comes in and is shocked when she sees all the tinkers. She goes to her desk nervously.

All the rest of the children are shocked to see the tinker children in their classroom. They whisper among themselves. They pass comments about the tinkers. The settled children are on one side of the class and the tinkers are on the other.

Mary Buckley doesn't look happy. Helen Conway points at Máirtín to look across the room at Mary. Mary doesn't respond. Máirtín smiles across the room at Mary, she ignores him, she is looking sad and unhappy. Teacher is anxious to start the class.

"Right now boys and girls settle down, ah, right well first you are all welcome to your first day at Ballycrackn school," says Miss Doherty referring to the tinkers.

"What you need to do first is to tell us all your names, right starting with you young man." She points at Máirtín.

"Now the rest of you regular pupils can familiarise yourself with our new arrivals." There isn't any response from the other pupils, they are nervous because of the tinker children in the classroom.

"Me, are you talking to me Miss?" asks Máirtín.

"Yes you, young man, what's your name?"

"Máirtín Ward is my name Mrs."

"And you?" asks the teacher.

She is pointing at the next boy beside Máirtín.

"Mrs my name is Willie."

Máirtín starts to introduce his sisters and brothers.

Teacher asks them all to sit down.

"Mrs, this is my brother Willie. He can't sit down because he was burnt in his arse with hot water a few days ago Mrs."

The settled children all laugh.

"My sister Katie,
my sister Diane
my brother Ollie,
my brother Johnny. He is a singer."

Again the settled children laugh and giggle.

"My youngest sister Moll,
my brother Jimmy, he's the youngest of the family Mrs."

"Mrs, there is a baby in Mammy's tummy," says little Jimmy.

She wonders with raised eyebrows because she knows their father is dead for over a year.

"Oh, ya," says Miss Doherty.

"There is a baby in mummy's tummy; mammy said that Daddy put the baby there before he went to heaven, so we could have another brother," says little Jimmy.

Miss Doherty smiles to herself, while the settled children laugh. None of the tinker children find anything funny, they look at teacher in confusion as to what is funny.

"And tell me this Jimmy," Teacher asks curiously.

She goes over to little Jimmy and goes down on one knee to talk to him. Little Jimmy backs off because he is afraid of Miss Doherty.

"How long is your father dead Jimmy?"

"'Tis just over a year Mrs why," says young Jimmy

The other children have a giggle at what Jimmy said. Helen Conway asks the teacher a question.

"Miss, that's weird, his mother is pregnant for one full year how could that be?" as Helen giggles with the rest of the class.

"All right, settle down the lot of ye, we will take a break till I sort out which room the younger ones are going into," says teacher, trying to keep a straight face.

"What does that mean Mrs," asks Máirtín.

"Well Máirtín this is fifth and sixth class, the older ones stay in this class and the younger ones go down to the lower classes next door, that's if ye want to come to school regularly."

"Mrs, we do want to come to school so we can read and write, but we all want to be in the one class together," says Willie.

The settled children have a laugh again except Mary.

"Quiet the lot of ye. If ye laugh once more you all will get extra homework tonight, is that understood?" says Teacher, annoyed with the rest of the students laughing and giggling at the tinker children.

The class takes a break while the teacher sorts out the class for the tinker children. All the children go out into the playground to play. The settled children are a bit cautious with the tinkers, after a while they all come together to play football. Máirtín is kicking football when he notices Mary walking on her own across the playground. He goes over to her and abandons the game of football.

"Where are ya off to?" shouts Johnny.

"Never you mind, 'tis none of your business," he shouts back as he goes over to Mary.

"Ah, I wouldn't mind we're winning the match," Johnny shouts over.

"Leave me alone, can't ye see I'm busy."

"Ary, piss off so, you ass," Johnny says, as he carries on playing football.

Máirtín goes over to Mary, she doesn't have anything to say.

"What's wrong with ya, I seen you in the classroom. You don't look happy, what's up with ya Mary?"

"I cannot be seen talking to you anymore 'cause my father said so. He beat me with his belt from his pants last night. Someone told him we were seen talking at the shop the other day." She puts her head down to cry.

"Well the rotten fucker, I will get him back for that one day, I will I tell ya, I will. If it's the last thing I will do." He gets into a rage.

"No Máirtín, stop, let it go, it's no good, my father will punish me for the rest of my life if we remain friends."

"No Mary, you can't let him talk to you like that, I like you and that's all that matters." They both sit down on the playground seats.

"I like you as well Máirtín, I know I'm only thirteen, but I do have feelings towards you, I do want us to remain friends."

It starts to rain. All the students are called into class by the bell.

"Mary, before we go back into class, I just want to say one thing. No matter what other people might say about us, will you promise me that you will stay friends with me forever," says Máirtín, with a tear in his eye.

"I sure will and that's one thing for sure," Mary replies, giving him a gentle touch on his cheek with her right hand and a gentle smile. They both go into the classroom to join the rest of the class. The rain falls from the heavens. Inside the class room, Máirtín and Mary are sharing the same school desk, they are happy to be in the same class together.

Helen looks on with amazement and shakes her head and gives

her best friend Mary Buckley a smile.

Three weeks later the tinkers are having a traditional open air wedding at Ballycrackn cross roads. Bridie's cousin from Tipperary decided to get married at Ballycrackn. It's the end of October and it's a crisp night. They are dancing around the camp fire, the couple that's getting married jump over the broom stick.

There are about one hundred and fifty people at the wedding. They play Irish traditional music, and sing rebel songs. The crack is good. All Bridie's children are at the wedding, and some of the local people are at the wedding also. There is Harry Lynch, Jim O'Sullivan and his wife Annie, Jack Conway, his wife Nellie, Father O'Breen who is pissed and is talking to some young boys who are sitting on their own on a limestone wall. There is plenty of fun and crack, plenty of food and drinks laid out on tables by the roadside. Mary Buckley sneaks out the window of her parents' house, so she can join Máirtín at the wedding celebration.

Chapter Three

Fourteen Years Later 1978
Ballinasloe Horse Fair

It's 1978 at the Ballinasloe horse fair, Johnny the Singer is now a vibrant young man married to another young traveller woman called Etna, who is a few weeks pregnant, and has gone to England to visit her cousins for a few weeks. Some of Máirtín's brothers and sisters are gone to live in England also except himself, Willie, Johnny, and Katie. Johnny and Etna have no children as of yet. Johnny loves singing especially rebel songs like his father before him, songs like, "The Men Behind The Wire," a rebel song which is connected with the troubles in Northern Ireland. Two years earlier when Johnny contacted the I R A to become a member of the I R A outfit, he was quickly informed that the I R A movement does not accept travellers, or anybody with a history of mental illness, or the Spanish. So Johnny sticks at what he is good at, which is buying and selling horses, nicking the odd car trailer, and as you can imagine, selling stolen goods at horse fairs around the country, with his two brothers Máirtín and Willie.

Willie is married to Margaret. They have three children, and Margaret is pregnant with their fourth child. Johnny loves singing on the street especially at horse fairs like Ballinasloe, where there are a lot of other members of the travelling community who gather around him while he sings. At the October fair there are hundreds of horses, ponies, dogs, cats, chickens and hens for sale all over the town. Johnny and his family don't live under a canvas camp covered with tar to keep the rain out, oh, no, he, and all the rest of the travellers as they are called now, live in luxury caravans or trailers as they prefer to call them, by the side of the road, off the beaten path between Ballinasloe and Athlone.

Their Mum is now a sixty five year old woman, well cared for by her three sons. She doesn't need to beg or put on the poor mouth any longer.

At the horse fair they have a lot of caravans and Hi Ace vans parked along the streets. Some travellers hang around the streets drinking. Others have stalls set up around to sell clothes and other items.

Máirtín is now twenty eight years of age, a handsome young man. He and his brothers, Willie and Johnny the Singer are selling a black stallion to a horse breeder called Johnny McCarthy. Máirtín is now known as Máirtín Dagger Ward because of the Dagger knife he carries in his brown leather cowboy boots.

"I tell you one thing for sure Boss you won't find a better stallion around Ireland or England, to beat this one, he's a mighty horse now you know," Máirtín says, to the horse dealer Johnny McCarthy, while he gets the stallion to stand up straight and pose.

"You might not believe this now Sir, but this stallion, he has sired about thirty mares this year so far on his own," says Máirtín.

Everybody is standing around watching Máirtín and having a good laugh at that statement.

"Each mare had the finest of foals I tell ya ha, that's true Sir. See that one over there Boss?" says Willie, pointing at a white pony tied to railings that surround a big oak tree.

"This is his father, I tell ya, you won't find better Sir," says Johnny the Singer, as he rubs down the stallion mane.

"I tell ya one thing for sure Boss, he is very strong, isn't that right Máirtín?" says Johnny the Singer.

Johnny McCarthy examines the black stallion, he checks his teeth for his age and checks his feet.

"Well Boss what do you think?" Máirtín says.

"Well Mr Ward I'd say he's not bad at all I suppose," says Johnny McCarthy.

"Watch this," says Máirtín.

As he puts his younger brother Willie up on the horse to ride him around, he gives the horse a lash with a stick to send him running.

"See that look, look at that Boss," says Máirtín, nodding his head.

"By damn he can run, no mare will get away from him, ha, ha, do ya think so?"

"I suppose you're probably right there Máirtín, about that, I'll tell you what I will do with ya young man, I'll give ya one hundred pounds for that stallion right now, take it or leave it, now I can do no better than that," says Johnny McCarthy, as he watches Willie ride the stallion around.

While Máirtín and Willie are making a bargain with Johnny McCarthy over the black stallion, two young traveller children are stealing from Kelly's V G supermarket in the town. They run out of the shop with biscuits and sweets under their jumpers, they lose some of them on the footpath while the Manager, Mr Kelly, comes running out of the shop after them with a sweeping brush in his hand.

"Come back here ye little fecks, I'll call the Police on ye, don't worry I'll get ya, ye little shits," yells Mr Kelly, who is very angry with the young travellers.

"Ah feck off will ya!" says one of the young travellers called young Johnny Barry.

He and his little sister Lizzy are sent into the shop to steal for his mother Fay Barry, who is a young widow. She is waiting for the children around the corner. Fay grabs the children and hide them under her long red coat and disperses into the crowd so the shop manager Mr Kelly can't catch them.

Around the town there are posters of Joe Dolan up on billboards and E.S.B poles. Joe Dolan is due to play at the Jack O'Reilly's pub in the centre of the town, it's the highlight gig at the October horse fair.

Brawl At Jack O'Reilly's Pub

There are at least two hundred travellers in the pub, it's a traditional Irish pub with wooden seats all round, wooden barstools, and a black mahogany counter.

Jack O'Reilly is behind the counter with a young barman called Brendan, who is serving up pints to the travellers, while the women and children are sitting quietly listening to Johnny the Singer, singing a rebel song, "Kevin Barry."

Everybody is in the pub including Máirtín, his sister Katie, Willie, Fay Barry and lots of children. There is silence while Johnny is singing his song, some travellers are saying things like:

"Good Man Johnny."

"Fair play to ya Johnny."

"By heck he can sing," says traveller Cathal Holms, from Dublin speaking in a Dublin accent.

When Johnny finishes the song they all clap. They are all looking at the band setting up their gear, they look disappointed because Joe Dolan isn't anywhere in sight. They notice Brush Shiels tuning up his guitar. One man calls a pint of cider for Johnny.

Cathal Holms ask Máirtín, how much did he get for the black stallion.

"£200 Boss, not bad at all now was it and look."

Pulling out a lock of the stallion's mane, he pulls out a long dagger knife up out of his right brown leather boot to show the lads how he cut off the horse's mane.

"'Tis good luck lads to keep a piece of horse mane, from the horse you have already sold, it can bring ya good fortune."

He takes out a crucifix that's around his neck.

"See that cross, my father gave me that before he died, he told me it would bring me good luck wherever I'd go," says Máirtín.

"Well you better buy us a drink so Máirtín, it might bring us all good fortune as well, ha lads what do ye think," says Cathal Holms.

He lives in a halting site near Ballymun flats which are built for a number of years now, and he is standing in front of Máirtín.

"By heck, if you got that much money for the black stallion, by feck I'd say you are loaded," says another man called Scar Face who is not a traveller and is watching everything that is going on.

"Be-Jesus lads I'm not loaded, but I will stand ye a drink either way lads." Máirtín calls over Brendan the barman to order a drink.

The barman comes over to Máirtín.

"Could we have three pints Boss and what ever the brother Johnny is having over there, and Sir, you might have one yourself."

"Ok Sir, that's three pints of cider, and a double scotch," says the barman Brendan, filling up a few pints of cider for the boys.

Brush Shiels and his Band are all tuned up ready to start playing, a man called Hattie the Swan, because of his long neck, shouts.

"Where is Joe Dolan? I drove here all the way from Mullingar to see Joe play!"

"Ah shut up you will ya Hattie, you know nothing you stupid fool, you didn't know that Joe was playing here till I told ya ten minutes ago," says Fay Barry.

"Testing, haon-dó, haon-dó, haon-dó-trí. Bhael tá brón an domhain ar Joe mar níl sé anseo Inniú agus tabhair sé an Irithscéal gibth agus tá siúl agam nil díomá a bith oraibh. I'm Brush Shiels," he says, nervously as the travellers look bewildered and confused of what Brush has just said.

"I hope my band and I can entertain you for the evening, haon dó trí."

The band starts to play, "Fields of Athenry," "Dirty Old Town."

"What was all that about, himself and his stupid Irish," Kate says, looking up at Brush on the stage.

"Don't mind that, I heard him play before, he's brilliant!" says Fay.

They all go out on the dance floor to dance.

Máirtín is having a drink at the bar with Cathal Holms who starts arguing with him over a car trailer. Scar Face looks on.

"You listen to me now Cathal, I sold that trailer to you in good faith now piss off will ya with that kind of talk," says Máirtín.

He turns his back to Cathal.

"No Máirtín you didn't and don't turn your back on me or I'll bust ya," says Cathal, grabbing Máirtín by the shoulder to turn him around to face him.

"I swear on my father's grave that there was nothing wrong with that trailer when I sold it to ya. 'Twas fine, sure wasn't I using it myself before I sold it to you. Now off with ya and don't be bothering me," replies Máirtín, getting annoyed with Cathal.

Jack O'Reilly looks on and warns the two men to calm down and carry their drink.

Cathal gets into a rage with Máirtín.

Scar Face is spitting on his hands.

"There will be a fight here soon I'd say Jack," Scar Face says. Cathal is furious.

"You're a proper liar, it was red rotten with rust and it fell apart on the side of the road on me," Cathal argues, hitting Máirtín in the face with his fist.

"For God sake lads will ye settle down will ye and carry your drink like proper men," Scar Face yells, as he tries to stop the two men from fighting.

"Get out of my way Scar Face will ya for God's sake, that's my brother you are talking to," says Willie.

Willie throws Cathal a punch in the face, Cathal falls to the ground, two or three of Cathal's friends join in.

"Will ye calm down for peace sake," says Jack.

Brendan and Jack are trying to console the men with no effect. The fight soon turns into a brawl, the inside of the pub is smashed up with bottles flying. All the travellers go out onto the street to fight, they are cursing and spitting. There is a lot of blood. The women and children are in tears shouting and screaming at the men to stop fighting. They fight until they cannot fight anymore. The local Sergeant Ricky Molloy and Garda Anthony Finell have arrived, with a few other Officers. They don't intervene until the travellers tire themselves out. It is a regular occurrence at the October horse fair.

When the fight is over most of the men who were fighting are sprawled out on the road. The guards move in, they make arrests. Willie and Johnny the Singer make a run for it and head off down the street to avoid been arrested.

"Who started this?" asks Sergeant Ricky." What's your name?" as he catches Máirtín by the arm.

"Nobody started it Boss, we're just having fun," laughs Máirtín, bursting out laughing with all the cider he has drank.

"Well I don't see anything funny, if that's the case we will take you all back to the Station."

He tells the Officers to put the men in the Garda van and take them back to the Station to give statements. Some of the travellers are put in the Garda van. Máirtín is bleeding from the forehead and mouth, so he is put into the ambulance and taken to the local hospital.

Back in the bar, Jack and Brendan and a few others are fixing up the pub after the fight. Broken glasses, broken tables and stools, broken mirrors, a pool table turned upside down, band equipment thrown around the bar. Jack is standing in the middle of the bar with Brush Shiels, lead singer with the band, who is bleeding from the forehead after getting hit with a flying bottle.

"What the hell happened to that shower of lunatics at all, what kind of animals are those turning into at all, you know you try and be nice and what do you get," says Jack, frustrated with what has happened.

"Look at this."

He looks around at the mess his premises is in after the fight.

"Oh, I don't know what I'm going to do at all. 'Tis worse it's getting every year," Jack says.

"Well Jack, I don't know what you are going to do, but this is the first and last time me and my band will play at this October fair," says Brush Shiels, wiping the blood off his face.

"I think I better go to the hospital to get a stitch on my forehead," he adds.

"Sure I might as well take you there myself, do you know something Brush, that cut looks deep, come on, lets go out of here before I lose the head."

Just as Jack and Brush are about to leave, Garda Anthony comes into the pub to take statements and to see who started the fight.

"Could I speak to Jack please?" says Garda Anthony, asking Brendan who is cleaning up the mess.

"He is down there with one of the band members," says Brendan.

"Thank you Sir," replies Anthony.

He goes down the back of the lounge bar to find Jack and Brush with Brush holding a tissue to his forehead.

"Well Jack they have done a great job this time I see."

He looks around at the broken furniture.

"You can say that again Anthony."

"Can you shed any light on what in the name of God has

happened here?" says Anthony.

He looks around, taking out his pen and pad to write his report.

"Well Anthony, they were all just drinking and having a good time, and then all of a sudden they started fighting," replies Jack.

"Who started fighting first?"

"Well, it's like this now, I don't know, I didn't see how it started," says Jack. He gives an eye to Brush.

"It happened so quickly I couldn't see who started fighting first."

"You're Brush Shiels the singer aren't you," says Anthony, shaking Brush's hand.

"Well, Brush have you seen who started this fight?"

"No Sir, I didn't, sure you couldn't see anything in here with the crowd of Knackers and the smoking, it would stifle ya in here an half an hour ago," replies Brush.

"Look lads the fight had to start somehow, somebody had to see something, ye are all not blind I hope."

"Sorry Anthony, if you wouldn't mind, I have to take poor Brush to the hospital to get a stitch."

"You better do that so Jack and if you can refresh your memory don't hesitate to give us a call. You have our number, hope to see you soon. Brush, now mind that head, you wouldn't want to lose your memory now would ya?"

Brush smiles back at Anthony, they leave to go to the hospital.

"Well that's it so," Garda Anthony mutters to himself.

He closes his note pad and putting it in his top pocket with his pen, he leaves the pub and goes about his other daily duties.

Six young travellers run back to the open park where the horse fair has been held to tell Uncle Martin that the lads have been arrested. They are excited about the fight in Jack O'Reilly's pub. They all hop into their Hi Ace vans and drive to the hospital, there are about fifteen travellers who go to the hospital and others go the Garda Station. There is panic, especially with the women. They are crying and panicking at the hospital, and the Garda Station.

Willie and Johnny the Singer are on the road making their way back to the park, Uncle Martin is driving the van. He stops to pick up the two lads. On the way to the hospital they pass on the road Jack McCarthy with Máirtín Dagger's black stallion.

Uncle Martin is driving the van, he talks about the stallion to Johnny the Singer who absconded from the fight, is sitting next to Uncle Martin. There are also two young children in the front of the van, and women and children in the back including Fay and her two children.

"Well there he goes, Johnny."

They pass Johnny McCarty walking with the black stallion on the side of the road.

"Do you know, he is a great breed of a horse," says Uncle Martin. He rubs his chest where he has been getting chest pain for some time now.

"He is, Uncle Martin, and that's one thing for sure, just look at the way he is built, by heck, ha, I tell ya something for nothing, that fella got a bargain with that stallion and that's one certain thing," says Johnny the Singer, letting down the window to shout at Johnny McCarthy with the black stallion.

"You got a bargain there with that one Sir!" shouts Johnny as he passes Johnny McCarthy with the horse.

He gives the travellers van a wave as they pass him by.

"I think Máirtín sold that black stallion too cheap I'd say," says Martin, driving the van to the hospital.

"Well, I suppose Uncle, if that's the case we could always steal him back and flog him somewhere else up the country," says Willie.

The children are listening to the conversation, they think it is funny. They arrive at the hospital to see how Máirtín is getting on.

Jack's Worried His Insurance Policy Maybe Expired

Jack is back after leaving Brush Shiels to the hospital. Himself and Brendan are cleaning up the mess after the fight, Jack is fuming with the state of his premises.

"I tell ye something Brendan, them lads will pay for this and that's one thing for sure," says Jack, looking frustrated.

He looks around and takes note of all the damage.

"Jack, let it go, it's only a few tables, you know what that lot is like," says Brendan, sweeping up the blood stained glass with a broom and putting it into a bin.

"You should be more worried about Brush Shiels suing you for that nasty gash in his head," says another man.

He gives a hand mopping the floor for a few pints as payment.

"'Tis all right talking but with the look of that cut I'll say Brush will definitely have a nasty scar there," says Scar Face, as he comes into the pub and overhears the conversation.

"Ha, that's all I need, do you know now that you mention it, I think I haven't renewed my insurance policy, it may be expired, I think it was up for renewal last month as far as I know."

"Well Jack, I'm afraid you could be in trouble there then, you wouldn't mind filling a pint of stout for me would ya Jack? This fighting is thirsty business," says Scar Face.

"I suppose you're right, pressing charges against them boys, oh I don't know, they might only come back and wreck the whole place again," Jack says anxiously.

He stops to think.

"Look lads, tell the Guards nothing, the best thing we can do is forget the whole thing all together." He goes behind the counter to fill a pint of stout for Scar Face.

"Sure wasn't it that Máirtín Dagger Ward and another man that started it. I don't know the other man at all, I seen him before somewhere I think he's from Dublin or up around that side of the country some where, I think," Scar Face says, picking up a barstool off the ground to sit on.

"Ary, look, lets forget it, it would probably cause more trouble than it's worth, look trying to take them lads to court, sure ya wouldn't get a penny out of them lads anyways. What do you think Scar Face?" Jack leaves the pint of stout on the counter.

"I'm saying nothing Jack," as he takes a drink of his pint of stout.

Mayhem At The Garda Station

Most of the travellers are out of control entering the Garda Station. A traveller widow woman arrives, called Nina Barry (herself and Fay were married to two brothers, who are dead now, whose father is Luke the bookie Barry). Nina lived in England for years with her husband and two children. She is talking to Garda Mick Walsh who is on duty.

"Sir, I demand to see my two boys Roger and Malachy, now where are they?" As she comes in the door, she hits the counter with her fist. "Sir I want to see my sons right now!"

"Calm down now Mrs, in a minute," yells Mick, at Nina Barry. He goes on the radio to call in other Guards for help.

"Base calling all cars, return to base as soon as possible."

"Now Mrs, what can I do for you?" he asks.

"Please Sir, I just want to see my two boys that's all," says Nina.

"In a minute now Mrs, look I'm doing my best, there are only three Officers on duty here, I'm on my own here while the other two Officers are taking care of the prisoners."

"Prisoners, is that what you call my boys, prisoners, oh my God over my dead husband's grave may God forgive ya, he died and left a widow and two children behind," Nina cries.

She blesses herself with a cross she has around her neck.

"My boys never were in trouble in their lives Sir and now you call them children prisoners."

"Look, Mam calm down. All right, can you follow me Mrs," says Garda Mick. He takes her to the back of the Garda Station to see her two sons. The rest of the travellers follow Nina.

"Look you all can't come back here it's only herself and nobody else, perhaps ye all might behave yourselves and stay outside the counter please." They are shouting and roaring.

Garda Mick tries to put down the hatch he lifted to let Nina through. They ignore Garda Mick and push their way into where the two boys and the rest of the men are held at the back of the Police station.

An Old Acquaintance Recognises Máirtín

All his family are around his bed at the hospital including his sister Kate, Fay, and his mum Bridie. He lay in bed, his face is black and blue with a broken nose and a black eye. His Mum is annoyed and upset.

"Oh my God, I didn't raise you to be like this, what were you fighting for anyways?" cries Bridie, sitting on the bed beside him and holding his hand.

"Look Mum, let go of my feckin hand will ya!"

He pulls his hand away.

"Leave me alone now, I'm all right I will be out of here in an hour or two, leave me alone will ya, for shit sake."

He plays with Fay's son young Johnny on the bed.

Fay comes in with sweets from the shop across the road.

"I see Brush Shiels is out there in the waiting room with a great big gash in his head."

"Ary, fuck Brush Shiels, if Joe Dolan came and played like he should, he wouldn't be in hospital now, ha, for God's sake," says Máirtín.

Nurse Mary Buckley, Garda Tim Buckley's daughter who is a nurse at the hospital and was forbidden to see Máirtín fourteen years earlier, comes to the room to give Máirtín something for the swelling on his face.

"Well what happened to you, what were you doing with yourself at all, I wouldn't like to see the other one, he must be in a terrible state all together," says Nurse Mary.

Some of the travellers have a laugh; some of them aren't too impressed.

"Right, you can take two of these."

She gives the pills to Máirtín.

"These will help take down the swelling in your face and help ease your pain for a while."

"Thanks Nurse. I thought you weren't going to give me anything for the pain at all, I asks for them earlier on, they told me the Nurse would come around with them later." He rubs his face.

"By heck Nurse you took your time, you wouldn't want to be

dying around here would ya," says Fay Barry, giving the eye to the other travellers and smiling.

"What's your name?" asks Nurse Mary, as she checks his pulse, and notices his name written over the bed.

"Dagger Ward, is that your name?"

"It is Dagger Ward, and this time next year I'll be king of the travellers."

He shakes his head and gives the eye to his mum. His mum turns her head away.

"King of the travellers my ass," she mutters.

Katie, his sister isn't too impressed with that statement either.

"Shut up will ya with your tough talk, that's nothing to be proud of, king of the travellers." says Katie, turning her head away.

It's obvious that Katie and Bridie don't want him to fight for the title king of the travellers because they fight bare knuckle and that can have it's repercussions.

"It's none of your business Kate, what I do!" he replies, getting annoyed, folding his arms in a huff.

"Don't mind them, I'll stand by you whatever you do, King of the travellers or not, it don't matter to me," says Fay. She goes over to sit beside him on the bed.

Mary is looking at him. He is beginning to look familiar to her, she gets a flash back to when Máirtín was outside Ballycrackn shop with her fourteen years earlier.

"Is that your real name?" she asks, looking at him in the face, so she can try and recognise him under the black-n-blue cuts to his face.

"It sure is Miss, why, don't you think that's a real man's name?"

He begins to fancy himself as a bit of a man.

"No, it's not a stupid name, Máirtín that's his real name, and he doesn't like to be called by that name either. He thinks it isn't a real man's name."

"Shut up you Katie you know nothing! Sitting there with a bull nose face on ya!"

Bridie is taking notice of the way Nurse Mary is looking at Máirtín, as Mary's eyes began to fill up.

"I see your name's Mary," says Katie, looking at nurse Mary's name badge.

"Oh, Máirtín was in love with a beautiful young lass called Mary one time you know, remember that Mum?"

She looks over at her mum for a comment. Her mum doesn't answer. She knows that Nurse Mary is Mary Buckley the Garda man's daughter from Ballycrackn Village.

"Katie, shut up will ya, you have a big mouth. Now shut up it's none of your business at all who his friends are," says Bridie.

She wants to quieten Katie in case Máirtín might discover who the nurse is, she doesn't want him getting involved with the Garda man's daughter again.

"He was so upset when we moved away, oh he wouldn't talk to anybody for weeks, love sick he was, I can remember that like it was just yesterday," says Katie giving the eye to her mum, as her mum snubs her.

"You have a big mouth on ya Katie. By damit I'll close it for ya if you don't shut up," says Máirtín, putting up his fist to Katie to shut her up because she is embarrassing him in front of the others.

"Máirtín Ward," Mary says.

She puts her hands to her face.

"Ya, and what's wrong with that. Do you have a problem with travellers or what?" he says, with a frown.

"Oh my God, it is you, I can't believe it."

Her eyes fill up with tears as she walks out of the room.

"Well, what's her problem," says Katie, thinking she said something to upset Nurse Mary.

They all look at each other, wondering what was the problem with the Nurse.

Fay looks jealous at the way Mary was looking into Máirtín's eyes. Bridie is worried that he might recognise who Mary is and might want to get involved with her again. Bridie is well aware of the complications that could occur if that romance between her son and the Garda man's daughter could spark off, especially with her father Tim Buckley, who forbids any member of his family being involved with travellers.

Back At The Garda Station

Garda Anthony releases the two Barry brothers, Roger and Malachy, from custody.

"Right lads I'm letting you go this time, but the next time you won't be getting away so handy, I've just talked to the pub owner and he is not pressing charges, you are free to go," says Garda Anthony, opening the cell door to let them out.

"Oh, isn't he such a nice Garda, well may God bless ya," says Nina Barry, getting up off the chair she is sitting on.

Garda Anthony gives Nina a sour look. While Roger is lying on the cell bed, Malachy is standing up looking out the window at the other travellers that are outside the Garda Station waiting for the two boys to be released.

"Now, if you come back in here again you won't get away so handy the next time, so just remember that now lads. Now, off with you and let me never see the both of you in here again," he says.

"Thank you Sir, and don't ya worry, you won't be seeing me in here again, isn't that right Roger," says Malachy, looking at Roger with a sarcastic smile.

"Right Boss we will see ya," says Roger. He shakes Garda Anthony's hand, as Garda Mick looks on.

The two boys sign themselves out of the Station by putting their signature mark-X on the Garda custody release book. The travellers that are outside cheer when the two boys are released, they go into their vans and drive away from the Station. They go back to where the Horse Fair is held.

There is a dark October chill is in the air. They sit around a campfire, where Máirtín, Willie, Luke the bookie and a few other travellers are drinking whiskey. Johnny the Singer is singing "The Men Behind The Wire," "armoured cars and tanks and guns came to take away our sons, but every man must stand behind the men behind the wire." Fay goes to join them, but when she sees her father- in-law Luke, she gives him a nasty look. She decides to go elsewhere. The others just raise their shoulders and take no notice of Fay.

They get drunk and decide to have a chicken fight; they bet on the cocks, there is a lot of shouting and betting. Luke the bookie is taking the bets, children are running around chasing cocks to give to the men to fight.

Máirtín and Willie, are drunk from drinking Poítin, they approach Luke to put on a bet. He has a betting stall set up under a high ivy wall to keep the cold night chill off of him.

"Well Máirtín Dagger, that is a fine shiner you got there," says Luke the Bookie. I tell ye one thing lads, ye got away light," he adds.

The two lads are standing looking at Luke, they cannot move with all the drink they have taken.

"Well now lads, are ye going to bet or what, ha."

"I might put a £1 on that cock there with the red neck, he looks like a tough warrior," mutters Dagger, as he can't stand up with all he has drank.

Luke takes the bet money off Dagger, while Willie decides to put on a bet as well, just as the two lads are about to stagger away from Luke.

"Willie how's your mother keeping these days, I haven't seen her in this long time."

"Sure she's fine Luke, sure she is, will I tell her you were asking for her?" Willie says. He gives a funny eye to Máirtín Dagger as they stagger away.

"I suppose you have the hots for my mum do ya Luke," says Máirtín.

He has a good laugh at Luke and walks away with Willie back to the campfire, they sit down and drink some more.

Chapter Four

Mary Buckley's Flat

Mary is in her flat; pacing up and down her sitting room, she is excited and bothered about meeting Máirtín that day in the hospital. She decides to call her old school friend Helen Conway to confide in her. Helen is in her house back at Ballycrackn, brushing her long blond hair. The phone rings. She picks it up.

"Hallo?"

"Helen, it's Mary how are you?"

"Mary Buckley, is that you, how are you? I haven't heard from you for months."

"I know Helen, I'm sorry, I was very busy at work and I didn't get a chance to call."

"Ah never mind Mary, it the same for me, I'm moving house anyways so I'm very busy also, how are you?"

"I'm ok, where are you moving to Helen?"

"You won't believe this, I'll be your neighbour now sure I will."

"Why you aren't moving to Ballinasloe are you?"

"I sure am Mary and guess what, I'm going to work in the bank there also, they asked me if I would transfer to the bank there, so I said why not, a break is as good as a rest isn't it? I knew you had moved there, so I said to myself why not?"

"Well, that's great news Helen, you'll never believe who I met today, who would you think?"

"Elvis Presley?"

"Not at all Helen, are you crazy, isn't he's dead, remember Máirtín from school?"

"Máirtín Ward, you mean," replies Helen.

"Yes, that's the one, I just couldn't believe it was him after all these years."

"Oh my God Mary, I better sit down and brace myself for this one."

Helen sits down on a chair and pours out a glass of whiskey for herself. Her mum is passing the sitting room she notices Helen drinking whiskey again. She is saddened and disappointed with Helen for drinking so much, and turns away annoyed.

"Where did you come across him?"

"He was brought into hospital today, with cuts on his face, I don't know what happened to him, I guess he was kicked by a horse at the horse fair."

"You were so crazy about him you know, remember Mary when he moved away from Ballycrackn, I really thought you were going to commit suicide, you were so heart broken after him that time, well, I suppose he is married by now with a half dozen children."

"I don't know Helen, there were a gang of children around his bed all right, I couldn't tell was his wife there or not. He had a child in his arms at one stage, I don't know was the child his or not." Mary lies down on her couch and puts up her feet.

"Ary, he probably is married, you know that lot, they get married at fifteen or sixteen probably to his first cousin or somebody like that I'd say."

" I don't know Helen, he looks so handsome, I am still so crazy about him you know."

"Now Mary stop that talk, you know the trouble that caused the last time." She takes a sip of whiskey from the glass.

"With my father you mean?" says Mary, with a frown as she is annoyed with that statement. She feels she doesn't have Helen's support.

"Ya, and you know how he feels about that lot don't ya, he will go off his head if he finds out."

"I don't care, Helen, about my father or what he thinks, we haven't talked much for years. Anyway, why are you so cynical, I thought you liked Máirtín's family."

"I did Mary, but I don't know, if you get involved with him

again your father will go crazy, I'm afraid of what he might do, see what he did the last time," Helen says.

"Let him do what he likes! Do you want to meet up for a drink or something at the weekend?"

"Ya Mary why not, that would be mighty I'm moving into the house on Friday, so we will meet up then. We have a lot to catch up on you know, and I want to tell you about my new house." She sips more whiskey.

"Did you buy a new house or what here?"

"I did, it was my aunt Maeve, she left me some money in her will and I bought myself a house. You knew Mum's sister Maeve don't ya, the one that worked in Jack Lynch's office in Dublin."

"Oh ya, I remember her, she had to let everyone know that she worked for Jack Lynch. Anyways Helen, I'm off; I'm only building up a gigantic phone bill, right, so does Friday night suit you to meet up?"

"No problem Mary, Friday night is perfect," says Helen.

"I will see you in Jack O' Reilly's pub, Friday night about eight o'clock, is that all right?"

"Eight o'clock it is then, I can't wait to see you, bye for now Mary. See you then."

"Bye Helen."

Mary leaves down the phone and sits on her own and watches TV.

Helen picks up the bottle of whiskey and fills her glass, her mum comes in.

"Well for God's sake, you're not drinking again, what in the hell will I do with you, your father and I are worried sick about the way you are drinking."

"Don't worry mum, in two days time I will be out of your hair forever, I have my own place now, so stop worrying about me. I'm a big girl now I'm well able to look after myself," replies Helen.

"That's what I'm worried about Helen, are you able to look after yourself, God only knows what you will get up to in Ballinasloe. Anyways I'm off to bed, your father went asleep ages ago, now I think you should go to bed as well and never mind your whiskey."

Helen sticks out her tongue at her Mum as she leaves the sitting room to go to bed.

She comes back again.

"I'm sorry to bring this up again but have you got any reply from Dublin yet?"

"No mum, that could take months."

"Look Helen I'm sorry we didn't tell you this earlier, maybe we should have told you when you were a child."

"Don't worry about it mum it's ok, I'm glad you told me."

As her Mum retires to bed for the night, Helen sits on the couch grasping her two feet tightly with her hands as she bursts into tears.

Mary Is Disappointed Máirtín Discharged Himself

Next morning, Mary goes into work. She go to reception to check the register and to talk to Nurse Celine who has been on night duty.

"I see Máirtín Ward has discharged himself," she says, checking the discharge sheet.

"Yes Mary, he discharged himself just after midnight, he said he was all right and that he would come back in a few days for a check up appointment."

"And how was he Celine, was he all right when he left?"

Mary is concerned about Máirtín's welfare.

"He seemed fine, a bit black and blue I suppose, but nevertheless I wouldn't be worrying too much about him, sure those guys are as tough as nails."

Mary looks at Celine and smiles putting her head down.

"Anyway I'm glad he's gone, it wasn't a pretty sight above in St Brendan's ward late last night. There was about fifty of his gang visiting him, looked to me like they were drinking all day. Drunk as skunks they were. I wouldn't mind some other Knacker then brought in a guitar for that singer, what's his face? Let me think, oh ya, Brush Shiels."

"That's right Celine, he was in casualty when I was leaving yesterday evening, I tell you something he's one funny guy. He had all the doctors and Nurses in stitches in casualty, when I was leaving to go home yesterday evening."

"You mean Mary, the doctors had him in stitches," says Celine with a good laugh.

"That's right, look I better get back to work before the Matron comes looking for me."

Mary heads back to her ward to attend to her patients.

It's Friday night and Mary gets ready to go out to meet up with her friend Helen. She puts on her makeup and nice clothes, sips a nice glass of chilled wine, lies down on the couch and listens to the Rod Stuart record, "First Cut Is The Deepest." As she lies back on the couch she gets flashbacks of Máirtín and her in school playing football out in the school yard, the boys against the girls.

"Come on Mary, pass the ball to me," Máirtín says, with his hands out to grab the ball.

Mary has the ball.

"Hey Máirtín, catch!"

She passes the ball to him.

Máirtín catches the ball. Mary looks happy to be playing ball with Máirtín. Helen is playing on the girls side, and notices how Mary passes the ball to Máirtín.

"Hey, that's not allowed," shouts Helen.

Mary has a tear in her eye while she is reminiscing about her fond memories in school with Máirtín. She finishes her glass of red wine and heads out to meet Helen.

Mary And Helen Meet Up At Jack O'Reilly's Pub

It's eight thirty, Helen is already in the pub waiting for Mary to arrive. The pub is quiet, there are only a few other customers. Helen is talking to Jack at the counter, Scar Face is sitting with a few other men playing cards. Mary comes in.

"Well hello there," Mary says.

She goes over to Helen.

"How are you Mary?"

They give each other a hug.

"It's so good to see you Mary, you are looking superb. Oh my God, it has been so long since I've seen you. You look so well, doesn't she Jack?" Jack nods his head.

"You are looking well yourself Helen, look at you, there isn't a pick on you, your hair got so long. I see you met Jack." Mary says.

"I sure did, isn't he a lovely man?"

"He is all right."

Jack is blushing and smiles at the girls.

"Come on Helen over here, lets sit down, we have a lot to catch up on."

They both take a seat in the nook, Jack comes up to the girls.

"Well ladies, what will it be?" he asks.

"You know something, I feel like a pint of stout."

"Bloody hell Mary, you can't drink that here, what will people think?" says Helen.

She looks around to see is anybody listening.

"Feck them I don't care, Jack I'll have a pint of Guinness please, if you don't mind."

"Well excuse me Mary, you're letting your hair down, my God you have changed," Helen says.

"And yourself Helen?" asks Jack.

"I will have a glass of Harp, thank you Jack."

"That's a pint Guinness for Mary and a glass of Harp for yourself Helen."

He goes to the bar to fetch the two girls' drinks.

"Anyways Mary tells us about him."

"Who?"

"Máirtín Ward who do you think I'm talking about?"

"Oh ya, wait till I tell ya, well I got the fright of my life when I seen him, there he was up in St Brendan's ward lying in bed, I could not believe my eyes. I got such a shock I was so overwhelmed. You know Helen, I was so crazy about him, you know I never really stopped thinking about him all those years."

Her eyes begin to fill up, as she picks up a table mat and fiddles with it.

"I know Mary, but after all, he is a traveller and have you taken that into consideration, have you, what about the way some folk are about travellers?" Helen says.

"I don't care, look, the travellers would not be the way they are now if only for the way we treat them."

"Well now Mary, they drew it all on themselves you know, just look what they did here a few days ago. While I was waiting for you here Mary, Jack O'Reilly-" looking up at Jack behind the bar.

"He was telling me what the travellers did here a few days ago, they smashed the whole place to pieces, sure they did!"

"I notice a change here all right Helen, look, new tables and stools."

Mary looks around and notices the changes. Jack leaves down the drinks on the table.

"I see, Jack, you had a bit of a face lift here."

"Ya Mary, the travellers smashed the whole place up the last day of the horse fair, they were here for a couple of days, and on the last day they went mad." Jack sits down at the table in front of the girls.

"I was inside the bar and Dagger Ward and another of his cronies started fighting. Brush Shiels had to be rushed into hospital."

"Well, is that right," Mary says, smiling to herself.

"And which of them is Dagger?"

Mary is sussing for information from Jack.

"That stupid feckin!.."

He picks up a table mat to fiddle with it.

"Máirtín Ward. Dagger he goes by now, he must think he is some kind of hard man or something, Dagger, ha, well did you ever hear the likes, sure 'tis only a traveller that would have a nickname like that," Jack says.

Mary gets embarrassed when she hears Máirtín's name mentioned.

"He was in and out of here with his mates all week and not a word and on the last day, bang, all hell broke loose, they all went mad. Why couldn't they have kept the peace without having to cause trouble and wreck the whole bloody place?"

He shakes his head with disgust.

"I know that's the way they are," says Helen, giving the eye to Mary. Mary puts her head down.

"You're right about that Helen, you can never trust them lads, one minute they are very nice to ya, and the next bang they smash everything, they would kick your head in as fast as they would look at ya," says Jack.

Mary looks embarrassed.

Máirtín Dagger and his brother Johnny the Singer come into pub, they go to the counter, Máirtín still has the black eye, and a plaster on his nose. He takes out the crucifix he has around his neck and kisses it. Mary notices this, she puts her head down and starts to smile.

"Ja-ses will ya look who's in, well for God sake, haven't they some neck coming in here!" says Jack.

He gets up from the table, goes over to the two lads that's standing at the counter.

"Look now lads, I don't want any more trouble in here, ye have caused enough trouble around here as it is, now off with ye."

"Will ya relax a minute Boss, we're not here to cause trouble Sir, my brother Dagger, he just wants to talk to ya, relax now Boss one minute, don't get excited now, we're not here to cause any trouble at all, I told ya," says Johnny.

"Go ahead lads what do you want to talk about, come on spit it out and be off with ye."

"I'm sorry for smashing up your place Sir." Máirtín says, holding his head up as bold as brass.

"I have £100 here, I sold an old horse I had at the fair, I will give the only money I have Sir for any damage that was done to your place, ok?" says Máirtín.

He notices Mary sitting in the nook and gives an eye. She puts her head down, and smiles to herself. Helen notices this.

"I don't know, I'd rather ye piss off now out of here all together and never return."

"Ok Boss, sure we will do that so all right, I'll leave the money here on the counter and we will be on our way, is that ok now Boss."

Mary is looking at Máirtín, she is blushing, her face is as red as fire.

"Come on Johnny, we are not welcome here."

They both leave Jack's pub.

"Flipping hell Mary what's wrong with your face, you make

out Tom Jones just entered the building," says Helen.

"Is that him, is that Máirtín?"

"'Tis Helen that's him, ha what do you think?"

"Well, there is no doubt about it, he is a fine looking Knacker all right."

They both laugh and drink to the occasion. Mary only takes a sip out of the pint, she leaves the money on the table for Helen to pay for the drinks.

"Look Helen, hang on you here a minute, I shouldn't be long." She rushes out the door to catch up with Máirtín.

"Wait a minute Mary, where are you off to?" says Helen.

Mary ignores her and keeps on going.

"Well, what am I supposed to do now?" Helen says to herself. She looks at the pint of Guinness, looks around to see if anybody is watching, and drinks the pint of Guinness. Scar Face notices this.

"Well Jack, do ya see that one, wasn't it her that didn't want her friend to drink a pint of stout, now look at who's drinking the stout herself, ha, isn't that a good one?"

"Sure isn't that women for ya, they say one thing and do the opposite," replies Jack. He puts the £100 he got from the two lads into his pocket.

Máirtín is walking down the street with his brother Johnny. It's dark and wet, and there are a few couples heading into the pictures across the road to watch a late movie. The two lads go into their white Hi Ace van. Mary follows Máirtín, and she calls him.

"Máirtín."

He turns around and sees Mary.

"Oh, it's that Nurse from the hospital, I wonder what she wants?" he says.

"How the hell do I know Máirtín, don't ask me, 'tis you she's calling, maybe you forgot your tablets or something," says Johnny.

They both laugh.

They are just about to start the van, when Mary comes to the window.

"Máirtín, I'm Mary."

"Mary who?"

"Mary Buckley. You know from Ballycrackn, remember?" she says nervously.

"Oh God damn it in hell, I don't believe it. Mary Buckley, the pig's daughter, what in the hell do you want?"

He starts his van to drive away.

"Máirtín wait, I want to talk to you for one minute that's all, please wait."

"Me, you want to talk to me, about what?"

He gets annoyed; after all it was her father that cleared his family from Ballycrackn.

"Máirtín, I need to talk to you alone, look I'm getting wet, will you please?" cries Mary.

Johnny looks at Máirtín.

"Well, it's up to you Boss. It's you she wants to talk to, not me."

Máirtín pauses for a moment.

"Ok so Johnny, but, will you stay with the motor, there is a lot of valuable goods inside, I will be back in a while," he says.

He turns off the engine and gets out of the van.

"Alright, give her one for me."

He puts up his right hand to Máirtín.

"Go way you Johnny, look, just take care of the van till I get back."

He gets out of the van to join Mary. They both walk down the street, there is a canopy left open outside Kelly's V G. Supermarket. They both stand under it for shelter from the rain.

Tim And Sheila Gives Mary A Surprise Visit

They have decided to go on a surprise visit to Mary. They are driving along the road in the Garda Squad car, just approaching the Town.

"I can't believe I let you talk me into this."

Tim is annoyed. He didn't want to travel to Ballinasloe, also his car has broken down along the way.

"Look Daddy, it's not my fault that the car broke down, anyways it's a heap of shit."

"Sheila for feck sake, will you mind your language, sorry I lost you there, what did you say was a heap of shit?" he asks.

"Your old car of course, look watch your own mouth, it's filthy sometimes," Sheila says.

Tim puts his eyes up to heaven with a sigh.

"Anyways, I'm glad the young Officer was able to pick up our car before thugs got their hands on it," Tim says.

"Who'd bother with it anyways, sure its not worth stealing."

They both smile at each other.

"Never mind, Mary will get a heck of a surprise when she sees us."

"I don't know Sheila sure she hasn't talked to me for months," says Tim.

He swerves to avoid a black cat that runs across the road.

"Oh God, will ya watch where you are driving, do you want to kill us both, that's a good sign having a black cat run across the road in front of us."

"I suppose," replies Tim.

They drive into the town. Tim looks unsettled. He's not sure what kind of reception he might get from his daughter Mary.

"Look Daddy you'll be all right, just keep your mouth shut, and you'll be fine, she can be hot headed as well you know, like father like daughter I suppose. The only difference between you and her is she is forgiving."

"God all mighty Sheila, will you stop calling me Daddy, anybody would think I'm your bloody father, I hate that," he says getting annoyed with Sheila, he bangs the steering wheel with the palm of his hand.

Mary and Máirtín decide to go for a walk when the rain subsides. They walk up the main street till they come to the church. Sitting on a wall outside the church under a street light, they talk about years gone by.

"You know something Máirtín, I never thought I'd see you again after all these years gone by."

"Me the same I suppose, Mary will ya call me Dagger, it's better than Máirtín, I hate that name sure I do."

"Why's that, I think Máirtín is a wonderful name."

She begins to blush.

"Did you think about me at all this last couple of years," she asks eagerly.

"Ah, I did alright, I thought about you a lot. Look Mary what do you want of me?"

"I don't know. I just wanted to see you again I suppose."

"It will do no good Mary, I can't be friends with you people, the settled people don't like travellers at all. They say travellers are not good enough, that's what they say."

"I don't care what they say, Máirtín."

She looks at him, she is getting emotional.

"Are you married?"

"Why do you want to know that for?"

"I was just wondering," she says.

"I was married one time for five years to Julia, she was the most beautiful woman in the land."

His eyes begin to fill up with tears.

"And are ye not still together?"

"No." He looks away, putting his head down.

"I'm sorry, I thought when you people get married you stayed married no matter what."

"Mary, I don't want to talk about it, anyways it's none of your business. I have to be off now, goodbye," he's annoyed, and upset. He hops off the wall to walk away.

Mary gets distressed.

"Wait Máirtín, I'm sorry I didn't mean to upset you like that!" she cries, walking down the street after him.

Mary's mother and father are driving through the town. They admire the parks, they pass a few Hi Ace vans, including Máirtín Dagger's with a few travellers having a chat with Johnny.

"Will you look at that shower, they are still here hanging around, I thought the horse fair was over a few days ago. What in the hell are they still hanging around here for?"

"Never mind them lads Tim, watch where you're going, do you want to crash," says Sheila.

"Hey, isn't that our Mary up ahead across the road," says Tim.

As he drives past the church, he notices Mary up ahead.

"Where is she?"

"There Sheila, look, in front of you, talking to some young lad."

"You're right it is her all right, stop the car."

Sheila lets the window down and calls out.

"Mary, yahoo, hello!"

"Oh shit, it's my parents, what in the hell are they doing here?"

She sees her mother and father across the road in the Police squad car.

"Oh shit if that bastard catches me talking to you, look I have to go, bye, see ya."

"Máirtín, never mind him he doesn't know who you are."

He walks away and heads down the street towards his Hi Ace van.

Mary goes across the road to talk to her parents.

"Dad, Mam, what are you doing here?" she asks anxiously.

"Your Daddy and I thought we would surprise you."

Tim is annoyed at Sheila for calling him Daddy.

"You did that all right." Mary replies.

She puts her hand to her heart, where her heart is pounding with fear of her father seeing her with Máirtín Dagger.

"Who was that sweet looking lad you were talking to?"

"Just somebody I work with, Mam."

"He looks like a tinker, is he one of them lads again, is he?"

"No Daddy he's not one of them lads again, will you shut up now?" Sheila says.

"Look woman, will you stop calling me Daddy I said, I'm sick of it! Daddy, you make out I'm your father or something the way you keep calling me Daddy. Stop it now for once and for all."

"Will you two stop arguing, anyways why are ye driving this car?"

"The Cortina is in the garage for a service."

"Don't mind him Mary, it's not, it broke down again, and one of your Daddy's colleagues was kind enough to give us this car."

Tim gives Sheila a sour look.

"It's cold out here, lets go into O'Reilly's for a drink, Helen Conway is waiting for me there, if she is not gone at this stage."

Dagger is driving along the road heading home, in his white Hi Ace, his brother Johnny is with him. It's very dark and wet, not a star can be seen in the sky. They are listening to Joe Dolan on the stereo — "The House with the White Washed Gable." Máirtín is in a world of his own.

"Feck me Dagger what's wrong with ya, you didn't say nothing since you came back from talking to that one. Anyway who was she, that one that wanted to talk to ya?"

"You wouldn't believe me now Johnny, if I told ya who she was now would ya?"

"I know she's the Nurse from the hospital. I seen her there when you were banged up."

"You wouldn't believe who she is now Johnny, would ya. Remember Mary Buckley, the pig's daughter in Ballycrackn?"

"By feck, well you're the dirty auld dog, bloody hell, she made a fine thing, ha, well I be dog gone," says Johnny with a yahoo.

He plays the drums on the dash board with his hands.

"Ara, she's all right," replies Dagger.

He drives his van back to the campsite with a smile in his face.

"Are you glad to see her?"

"I think so Johnny, I think so," Dagger replies joyously.

He taps the steering wheel with his fingers to the music as he drives.

Back At Jack O'Reilly's Pub

Mary and her parents come into the bar. Helen is on her own waiting for Mary to arrive. She is highly intoxicated; not alone has she drank her own alcohol, she has drank Mary's pint of Stout as well. Scar Face is looking at her with pity.

"You know something Jack, I hate to see a woman in that state," Scar Face says.

"Well I wouldn't blame you, sure wasn't it a drunken woman that did that to your face?" replies Jack.

With a suspicious look on his face, while he washes the pint glasses in the sink.

"Say no more now, Jack, say no more."

Scar Face gets embarrassed with that statement from Jack, rubbing the scar on his face with his right hand. A few other customers look at Scar Face and snub him.

Mary and her parents arrive into the pub. Mary goes straight over to Helen where she is still sitting in the nook.

"Sorry Helen for being so late, I got held up. I know you we're in good hands with Jack up there."

Mary gives a pungent look at Scar Face, as he looks at Helen in disgust.

"Remember my mum and dad?"

"I haven't seen ye two in this long time, how are ye, and how's Timmy, I heard Tim you got promoted, what are you now, Sergeant I believe," says Helen, with a drunken stammer. Tim is embarrassed, gives weird looks at Helen as they take a seat.

"Anyway, we are all proud of Daddy aren't we, with his promotion and all," Sheila says. looking at Mary proudly and tapping Tim on the shoulder.

"Will you stop calling me Daddy, do you hear that woman, do you know something that woman has never grown up at all!" says Tim, getting annoyed with Sheila.

"Any—any-way Mary, di- did you catch up with your friend Máirtín?" Helen stammers her words. Tim and Sheila look at each other in wonder. Where did they hear that name before?

"Where have I heard somebody by that name before? Máirtín?" says Tim. He sits and wonders.

"Máirtín, gee what a nice name, huu, Máirtín," Sheila thinks.

"Do you know something I like that name, Mary and Máirtín what do you think Tim?" Mary is getting embarrassed and starts to blush.

"Will you shut up the lot of ye, you're embarrassing me, oh my God Mum, you're such a child sometimes I can't believe you."

"Who is this Máirtín fella, was that him we seen you with a while ago?"

"No, Dad it was not, anyways you wouldn't be interested. Now can we change the subject please, and talk about something else," says Mary, with a sigh of relief.

"Ary, I'm sitting here long enough I think I will have a pint."

Tim gets up off his seat and goes towards the bar to call a drink.

"A stiff whiskey for me while you are up there Daddy," says Sheila.

"And me too Daddy," says Mary.

Tim looks back at Sheila and shakes his head with annoyance because she called him Daddy again. Sheila smiles and turns her head away.

"Well Helen how are you love, I haven't seen you in ages, how are you at all?"

"I'm fine Sheila, and don't mind me, I don't need any more drink I'll soon be off now."

"I'm sorry Helen, I didn't think you wanted a drink, you have a full one in front of you," says Mary.

Mary goes up to her father to order a drink for Helen. Sheila looks at Helen, as if Helen didn't have enough drink taken all ready.

Helen finishes off the drink she had in her glass.

Tim returns with the drinks; they all sit and chat for a while.

Uncle Martin Has Passed Over

Martin Ward dies at the age of sixty six, in his bed during the night while Bridie sleeps beside him. He dies from a heart attack, he hasn't been well for some time now. He helped Bridie raise the children when her husband died. When she wakes up she finds him dead.

"Martin wake up, oh what am I going to do now?" she cries.

There is no response from Martin.

"Wake up Martin will ya please, oh my God all mighty somebody help me!"

She begins to panic checking his pulse, he has no pulse and is cold as ice, she gets a terrible shock when Martin is dead.

"Oh God and his blessed mother look down upon us."

She runs out from her trailer to call Máirtín and the rest of her family, and blesses herself at the same time. All of her family come out of their trailers dressed in their night gowns and pyjamas.

"Mother what's up with ya?" yells Máirtín.

"It's your Uncle Martin. He has passed over, oh my God and his blessed mother what am I going to do?"

She blesses herself again.

The whole family are devastated, especially Johnny the Singer. He was the closest to Uncle Martin. He looked up to him.

Bridie, Willie, Máirtín, Fay, her two children and Katie kneel around Uncle Martin's death bed to pray. Johnny the Singer sings a Sean-nós song and cries.

Two days later Martin Ward's coffin is taken to the local cemetery for burial. Some of his nieces and nephews have been living in London for the past couple of years. They are home for the funeral. It's the biggest funeral the town has ever seen.

Travellers come from all over Ireland and England, including Northern Ireland. All the shops, pubs, hotels close down in the town for two days in case of trouble, while the funeral is taking place.

There is no trouble in the town during the funeral. Martin is laid to rest in a cemetery two miles outside the town.

Chapter Five

Christmas 1978

It's two weeks before Christmas, Dagger and his brothers Willie and Johnny are stealing Christmas trees from a local forest. It's the dead hours of the morning, the night is still, they are cutting the trees with a handsaw and loading them into their white Hi Ace van. It is a bright frosty winter's night with a bright moon. Foxes can be heard from a distance howling. There are sounds of hooting owls heard high up in the trees while the three lads cut down the Christmas trees.

"How many trees do ya think we need Dagger?" Willie shouts.

"Will ya keep your big mouth shut, do you want the whole place to hear us," says Johnny, cutting down a tree with a hand saw.

"We need about fifty or more, now will ye two keep your big mouths shut and hurry up!" replies Dagger, as he pulls a Christmas tree behind him to take it to the van.

"Ok Man don't shit on yourself," says Willie.

"I tell ye one thing lads if we get caught by the Police we will do six months for this," says Dagger.

"Well then lets be quiet so. I see over there at that farm house there is a light after coming on, lads can ye see it?"

"Well Willie, lets load up and we will be getting out of here fast before somebody hears us," says Dagger.

They load up the van with Christmas trees. They hear a gunshot away in the distance.

"What in the hell is that," says Willie.

He ducks down to avoid being shot.

"Don't mind that," says Dagger.

"That's the local farmers around here, they do be hunting for foxes this time of night you know."

He puts the last tree into the back of the van, fastening the back doors with baling twine to make it secure, as the Christmas trees are too long to fit full into the van. They are sticking out through the back doors and are clearly visible. Dagger is conscious of this.

"Dagger how do you know it's farmers that's doing the shooting?" asks Willie.

"Lads I've been staking this place out for the last few months, I know everything that's going on around here," he says.

"If they catch us they will shoot us and that's one thing for sure," Willie says apprehensively. He gets into the van.

"Right lads lets get out of here before we are spotted," says Dagger.

The three lads get into the van and drive off.

Gardai Give Chase To Van Load Of Stolen Christmas Trees

Garda Officers are on night duty at the Station, it's early hours and they are having a well earned tea break. Garda Mick Walsh, Garda Anthony Finell and Sergeant Ricky Molloy are discussing the horse fair.

"Do you know something men, didn't Martin Ward's funeral go off very well?"

"There is one thing about the travellers, Sarge, they respect the dead. I was watching the way they walking behind the horse drawn wagon that carried the coffin, not a sound, just praying they were, and I will say this about Martin Ward, he was one hell of a respectable man sure he was," says Garda Anthony.

"He was that all right," replies Sergeant Ricky.

"I will tell you one thing is for sure, I'm glad that horse fair is only once a year," says Garda Mick.

"You had a mighty fine wage packet after that week Mick, and that's one thing for certain."

"Well, Sarge I suppose you're right."

"You know something lads, I can't believe this, you know I worked sixty five hours that week, that's almost double the hours I normally work," says Garda Anthony, totting up his work hours on his note pad with his two feet up on a table.

"You mean that's treble the hours you normally work, as far as I'm concerned Anthony, you only work twenty five hours a week, sure you're never here, anyway your always talking about wages; is that all you are concerned about, how much wages you made during the Horse Fair? That's two months ago now, the festive season is coming up, I want all the Officers I have, on duty; mark my words, all the travellers will be back on the streets in full force again this year," says Sergeant Ricky. He sits across from Anthony reading the newspaper and drinking a mug of tea.

"Well now Sarge for your information I spent fourteen hours a day on duty during the Horse Fair in case you haven't noticed," says Anthony.

Ricky and Mick look at each other and raised their eyes up to heaven.

"Well, I hope that lot will behave themselves and not cause trouble like they did at the horse fair," replies Mick.

The phone rings. Tina Mulryan is on the line in distress, her car is broken down. She is left stranded on a lonely country road in the middle of nowhere. Sergeant Ricky Molloy answers the phone.

"Hallo, An Garda Síochána."

"Yes, yes."

"Slow down Miss, whereabouts are you located?"

"Ok, fine."

"Right, right Miss, now go back to your car and stay there, I will send one of our Officers around to you straight away."

He writes Tina's whereabouts on a sheet of paper.

"Somebody in trouble Sarge," asks Mick.

"Tina Mulryan, her car is broken down. Just left at Griffins Cross."

He hands the sheet of paper to Anthony.

"Now off with you, she is a half a mile on the far side of the telephone box, just past Griffins Cross, she will stay in her car till you get there, now off with you and don't be long."

"Sarge, I have to finish this," he says, referring to his last months hours.

"Listen up Anthony, remember this is an Police station not an accountancy agency, I'll tell you what I will do, the both of you can go while I hold the fort, now how's that."

"Well, Sarge I suppose we have no choice in the matter," replies Anthony, putting his note pad away and getting up off his chair as he finishes his mug of tea.

"Right Mick, lets be off."

Anthony and Mick leave the Station to pick up Tina Mulryan. They drive through Griffins Cross to find Tina sitting in her car smoking a cigarette. They are on their way back to the Police Station, Tina in the back seat. She is under the influence of alcohol, her makeup is messed up, she is not a pretty sight.

Anthony notices a white Hi Ace van full to the brim with Christmas trees coming towards them.

"Will you look at that, well I wonder where do that lot think they are going this hour of the morning," says Anthony, referring to the Ward brothers with the van load of Christmas trees, which are sticking out the back door of the van and up on the roof rack.

Dagger is driving the Hi Ace, he spots the Police coming towards them.

"Oh shit lads, look at this, where in the hell did they come out of?"

He swerves to avoid hitting the squad car. The squad car swerves to avoid hitting the van and stops when the van speeds past them.

"Oh shit I'm dead," screams Tina, hitting her head off the window.

Máirtín drives faster, so he can go out of sight of the Police car.

"Well, could you be up to them lads, well for God sake, I wonder where did they get them trees this time from, I hope it wasn't from Paddy Finnegan. I tell ya something for nothing Mick, they won't get off as handy this year as last year."

"Well, wasn't it old Paddy Finnegan that they got the trees off last year, didn't he say he sold the trees to them, and I know well they bribed him. Sure didn't Jack O'Reilly say down in the pub that poor old Paddy was terrified of them lads, well, that won't happen this year and

I will make sure of that," says Anthony.

They turn the squad car around to give chase to the lads.

Willie looks back to see can he see the squad car. He tells Dagger that the Police car might be doing a U-turn in the middle of the road to give them chase. Dagger, driving at high speed to get away from the Police, switches off the lights so they can't be seen.

"Do you know something boys if we are caught this time we're damned, we won't get off as light this year, Paddy Finnegan won't take a bribe this year I'd say," says Dagger, driving down a narrow lane to a disused farm house.

The Guards have turned their car around; they are driving along the road but there is no sign of the white Hi Ace van to be seen.

"Where in the name of hell did they disappear to, not a sign of them. Turn off the lights Anthony to see can we spot their lights."

Anthony turns off the lights. They both look out for the lights of the van.

"Could you beat that Mick; where in the hell did they go, ha, I'll stop the car so we might hear the noise of the van."

Stopping the squad car Anthony and Mick get out of the car to see can they hear the noise of the van's engine.

"Nothing, not a budge, lets go back, we just passed a laneway a half mile back. lets check it out," says Anthony.

They turn the car around and drive down the narrow lane.

"Sorry to bother you now Garda, shouldn't you be leaving me home first? I don't think this is an appropriate time for me to be sitting in the back seat of a Police car while it's involved in a high speed pursuit."

"Don't worry Tina, you will be fine, there is nothing to be worried about," replies Anthony.

Tina sits in a huff with her arms folded. They drive up the lane till they come to Pa Tyler's old farm house. Pa is in an old folks' home for the past four years.

"I think Anthony, they might be hiding out here, you couldn't be up to those lads, they had to go somewhere they just didn't disappear, there is no way they stayed on the main road, they have to be here somewhere," says Mick.

The boys are hiding the Hi Ace van behind a shed behind Pa Taylor's old farm house.

"Hi Dagger, I wonder have we lost them?"

"Shee, Willie, I hear something, look there is lights coming."

"Oh fuck, Dagger what will we do?"

"Look Johnny I'm trying to think."

The Guards drive around to the back of Pa Taylor's farm house. They notice the shed. They get out of the car and shine their torches into the shed, there is nothing there, only Paddy Finnegan's Massy Ferguson tractor he stores in there during the winter months.

Tina gets frightened left in the car on her own.

"Sorry to bother you now Garda but are you going to leave me here alone, it's not safe out here you know, anybody could be hanging around out here," says Tina.

She is peeping out the window into the dark of the night.

"Shee be quiet you, we're not going far," replies Mick.

The two Officers shine their torches into the shed and surrounding areas, there is no sign of the travellers or their van.

"Mick look over here, there is fresh tyre tracks, I'd say we are on to them now the tracks are going behind the shed. Come with me!"

They shine their torches at the tyre tracks and follow them around to the back of the shed. In the meantime, the three lads are hiding in the bushes and notice the two Officers coming to the back of the shed.

"Shee now lads, here they come, don't make a sound, not even a fart," says Dagger.

Willie finds that statement funny and starts to snigger.

"Shee, for fuck sake Willie shut up will ya!"

Dagger gets annoyed with Willie and raises his hand to him.

The two Officers go around the back of the shed and notice the Hi Ace van full of Christmas trees, but no sign of the three boys. Tina is frightened in the Squad Car on her own, so she gets out and goes around the back of the shed to where the two Police Officers are. She startles the two Officers as she approaches them.

"Who's there?" asks Mick.

He gets a fright when he notices a figure in the dark coming towards him.

"Don't shoot, it's only me!"

Tina gets startled when she notices Garda Mick move in the dark.

"Shit, for God sake Tina, I thought I told you to stay with the car, what brings you back here it's not safe here."

"Woops, I'm sorry did I startle you? But it's not safe in the car either," Tina says, breaking a strap on her high heel shoe as she walks.

"Oh my God look what you made me do now," she yells.

She takes off her broken shoe as she staggers her way back to the Squad Car. The three lads are still hiding in the bushes.

"Shit, they have found the van," says Dagger. "Damn it what will we do now, shit, that's it, we're finished now," he adds.

Garda Anthony and Garda Mick are at the van; they open the door to notice it's occupants have absconded.

"I wonder where they disappeared to, they couldn't have gone far," says Garda Mick, shining his torch around the surrounding areas. He walks over to the bushes where the three travellers are hiding. Johnny spots Garda Mick walking towards where they are hiding.

"Shee, be quiet now lads, here comes one of them, not a sound lads."

Garda Mick approaches the bushes shining his torch into the bushes but doesn't see anybody.

"There's nobody here, they must have absconded across the fields, anyway, lets take this van back to headquarters."

"Look Mick, they're not as smart as they think they are, look they left the keys in the ignition, and their fags behind," says Anthony

"Right it's getting late, I'll drive back the van Mick while you take Tina home, right?"

Dagger overhears Anthony talk about the keys of the van.

"Shit, I forget to take the keys out of the ignition, frig-it, they will take the van now, I don't believe this!"

He accidentally makes a noise.

"Shee?"

Mick hears the noise.

"What's that, did you hear that Anthony?"

They both listen for a moment.

"I didn't hear nothing," replies Tina.

"For the love of God Tina; I thought I told you to go back to the car," Mick says.

"I'm too scared, come on, leave me home," she replies.

"It was probably a fox or something Mick, never mind, come on, we have enough time spent here, lets be off," says Anthony.

They take the van and car and drive off. The three lads come out of the bushes surprised they weren't caught by the two Officers.

"By hell lads that was close," says Johnny, with a sigh of relief.

"Come on boys, lets go home," says Dagger.

The three lads go into the shed and steal a small Massy Ferguson tractor belonging to Paddy Finnegan to take them home.

Bridie Worries About Her Boys

It's five thirty am and Bridie wakes up again. She checks to see is Máirtín's van home. She goes outside and goes over to Willie's trailer to see is he home, knocking at the door. Margaret, who is pregnant and is expecting their fourth child in a couple of months, wakes up, her children also wake up. She notices the time and her husband isn't home. She opens to the door.

"What's wrong Bridie, what's up?"

"Margaret, Máirtín isn't in his trailer, is himself home?"

"No Bridie, there isn't any sign of him. Maybe the van broke down again, sure anyway it takes hours to cut down a van load of trees, don't worry they will be fine."

"Oh I don't know Margaret, I woke up earlier and didn't see Máirtín's van and he wasn't in his bed either, I wonder Margaret, where are they?"

She looks very worried.

"Well Bridie, it's not the first time they didn't come home, never ya mind. You must be famished, come on in and I'll make a nice cup of tea for ya."

"Oh thank ya Margaret, and God love you, with you carrying your fourth child."

They both go inside where they have a good strong mug of tea. Bridie admires how well Margaret has the trailer decorated for Christmas.

"Are you looking forward to Christmas Bridie?"

"Not really, till be a sad Christmas without Martin, he always gave us a good time for the holy season sure he did."

She is sad and lonely and puts her head down.

The three lads are on their way home with the Massy Ferguson. Willie is driving, Johnny is sitting on the mud guard singing a rebel song. Dagger is standing behind Willie, they are freezing with the cold.

"Hi, Willie have we far more to go, I am freezing."

"Not far now Johnny, just hold on."

He pulls back on the throttle.

"Anyway what kind of question is that, don't you live around here just as much as we do, now shut your mouth and keep singing."

"Sure how can he do that Willie, I thought he would have to open his mouth to sing?" laughs Dagger.

The three lads have a good laugh as they drive along the road.

"Willie, I'd say Margaret will soon give ya your fourth child I'd say. What do you think Dagger," Johnny gives a wink to Dagger.

"You know, I miss poor Uncle Martin, he'd love this now lads wouldn't he?"

"I know Johnny, I was just thinking of him, I tell ya one thing for certain he took care of us well when the auld man died," says Dagger, with grief in his voice.

Gardai Call To Travellers Halting Site

The next day at the Police Station, it's three pm. It's a bright, frosty, still December's day with Christmas approaching. Sergeant Ricky is going through the books, Garda Anthony and Garda Mick come in looking very tired after being out all night.

"Good afternoon men, I'm sorry I wasn't here when you got back last night or should I say the early hours of the morning. I see here you certainly had a busy night, that's a fine load of Christmas trees you have out the back there, my heck you are starting Christmas early this year. Sure it's not for two weeks yet," says Sergeant Ricky, joking with the two Officers. He goes to the window to look outside at the van load of Christmas trees.

"Well Sarge, we were very busy, as a matter of fact we caught the Ward brothers in the act after we picked up Tina Mulryan. We followed the van and found it on Pa Tyler's derelict farm. By the time we got there, they absconded, anyways we have the evidence, it won't be long till we have the culprits in custody also," Garda Anthony says.

"Very good men, now you both might go round to the travellers' halting site and see are they missing a van and some Christmas trees, you be careful over there with that lot, we might as well eat the bun while it is still hot."

The two Officers look at Sergeant Ricky, they aren't too impressed having to visit the travellers' Halting site, but they have no choice. They head off in the Squad car to the travellers site.

When they get there they go to Bridie's trailer. They knock at the door, Bridie comes out.

"Oh ya, what do you lot want?" she says, with an unpleasant reception for the two Guards.

"Good afternoon Mam, we just want to know what your lads were up to last night," asks Mick.

"Nothing, I swear to the almighty God, my boys never left here all night long, why what's up, has something happened?"

Inside the caravan the lads are having a good laugh at the two Officers.

"Well, we would like to talk to the boys anyways, are they home?" asks Garda Anthony.

Dagger and Johnny come to the door Johnny is singing a rebel song again. "The Men Behind The Wire".

"What brings you around here?"

"Look Máirtín, we are just doing our duty, where about were you two lads last night?" asks Anthony.

"We were here all night Boss, now just get that straight and whatever trouble or anything else that has gone on in the town last night, leave us out of it, 'tis nothing to do with us, anyway what have we supposed to have done Boss?" says Dagger.

"Don't talk to me like that young man, a white Hi Ace has been involved in a serious crime last night, that we now have in our custody, and we know the white Hi Ace van belongs to you Máirtín Ward," says Garda Anthony.

"Now Boss, call me Dagger. My name is Dagger Ward to you Sir."

"Well Dagger," says Garda Mick, as he looks at his colleague Anthony.

"Dagger Ward we know it's your Hi Ace."

"Hold on one minute Sir, I don't know anything about that kind of motor," he says, getting annoyed with the Guards.

"I'm sorry Dagger, we know well it's your van, we noticed you driving it at the horse fair."

"Ah, ye seen me driving it all right, I only borrowed the van from my cousin in Mullingar, that doesn't say it's the van you have Boss," says Dagger.

"What's your cousin's name?" asks Mick.

He takes out his note pad to takes notes.

"Willie Ward," replies Dagger.

"What's his address?"

He starts to write on the pad.

"On the side of the road Boss, near Mullingar."

"Where in Mullingar would that be now?" asks Mick, while Johnny is still singing, and Willie is sussing out the two Gardai.

"Well, I tell you now, if ye drive there, you can't miss the trailers on the side of the road Sir, just outside Mullingar town on the Athlone road."

"Does that lad ever stop singing?" asks Mick, getting agitated with Johnny's singing.

"Johnny, shut up will ya, you are annoying the nice Garda."

"Right Dagger, sorry Sir," says Johnny.

"Thank you, now, what was your cousin's van doing in Ballinasloe do you know?" asks Anthony.

"We don't know nothing."

"And what's your name young man?" asks Garda Mick.

"Willie."

"Willie who?"

He starts to write in his note pad.

"Willie Ward, Sir."

"Are you the Willie Ward that owns the van in question?"

"No, that's my cousin Willie in Mullingar, Boss."

"All right, whichever Willie Ward owned the white Hi Ace van, it's not registered and it has no tax or insurance, and as you know quite well that's a serious offence in this country," replies Garda Mick.

"The van goes better without them Sir," says Johnny.

"Now what van would that be young man?" asks Garda Anthony.

"Any van, anyway, off with ye and leave us alone, we have nothing to do with whatever happened last night," says Dagger getting annoyed.

"Right; we'll be off but from now we will be keeping a close eye on you lot, isn't that right?" Mick says.

As he looks at Garda Anthony, they start to leave the halting site.

"Good riddance to you Sir and don't come around here again if you know what's good for ya, now piss off the both of you, ye heard me now," says Dagger

The two Officers go into the car and leave.

"Well Dagger, what do you think?"

"Ara, feck them Willie, I don't care as long as they stay away from here, come on boys and help me put a saddle on this new mare I bought last week."

Chapter Six

Máirtín Having A Nightmare

Máirtín's is in bed having a bad dream about his wife Julie and two children, Frances aged two and Catherine aged four and a half. He is perspiring heavily. They are in their trailer watching Frank Hall on the Television. Catherine is hungry.

"Mam, can I have a slice of bread?"

"Of course you can lovine, help yourself, you know where the bread is."

Julie is giving young Francis his nightly feed, Máirtín is admiring his wife and children. He is proud of them.

"Do you know something Julie, she is the spitting image of her grandmother."

"What are you saying Máirtín she doesn't look anything like my mother."

They both admire their daughter Catherine.

"I'm not talking about your mother, I'm talking about Bridie."

"May God forgive ya, Catherine looks nothing like Bridie, she is cut out of meself, what's on ya."

She picks up a pillow and throws it across at Máirtín, they have a laugh.

"Look Julie, I think I will go down to McBride's for a packet of fags, can I get ya anything?"

"Do so and get me something for this rotten flu I have, and something for a cup of tea before we hit blanket street, anyway you should be giving up them fags, look what they did to Fay's husband."

"Anyways Julie, twasn't the fags that killed Fay's husband and you know that bloody well fine," says Dagger.

"What's that supposed to mean?"

"Look, I'm off, I'll tell ya when I come back."

He leaves to go to the shop.

His daughter Catherine climbs up on a chair to fetch a slice of bread from the cupboard. She finds a box of matches, turns on the gas cooker and tries to light the gas.

Arriving at McBride's V G food store Máirtín goes into the shop. Dennis McBride is behind the counter.

"Well Mr Ward, what can I do for you?"

"I tell ya now Dennis what I'm after. I'll have a packet of them nice biscuits you have there." pointing at the chocolate gold grain.

"And twenty major, oh ya, something for Julie's flu as well please."

"What way is she complaining?"

"Complaining Dennis, I say this to ya now, she never stops complaining, and if she is not doing that, she is nagging!"

Mrs McBride comes out from the back room. She overhears the conversation between the two men.

"I tell you something Mr Ward, you have a good woman there, you should be proud of her. You will go a long way before you will find a woman like Julie, sure you will and that's one thing for certain."

"I suppose you're right Mrs" he says. He gloats, with a pleasant smile.

Back at the trailer, Catherine is trying to light the matches, so she can light the gas. Julie is too busy watching the Television and doesn't notice Catherine trying to light the gas cooker. She cannot smell the gas either, because of her blocked nose. Catherine cracks the match, she blows up the trailer to pieces.

Máirtín drives into the site; he sees the fire, he goes hysterical.

He calls out for his wife and children.

"Julie, Oh my God, Julie, Francis, Catherine, what in the name of God has happened?"

He gets out of his van, and runs towards the trailer. All the other travellers at the site come running out of their trailers to see what happened. They watch the trailer go up in smoke.

Máirtín runs towards his trailer to save his family. His mother and Johnny go to stop him, everybody is hysterical, there is nothing they can do.

He falls to the ground, his mother consoles him by putting her arms around him.

"Oh God how has this happened to me?" he screams.

He wakes up, sits up in his bed covered in a cold sweat, holding his head.

Next day, Sergeant Ricky Molloy at the Station, taking care of some paper work he has to catch up on. He hears the phone ringing and picks it up.

"Hello Ricky, this is Tim Buckley."

"Well hello Tim; I haven't heard from you for a long while, how are you?"

"Sorry about that Ricky, I often meant to call and see you, do you know I was down your way a few weeks ago and I meant to call into see you?"

"I heard that Tim all right, that you were in town, was it business or pleasure?"

"Mary, my daughter, is working as a Nurse in the hospital there. You know Ricky you have to take care of family business," says Tim.

"I never knew she was working in the hospital, how long is she working there Tim."

"A few months. Look, that's why I am ringing you, it's about Mary. You might keep an eye on her, I want to know what kind of company she is keeping. I'm a little bit concerned about her you know, with her being in a strange town."

"Leave it to me Tim, I'll be going to the hospital to visit a neighbour, Pa Tyler, during the week. He is in the old folks home there for the past few years. I'll watch out for her, you can rest assured there Tim."

"Thanks Ricky, we must have a pint one of these days."

"By the way Tim congrats, I believe it's Sergeant Timothy Buckley now."

"Indeed Ricky, anyway thanks and I will be talking to you." He hangs up the phone.

A few days later, Máirtín Dagger is still upset over the dream he had about his wife and children, he feels alone in the world with no partner in his life. He is thinking alot about Mary and how they both have feelings towards each other, he decides to go to the hospital to visit her. When he gets there he asks the Receptionist, Celine, if he could see Mary Buckley, he admires the twelve foot Christmas tree that's set up in the corner of the reception room.

"Wait till I see, who will I say is looking for her?" asks Celine.

"Just a friend," he replies nervously, he thinks that the staff at the hospital might judge him because he is a traveller.

"Would Nurse Buckley come to reception please?"

She calls Mary on the intercom.

"You were in here a few weeks ago yourself weren't you?" asks Celine.

"I was so, I was in a bit of a brawl and I got a few punches, isn't it well now you remember me ha," says Máirtín.

Mary arrives at reception.

"Ah, here's Mary now," says Celine.

"Hello there, what brings you here, are you sick or something?"

"No Mary."

His eyes fill up when he sees her.

"Can we talk somewhere?" he says.

"Ok, I'm on a break anyways. We will have a coffee in the staff canteen," says Mary.

They both go to the canteen. Celine gives them a funny look.

"Well, everybody to their own." Celine says, to herself.

"Look Mary, I don't know, can I go in there, the people that work there might not like to see a traveller in there."

"Never mind them Máirtín, you're with me."

He takes a seat while Mary gets two coffees. He is nervous sitting on his own, the others in the canteen are giving him funny looks. When Mary joins him he says.

"Mary, I feel awful in here."

He looks around at the others staring at him.

"Will you just relax, you'll be all right, anyways what's up with ya?"

"I don't know, I been thinking a lot about things lately," he says.

"What kind of things?"

"I don't know, things about the past I suppose, you know when we were youngsters and meeting you the other day started me thinking about you again. I'm a long time on my own Mary."

"I know Máirtín, you told me that, five years is a long time to be alone."

"Ya, 'tis, five years Mary, but I don't want to be with anybody else; there was only one woman for me, Julie, she was my Mrs, I can't have anyone else you know, it's not right."

"Is there something wrong Máirtín? Tell me what's bothering you, what's on your mind?"

"Mary, I don't know what's wrong with me, I think I'm going crazy ever since Julie and the children died, my life has never been the same."

"I'm sorry Máirtín." She puts her hand on his hand, he pulls away.

"I'm so angry and sick of this life, why did God let this happen to me and my family?" he says.

He rubs his face with frustration.

"What happened, what did happen to your family, just tell me Máirtín, I want to know."

"I can't Mary, it hurts too much to talk about it," he says.

"I'm listening just let it out," says Mary.

He sits with his head down for a moment.

"There were an explosion in the trailer, and Julie and the children died. They didn't have a chance, they were blown to pieces."

"How did the explosion happen, was it a bomb or something?"

"No Mary, it was gas that caused the explosion, forensic examined the whole place and the conclusion was that Catherine my little girl was playing with matches, the gas must have been turned on or something at the time, the three of them didn't have a chance, I was at the shop and when I came back they were blown to pieces," he cries.

"Oh my God, I'm so sorry, you must be going through hell, oh Máirtín I had no idea." Her eyes fill up.

"Mary, I think about you now all the time, you were the first person that was ever kind to me, I don't mean that I want you to be my wife or anything like that, it's nothing like that, I just need to talk to someone, and I think a lot of you." Máirtín says.

"I'm listening go ahead, let it out," says Mary.

"I went to the shop for fags, and when I came back the trailer was in flames. Julie died in my arms, Johnny and Willie and a few of the others pulled her out, they couldn't find the children, they were gone, burnt in the blaze. Julie died in my arms, Mary, she was black as smoke, all her body was burnt." he starts to cry.

"Oh Máirtín, I'm so sorry, I heard about that. I read it in the paper you know, I'm so sorry it was you," says Mary.

"It was on the news as well," he says.

"That's right and that was your family, I had no idea," Mary cries.

"The brigade and the cops arrived and the priest, it was the one of the worst things I ever had happen to me or my family," he cries.

"What could be worse than that?" asks Mary.

"A few days later, we destroyed everything that belonged to Julie and the children, it's our tradition you know, the travellers are doing that all their lives, we burn everything; clothes, furniture, jewellery, everything. I don't know where I go from here. I can never be with another woman again, not after Julie, a traveller never gets married again Mary you know, if the man or woman dies that's it, whoever is left stays on their own for the rest of their lives, we believe our souls will meet up again one day in heaven."

"And why's that, why do you have to stay on your own?" asks Mary.

"That's the way it is, when my father died my Ma never married again, my Uncle Martin God rest his soul, he looked after us. I don't know, I'm not afraid to be alone, but sometimes it's very hard, Julie was there for me all the time Mary, she looked after me and the children and I looked after them," he says.

"You know something, the way people talk about the travellers you make out they have no feelings at all," says Mary.

"We do, we are human just like everyone else, we breath the same air as your people, Mary, the travellers are as Irish as everybody else in Ireland. Your people give us a hard time sure they do and there's no need for that at all. Anyways, I'm sorry for bothering you, and I have to go now."

He stands up to go.

"Look Máirtín, I'm glad you came to confide in me and don't

feel bad at all for talking to me, I have a lot to tell you too; you know, sometime we will talk again," Mary says, with compassion.

"Sorry Mary, I have to go now."

"Why do they call you Dagger? I was looking through the files and you were down as Dagger Ward?" asks Mary.

"Ah, I tell ya again some other time I must go now," he replies.

"Bye Máirtín, I'm here anytime you need to talk," Mary says.

Just as Dagger is about to go Sergeant Ricky comes into the hospital and passes by the canteen. He notices Dagger with Mary. He calls another Nurse, to see who is the lady talking to Dagger.

"Excuse me Nurse, sorry to be bothering you, but who is that young Nurse in the canteen with your man there?" asks Sergeant Ricky. He is pointing at Mary and Dagger in the canteen.

"That's Nurse Mary Buckley," replies the Nurse.

"Well, is it now, so that's why her auld fella told me to keep an eye on her, well I'll be dog gone," Ricky mutters to himself.

"Sorry Sir?" asks the Nurse.

"Ah, nothing miss," replies Sergeant Ricky. "I'm just thinking out loud."

Mary Confides In Helen

Mary is in her flat. She is agitated, and cannot settle or concentrate on anything, pacing up and down her living room, to keep herself amused she puts up the Christmas decorations. She eventually picks up the phone to confide in her friend Helen about her feelings towards Dagger.

"Hello Helen, it's Mary, how are you?"

"Hi, Mary, how are you?" she says, with a sigh.

"Helen I will get straight to the point, I cannot stop thinking about Máirtín Ward."

"I'm listening Mary," says Helen, as she polishes her nails.

"I'm thinking about him night and day, from once I get up in the morning until I go to bed at night, I even dream about him," says Mary.

"Jesus Mary you have it bad."

"I know, it's not funny Helen, I just cannot switch off, he's on my mind all the time."

"I know Mary, you have the hots for him, but this is crazy, do you realise how complicated that could be for you if ye were together?" Helen says, concerned for Mary.

"Look, I don't want to discuss anymore of this over the phone, they might be listening down the post office. You know like Miss Finell, she will have it all over the town in the morning, people say she listens to everybody's conversations that's why it's so hard to get a call out. I suppose, sure what other way would she be, isn't that her husband Garda Anthony Finell down at the station."

"Are you serious, well now Mary you learn something new everyday." She takes a drink from her glass of brandy.

"Look Helen, I will call around to your place."

"Don't bother Mary, I was going into town anyways so I will call to your place, put on the kettle I'm all ears," she replies.

"Oh Helen thanks, see you soon so, bye."

Kelly's V G Supermarket

Four or five young travellers go into Kelly's Supermarket, they robbed it before, during the horse fair. Wearing long trench coats with a lot of pockets, they fill their pockets with food, sweets and biscuits from the store. The manager Mr Kelly, is decorating the shop for Christmas with a shop attendant and notice the youngsters filling their pockets with food. He approaches them.

"Hey, what are ye up to ye little scutts?" shouts the manager Mr Kelly. The travellers run off.

"Come back here ye little shits, by feck if I catch ye I'll kill ye," he shouts

They run out of the supermarket and down the street. Mr Kelly run's after them and catches one of them, young Johnny, who is the smallest and cannot run very fast.

"Ha, ha, I caught you, you little scutt, you won't get away this time you're coming to the Police Station with me now sure you are, 'tis the last time you will rob from my shop again and that's one thing for sure."

"Mister, let me go, my Ma will kill ya when she catches ya, you'll be sorry, now let me go and I won't tell her on ya," says young Johnny.

"Ah shut up! You little shit we will see who will be sorry," says Mr Kelly, holding young Johnny by the collar and marching him down to the Police Station.

There is one Garda Officer on duty, Sergeant Ricky. Mr Kelly goes into the Station with young Johnny; he has him by the collar of his coat.

"Come on in here you little shit. Well Officers, I caught this little rascal stealing from our store, and 'tis not the first time he has stole in my shop either, the other lot that was with him got away," says Mr Kelly, as he goes in the door of the Police Station.

Sergeant Ricky raises his eyebrows when he sees Mr Kelly coming into the Station with the young traveller boy Johnny.

"Well young man, what did you steal?" he asks.

"Nothing Sir, I swear I didn't take anything, Will you tell this asshole to let go of my collar?"

Mr Kelly lets go of young Johnny's collar.

"Right, what's your name young man?" asks Sergeant Ricky.

"I'm not telling you Sir." replies Young Johnny.

"Ok, how do you mean you didn't take anything from the store."

"I wasn't in his store at all, I didn't go near his stinking place, he has nothing in there anyways Sir," he replies, with his pockets bulging, as Sergeant Ricky and Mr Kelly look at each other with astonishment.

"What?" asks Mr Kelly.

He hits Johnny in the head with his right hand, holding him again by the collar.

"Tell the truth, you know well you were stealing from our store, now come on now, tell the truth before I kick your arse!"

"Calm down now Sir, there be no need for that. I'll deal with this. Now young man, I will ask you one more time, what's your name?" asks Sergeant Ricky, bending over young Johnny.

"I don't know Sir."

"Look lad I'm losing my patience with you, I have a busy day ahead of me, I'll ask you again, what's your name?

"Tell the Sergeant your name or I'll redden your arse for ya."

"Look, Mr Kelly. Just leave it to me."

"Willie Ward Sir, that's my name."

"Ah not another one, how many Willie Wards is there, and where do you live?" asks Sergeant Ricky with a smile, looking at Mr Kelly.

"No fixed abode Sir. I don't live anywhere, only here and there Sir."

"I don't believe this, come on you little tinker tell us the truth or I'll burst ya," says Mr Kelly, getting furious with young Johnny.

"They are training you well, come on young man empty out your pockets," asks Sergeant Ricky.

Johnny takes out sweets, biscuits, and pots of jam, cheese, bananas and a dagger knife.

"What's this?" asks Ricky, as young Johnny takes the knife out of his inside pocket.

"Where did you get this?" asks Sergeant Ricky, taking the knife off Johnny.

"I got this knife from my uncle, you wouldn't want to see the one he has, 'tis about that length," says Johnny, holding his two hands up about a foot apart.

"What's your uncle's name?" asks Sergeant Ricky.

"Dagger Sir, Dagger Ward, and he will kill you when he finds out I am here," he says, referring to Mr Kelly as he stares into his eyes.

"Well is that so now, well I'm afraid I will have to have a word with your Uncle if that's the case, and that would be Máirtín Ward wouldn't it?" asks Sergeant Ricky.

"It sure would and some day he is going to be king of the travellers, he can fight anyone with his bare fists sure he can."

"Well young man, I've heard enough so off you go and tell your Uncle I will be giving him a call."

Young Johnny takes off running out the door, where his mum Fay is waiting for him to take him home. She stays well clear of the Garda Station so she could teach young Johnny to stand up for himself and fight his own battles, and how to talk his way out of trouble with the Gardaí.

Inside the Garda Station, Mr Kelly is fuming with Sergeant Ricky for letting the young traveller boy off Scot free. Sergeant Ricky tells Mr Kelly that he got his supplies back and from now on watch the travellers as they enter his store or bar them all together. Mr Kelly leaves the Police Station disappointed with Sergeant Ricky's way of dealing with the young traveller boy.

Helen Gives Advice To Mary

Helen knocks at the door of Mary's flat. Mary opens the door to let her in. She is glad to see Helen. They sit at the table. Mary opens a bottle of vodka, she fills up two full glasses, she has a glowing turf open fire on, the flat is warm and cosy. Helen drinks down half of the vodka in one go as Mary tells her the story about Máirtín.

"Here Helen, I'll top up your glass for you again," says Mary, taking notice of how fast Helen drank down the vodka.

"Not much now Mary, I am driving, you have the place looking fabulous with you're beauty decorations, anyways you were telling me, and did your father recognise him?"

"No Helen, I don't think so, but he looked curious all the same."

"I don't know Mary, look I don't want to give advice or be judgemental or anything like that, but do you know what you are getting yourself into? Do you know the gossip that this will cause, can't you imagine the tongues wagging," says Helen, with a worried look as she is still concerned for Mary's welfare.

"I know Helen, I thought about that and do you know what, I don't think I care, I don't care what people think, this is my life not anybody else's."

"And what about your job?" asks Helen.

"What about it?"

"Do you realise that when your employers find out about this they might let you go? Have you thought about that?" says Helen.

"I know, I thought about that all right."

She starts to think.

"And?" says Helen, with concern.

"I don't care," replies Mary.

"Are you sure you are in love with this man, or maybe it's just an infatuation or something else."

"Helen, I'm very much in love with Máirtín and nobody knows that but me, what do you think I am some kind of mental case or something," Mary replies, getting annoyed with Helen because she feels she doesn't have her support.

"Oh, I don't know Mary, that's like the Catholics and the Protestants getting married, it's a mixed marriage you know. Oh Mary, it will cause so many complications for you in the future," says Helen.

"I know and I have taken all that into consideration but when you are in love with someone nothing else matters," Mary replies.

"I'm not picking your brain but what do you love about Máirtín Ward?" asks Helen, pouring more vodka into the two glasses.

"Why do you say that, do you not trust my judgment or what, Helen?"

"Judgment, now Mary, a traveller, now hold on a minute I ask ya, I wouldn't call that judgment?" says Helen.

"Do you know something, I feel you have a thing with travellers, I hope you're not racist, now are you?" asks Mary.

"Look it's not that I'm racist," says Helen, getting up out of her seat to look out the window to avoid making eye contact with Mary.

"It's just I have a thing about travellers, and so does the whole country, sure all they do is rob from us, they don't work or anything, all they do is live off the tax payer that's all they do and that's what annoying about them. They don't even pay tax," says Helen.

"Look now, they wouldn't be half as bad if they we're treated half right by society, sure they get a hard time wherever they go, they're not allowed into the dance halls, the pictures, they cannot even book a hotel for a wedding," replies Mary, getting annoyed at Helen's comments.

"Mary, will you stop, how can you treat them half right, sure if you let them into a hotel or anywhere else all they do is wreck the place, and rob everything before and after them."

"Well Helen, now it's like this, years ago the tinkers, as they we're called back then, they were no different than the rest of us, we all lived on the side of the road at one stage you know. The only thing between them and us, is we live in houses now, and we have full time jobs and we pay taxes, that's all," replies Mary. She gets defensive.

"Well, I tell you one thing is for sure, we don't rob like them, and if we did well God help us," says Helen, as she goes over to sit down again.

"What are you on about, sure look at the Hagarthy's down the road from our house at home, they would rob the milk out of your tea and come back for the sugar," Mary says defensively.

"Ah well, Mary, I don't know, look just be careful, here have another drink."

"Helen I think you have a problem with the drink anyway," says Mary. Helen is surprised with that remark.

"Have I now, well Mary, I'd rather have a drink problem, than the problem you are getting yourself into now how's that, and don't be getting on to me just because I don't approve of you with that traveller lad, anyway I'm only concerned for you that's all, I don't want you to make a mistake, now that's it," says Helen. She folds her arms and turns her head away.

"I know that Helen and I much appreciate that, I'm a big girl now and I'm well capable of making my own decisions thank you very much."

They both finish off the bottle of vodka.

Helen is getting tipsy.

"Ma—ry there is one th—ing I will say to you?" Helen mutters.

"Look Helen say no more, I have had enough, I think we should talk about your drinking. Look at you, you're pissed all ready," says Mary.

"There is not—nothing wrong with my drink—ing, I don't drink anymore than anyone else," says Helen.
She is so pissed, she slurs her words. She can barely sit up straight.

"This is the third or fourth time I have met you in the past few weeks, and each time you are pissed, why's that?" asks Mary.

"Ary, who cares?" says Helen, falling off her chair laughing.

"I can't believe this," Mary says, in disgust.

Chapter Seven

Mary Gives Halting Site A Visit

Mary is driving along the road in her blue Datsun car to the Halting site. She stops to ask for directions to the travellers' site from an old man who is out walking along the road with his dog.

"Excuse me Sir, would you tell me where I would find the travellers' site around here?" The old man goes over to Mary.

"What are you a social worker or what?"

"Look never you mind, I'm just giving them a visit," replies Mary.

"Have you money or butter vouchers for them or something like that, ha?" says the old man, with an inquisitive look in his eye.

"No Sir, I am from the prize bonds office in Dublin, now all I want to know is where the traveller site is, Sir, Mary says."

"I'd say they must have won the prize bonds so, did they ha," says the old man.

"They sure did," replies Mary.

"Ok so, just drive down there, take the second turn on the left, go down there for about half a mile, you will come to a bridge now go slow because the bridge is narrow, go down there for a few hundred yards and you will come to a fork on the road, turn right there and about two hundred yards, there are on the left hand side of the road, anyway how much did they win?" he asks.

"Twenty thousand pounds," she replies, she drives off with a gloating smile, the old man looks surprised.

"That's the stuff for ya, now mind your own business," she mutters to herself.

She drives to the travellers' site following the old man's directions. Driving into the halting site, she sees about fifteen children, four or five women and men are standing around a barrel full of wood, they set it alight to warm themselves.

All the children gather around Mary's car. She lets down the window to asks one of the children where she would find Máirtín.

"Could you tell me where I would find Máirtín Ward please?"

Fay Barry, who is in love with Máirtín, overhears Mary ask the children for Máirtín.

"What do you want him for?" asks Fay.

"I would like to talk to him," says Mary.

"Why? What about?" she asks sarcastically.

"Is he here?"

"No, he will be back in a little while, you can come into the trailer and wait for him if you like," says Fay with a suspicious look, as she is inquisitive to know what Mary wants with Máirtín.

"All right so, I will," replies Mary.

She feels apprehensive because it is her first time at a traveller site. She doesn't know how they are going to react to her. They go into Bridie's trailer, where there are no Christmas decorations because of respect for the dead. There is a little boy about four years of age, in the corner with twine around his waist, so he cannot roam around the trailer. Katie puts on a pot of tea on the electric stove. Bridie and Katie make Mary welcome. Fay is suspicious, and doesn't trust Mary, because she recognises her from the hospital.

"You're the Nurse from the Hospital aren't ya, and why do you come around here to see Máirtín for?" she asks.

"Ah, nothing special," replies Mary, getting embarrassed with all of the children staring at her.

Luke The Bookie's Place

While Mary is waiting for Máirtín, he and his brother Willie are with Luke the bookie Barry, in Mullingar. He is Fay's father-in-law. Dagger looks up to him. They are all inside a large trailer, where there is about twenty male adults. There is a lot of frustration and outrage amongst the traveller community towards the settled community.

"Well lads, it is very clear to all of us, that the settled people hate the travellers, and there's one thing for feckin' sure, my family have enough of it," says Luke the bookie.

He is angry and hostile towards the settled people, sitting at the head of the table chairing the meeting.

"Now Luke. It's not our fault, we mind our own business, sure we don't bother anyone," says Hattie the Swan.

"Yea, it's them that hate us Grandpa, sure we don't hate them at all, remember the fight in Ballinasloe, you know we were arrested for fighting in the street, and we were let go without them charging us at all. I know I don't hate them anyway," says Malachy Barry, Luke's nephew.

He looks around at the others to agree with him, some of them just raise their shoulders.

"Hi Luke, I remember when we were children and in my father's time the tinkers were best of friends with the settled people. Now I swear to God on that, on my dead father's grave and that's true," says Willie, shouting loud with frustration.

"I tell you one thing, you're dead right there Willie, even in my father's time there wasn't any hassle, the tinkers were always working for the farmers. They were paid with food and sometimes money. I remember my father telling me never fall out with the settled people, you'll never know when you might need them. Even when my mother died, Lord rest her soul, may she rest in heaven, it was the farmers that helped us and I always remember that," says Luke.

"That's for sure, yah, and I remember the time when there would be bags of turf left outside our trailer when we were children, isn't that right grandpa?" says Roger Barry, speaking in an English accent, turning to Luke at the head of the table.

"And how come the tinkers never owned their own land, that's what I can't understand."

"Look Roger me boy, you're too young to remember, there is one thing ye must understand, it's because we didn't want land at the time, we were moving from village to village and we never wanted to settle, the land would only stop us from travelling," says Luke, taking off his hat to scratch his head.

"And now we want land and they won't give it to us, ha, isn't that a good one, and tis the same way in England, they wouldn't give you the steam of your piss over there," says Hattie.

"Hattie, you were with me when I tried to buy land last year from a farmer just outside Tullamore and he wouldn't sell it to me, because I was a traveller, he told me that straight up to my face sure he did," says Máirtín Dagger.

"That's right Dagger, and do you know something, there is a traveller family living in a big mansion of a house with ten acres of land down in Mayo somewhere, do ye know that now lads, ha," Hattie says, looking around at the other lads.

"Now, I wonder how did they get the land, I'd like to know," says Luke.

"I would like to have land of me own, but I can't get it anywhere, I've tried the whole country and not a blade of grass could I buy anywhere, now how about that!" says another old man.

"Hi, look at this," says Willie, jumping up on the table pulling down his pants and shows his arse to the rest of the lads.

"Look lads what they did to me when I was a little lad; I was shot in the hole! You remember that Dagger don't ya?"

They all have a good laugh at Willie.

"Wait till I tell ye this lads, he was out robbing eggs one Saturday night, and one of the farmers, what was his name at all?"

He thinks.

"Oh ya, Jim O'Sullivan thought it was a fox that was at his hens out in the hen house. The farmer heard the hens making noise around the place, and got the gun and let fire and shot Willie in the ass and the next morning at Mass the priest was giving a sermon from the altar, warned the farmers that there were foxes about and to keep an eye on their chickens and hens," says Dagger, with a good laugh.

"Ah ya, it wasn't funny for me, the priest told me to sit down and I couldn't with the pain I had in my arse."

There's more laughing from the rest of the lads.

Mary is getting impatient waiting for Máirtín to return home.

"Look I must go it's getting dark. You might tell him I called."

"Hang on, I will give Luke a call, he might know where he is," says Bridie.

Fay turns up her nose, when she hears Luke's name mentioned.

Bridie goes into the bedroom to make the phone call. The phone is connected from the telephone pole illegally; the telephone wire is going from the trailer to the telephone pole.

"I cannot see a thing here," says Bridie.

She is trying to dial the number in the dark.

"Will one of ye put on the lights there will ye?"

Katie switches on the lights, and like the phone, the electricity is connected to the ESB pole illegally.

Back at Luke the bookie's place, the phone rings. He picks it up.

"Hello, oh hello Bridie, I haven't heard from you for this long time, what's wrong?"

"Nothing's wrong Luke, is himself there?"

He gives the phone to Máirtín.

"It's for you."

"What's wrong Mammy?" The rest of the lads snigger.

"Nothing's wrong, why does there have to be something wrong, look, Mary Buckley is here to see ya, remember her? She's the policeman's daughter from when we lived near Westport, the one that's works in the Hospital," says Bridie.

"Oh ya, look tell her I will see her again, I'm busy now. I'll be home later, bye now." says Dagger.

He puts down the phone. The lads slag him.

"Who's the woman Dagger?" asks Hattie.

"Shut up, mind your own business, now what will we do about the way we are treated by these bastards?" says Máirtín Dagger.

"They don't like us anyways so we'll never change that, and that's one thing for sure," says Willie.

"You're right there Willie Ward, I think we should rebel against them as much as we fecking well can," says Roger Barry.

"Ya, lets rob them right left centre, anyways they have too much, by heck it will quieten them, sure it will," says Dagger.

While the rest of the men agree Dagger opens a bottle of whiskey. They all drink to that.

Gypsy Prostitute In Town

A couple of days later, there is a Gypsy woman prostituting herself on the streets. She is prowling up and down the street trying to pick up clients; Garda Anthony and Garda Jim, a new Garda Officer down from Dublin, come along in the Squad car. They stop to talk to the woman.

"Excuse me miss, can I ask you what are you doing here?" asks Garda Anthony.

"Nothing Boss, mind your own business, I don't come around you, so don't you come around me," says the prostitute.

"Sorry now miss, but you know that prostitution is illegal in this country," says Garda Anthony.

They get out of their car to talk to her.

"What is your name miss?" asks Garda Anthony.

She recognises Jim from Dublin.

"Be damit it's yourself that is in it Jim! I heard you were transferred from Dublin down the country somewhere all right, so this where you are. Oh, you are so handsome you know," says the prostitute, as she rubs Garda Jim's collar. Anthony is looking at Jim in suspicion.

"Do you know this woman Jim?"

"Not at all Anthony," replies Jim.

"Oh, don't worry Garda, he knows me all right, in fact he knows me very well, isn't that right Jim?" She winks her eye at him.

"What's your name miss?" asks Anthony.

"Bridget Holms Sir."

He writes her name down.

"Are you related to Cathal Holms?" he asks.

"I could be, why do you know him?"

"It doesn't matter, anyways we let you go this time, but don't worry, we will be keeping an eye on you from now on. By the way, just for the record, where in Dublin do you come from?"

"Never you mind Garda, you don't need to know that, isn't that right Jim?"

She winks one eye at Jim again and walks off. The two Officers look at each other, and raise their shoulders.

Dagger and the two Barry brothers are stealing a car trailer.

They are in the front of somebody's house hooking up the trailer to a blue Ford transit van. They drive away as fast as they can.

"This trailer must be worth £300 at least I'd say," says Malachy.

"We'll split the profit three equal ways, right, Dagger?"

"Right Roger, that's a deal, I have a buyer in Roscommon waiting to buy this trailer off me," Says Máirtín.

He is driving the van at high speed to get away quickly before they are spotted.

"Leave it there lads," says Malachy.

He spits on his hand. Dagger and Roger both hit Malachy in the palm of his hand to agree on dividing the profit of the car trailer.

"Before we go home I have a small stop to make," says Dagger.

"No problem," says Malachy.

"Were ye watching Alias Smith and Jones last night lads?"

"We sure were Dagger, I tell ye something they know how to rob a bank don't they?" says Roger.

"Do ya know something lads, we might rob a bank like that some day, ha, what do ye say to that?"

The two brothers look at each other not knowing whether Dagger is serious or not.

Sergeant Ricky Investigates Gypsy Prostitute

Garda Jim and Sergeant Ricky are on duty. The phone rings. Sergeant Ricky answers the phone. There is a concerned citizen on the phone reporting that there is a prostitute on the main street.

"Hello, An Garda Síochána, can I help you."

"I wish to let you know that there is a woman on the main street, now look as far as I'm concerned I think she is selling herself, maybe a prostitute," says the woman.

"And how would you know that?"

"I've seen her going off in cars, at least four or five cars pulled up and brought her away, that was only in the past few hours and I know she is there all day. I live across the road you see, so I can see her from my sitting room window."

"Ok Mam, I will send a car around right away."

He hangs up the phone.

"Right Jim, she is on the prowl again, come on lets see to it," says Sergeant Ricky.

"Who will look after the Station Sarge?" asks Officer Jim.

"It will be ok, I will lock the door, sure anyway who would be interfering with anything in a Police Station, anyways Anthony will be back shortly."

"Well, you would be surprised Sir," replies Jim. They both leave in the squad car to check out the prostitute.

Arriving where she is supposed to be on the prowl, there is no sign of her. They pull onto a laneway and wait.

"Well Sarge, would you fancy a coffee?"

"Brilliant idea Jim, I could murder one, that will be with two sugars please," replies Sergeant Ricky.

Jim gets out of the car and goes into Sheppard's coffee shop, which is decorated for Christmas. He asks the attendant behind the counter for two coffees.

"Milk and sugar?" asked the attendant.

"Yes please," he says.

She looks at Officer Jim and blushes. He smiles and gets embarrassed.

"Now there you are Sir, you must be the new Garda," she says.

"I am surely," replies Jim.

"What's your name?"

"Officer Jim to you Miss."

"Are you married?" she asks.

"Not yet Miss."

Ricky calls Jim on his radio.

"Sorry love, excuse me a minute," says Jim to the attendant.

"Yes Ricky, what can I do for you?"

"Can you get two donuts as well please, good man," says Sergeant Ricky.

There are about ten other customers in the coffee shop and they all hear the Garda radio, some of them laugh and others just look at each other.

"Now Jim there you are."

She leaves the donuts and coffee on the counter.

"How much do I owe you?" asks Jim.

"It's all right love, they're on the house," she replies.

"Thank you Miss, I appreciate that, thank you, see you again soon."

"Bye now, see ya Garda," says the attendant.

He leaves the coffee shop, and goes back to the car; they sit in the car and have their coffee. Jim leaves his coffee on the dashboard. Dagger, and the two Barry brothers pass in a blue transit van, with the large car trailer they stool earlier on.

"I wonder where they are off too now Sarge?"

"Probably up to no good I'm sure."

Bridget the prostitute gets out of a Ford Capri across the road from where the squad car is parked down a laneway.

"Well now, look Sarge, there she is!"

Ricky starts the car and drives towards the Ford Capri, the donuts and coffee end up down on Jims lap, they both get out of the car, with Jim's trouser soaked in coffee. They approach the driver of the car, Jim on the passenger side of the car, and Ricky on the driver's side.

"Leave it to me now Jim," Ricky says.

"Well Sir." He questions the driver of the Ford Capri.

"Can you tell me what you two are up to?"

"Nothing Officers, why did we do something wrong?" asks the driver innocently.

"What is your name?" he asks, taking out his note pad to take notes.

"Sam," replies the driver.

"Sam who?"

"Look Officers, what did I do wrong?"

"Do you know Sir that this woman is a prostitute?" asks Ricky.

"And what proof do you have to say such a thing? You can't piss now around here but you would get arrested for it," says Bridget.

"I have enough proof to arrest the both of you for illegal sexual trade."

"Look Sir, I only gave her a lift, she was thumbing on the road and I picked her up, sure that's no crime now is it?"

"Is that right Mam?" asks Ricky.

"That's right Sir, and I wouldn't go around with this buffer for all the tea in china," Bridget says.

Jim has a smile on his face.

"Look, go away and let me never see the both of you here again, now clear off the both of you before I change my mind," Ricky says.

"Happy Christmas to you Sir," says the driver.

They both drive off.

"I wonder was he telling the truth?"

"I don't know Jim, we will soon find out what she is up to, she is up to no good that woman is, come on lets go back to headquarters," replies Sergeant Ricky.

Stealing Back The Christmas Trees

It's about twelve midnight and Dagger, and the Barry brothers, are robbing the trees back from the van at the back of the Garda Station. They have pulled the van into the car park behind the Station. They take the trees out over the wall. There is a light on at the back of the Station. The two Barry brothers are talking out loud.

"Shag it lads, for feck sake will ya keep it quiet in there, bloody hell if we are caught we won't have a tree ever for Christmas," says Dagger.

The two lads are throwing the trees out over the wall to Dagger and he puts the Christmas trees into the large car trailer.

Inside the Station, Officer Anthony is on duty, he hears a noise. He goes to the back window to check, opening the window and shines his torch around the backyard. He sees nothing. The two lads spot Officer Anthony at the window. They duck down. Officers Anthony closes the window and attends to his work as usual.

"For God's sake lads. If we are caught we're finished," says Dagger.

They continue throwing the trees over the wall. When they have all the trees loaded into the Ford Transit and trailer they sneak off quietly back to where they live and hide the Christmas trees.

Selling The Christmas Trees At The Market

A few days later, the Barry brothers, Malachy and Roger, sell the Christmas trees at the market in Mullingar.

A car drives up; the driver lets down the window of his car and asks Roger how much is a Christmas tree.

"£4 to yourself, Boss,"

"I'll give you £2," says the driver.

"No way, £4 Boss, or piss off ya stupid asshole," shouts Roger.

"No, too much, I can buy them up the road for £2," says the Driver. He drives away.

"Well piss off so, ya bollix ya, and buy them for £2 so," shouts Roger, following the car down the road with a hatchet he picked up that was on the ground. He comes back to his brother Malachy.

"I'll kill that fecker," he says.

"Ary, don't mind that shit, he probably hasn't even a house to put it into to," says Malachy.

Another car pulls up.

"How much for the Christmas trees Boss?" says the driver.

"£2 Sir," says Roger. He looks at his brother Malachy.

"Ok, I'll take two, one for my mother in-law as well."

The man gets out of his car to put the trees into the boot.

"You must like your mother in-law Boss," says Malachy.

"I do, because she is paying for them."

"Ah, you're a queer one," says Roger, as he puts the trees into the back of the car.

The man pays Roger for the trees, as well as a tip.

"By heck you're a gentleman, well fair play to ya, and happy Christmas to you Sir."

Roger puts the money in his pocket, as the man drives off with a bargain.

Officer Anthony and Sergeant Ricky are out in the back yard of the Police Station, where there are about five or six old cars impounded, with a couple of bicycles.

"Anthony, do you notice anything missing that should be here?"

"No Sarge, why is there something missing or what?"

"Yes, the traveller's van, it's gone!"

"You're dead right Sarge, it is gone. Well could you beat that."

"I know Anthony, it was bad enough they took the Christmas trees last week, but they have to come back for the van as well. I want this place dusted for finger prints and foot prints right away," says Sergeant Ricky, taking off his cap to scratch his head.

"I'll get on that right away Sarge."

"Any word on the fingerprints on the Hi Ace Van before they nicked it back?"

He shakes his head with frustration.

"Not yet Sir, I'm expecting the results back from forensic any moment now."

"Look, them prints we're taken a week ago. The Christmas trees will be well sold by now. I want them finger prints on my desk first thing in the morning." says Sergeant Ricky.

"Right Sir," Anthony replies.

Chapter Eight

Helen Conway Travels To Dublin

Helen decides to go to Dublin on family matters and also does some Christmas shopping. She goes for a site-seeing walk along the Quays, and O'Connell Street.

She also goes into a lounge bar somewhere off O'Connell St, where she meets up with Cathal the Stud Holms. Helen has had it in her head to try out sex with a traveller man for some time now. After having a few brandys, she approaches Cathal.

Later on that night she ends up back at Cathal's Caravan at a traveller halting site near Ballymun Flats, where she stays the night with Cathal and they have sex.

"Oh, feckin hell, that was good, now I know what Mary is talking about," says Helen.

"Well they don't call me the Stud for nothing you know," says Cathal. Helen puts her arms around him to give him a kiss.

Later on that day Helen and Cathal decide to go to the cinema to catch an afternoon matinee, and then they meet up with Cathal's family in a pub near Ballymun. Helen is so excited with herself that she decides to phone Mary.

"Mary, you wouldn't believe what I got up to last night. I had sex with a traveller last night and guess what, his name is Cathal the Stud, ha what do you think Mary?"

"You did what?" asks Mary, putting her hand to her mouth with total shock.

"Indeed I did, and it was fantastic Mary, now I know what you are talking about. I was wondering why you were so keen on that traveller," says Helen.

"Helen I never had sex with Máirtín or any other traveller either for that matter. Oh, I can't believe this, what in the hell did you go and do that for? Helen are you crazy or something?"

"Mary, I thought you were into Máirtín because of the sex."

"Sex, is that why you did it, because you thought I was having sex with Máirtín, Oh my God I'm not hearing this!"

"Ya I did, sure you were so excited I thought that was because of the sex," she feels disgusted with herself for what she has done.

"Where are you now Helen?"

"I don't know really, some pub in Dublin, feck it Mary, you make me feel so bad now," says Helen.

"Ok, I'll talk to you when you get back, good bye," says Mary.

She hangs up the phone; Helen is in the pub with about fifteen traveller men and woman and a load of children. The pub is sleazy and shabby.

Helen is ashamed of herself for having sex, she goes back to Cathal to tell him she must leave.

"I'm sorry, I have to go now, something has come up at home, I must leave now."

"Ary, stay for another while why don't ya," Cathal says, disappointed because Helen has to leave.

"No, I have to go now."

"Do you want a lift anywhere?" he asks.

"No, you're all right, I will get the six o'clock train."

"Hold on a minute," says Cathal, as he smokes a cigar.

"Where is Seamus?"

He looks around the lounge.

"Hey Seamus, will ya take Helen to the train for me, I'm tied up here."

He is playing a game of pool.

"Ah, no you're all right, I'll get the bus into the Train Station, I don't want to put you out," replies Helen.

"Here's the keys, look after her now for me, do ya hear me now Seamus?"

He gives him the keys of the van. Helen is embarrassed. Herself and Seamus leave to go to the Station to catch the six o'clock train.

Fun Fair Comes To Mullingar

The travellers' funfair is coming to Mullingar town, there are about twenty to thirty vans, trucks, and caravans coming to town. All the travellers from Ballinasloe, Galway, Dublin, come to Mullingar, to join the funfair.

Dagger and his family go to Mullingar to work in the fun fair, they are driving in convoy, there are a lot of people on the route into town greeting them.

It's Christmas time, with high spirits and excitement in the air, as the fun fair passes a school. All the children are playing in the playground getting excited when they see the Fun Fair, it's also the last day before they get their Christmas holidays, there is a good atmosphere around. A man and his wife on the side of the road watch the convoy pass by.

"Well, here they come; I tell ya one thing, there will be riding going on in town tonight and that's for sure," says the man to his wife, taking off his cap to greet the fun fair.

There are about ten men working on a building site. They see the convoy coming, they stop working.

"Is it that time of year again," says one of the men.

"Tie up your daughters, the boys are back in town again," says another man. The lads have a laugh.

"Remember last year, two weeks they were here, they took over the whole town. I tell ya one thing is for sure, the cops will be busy now sure they will, didn't the Joker McTigue join them last year, and he went all over Ireland and England with them," says one of the Men.

"He sure did Boss, sure the Joker would try anything, sure he is cracked as a badger," says another man.

All the men have a good laugh as they take off their caps to welcome the fun fair convoy to the town.

Ricky Goes For A Well Earned Pint

Ricky Molloy is off duty and he is going for a pint to Jack O'Reilly's, which is well decorated for Christmas. There are about ten other people in the bar including Jack and Scar Face. Sergeant Ricky walks into the bar, he goes to the counter.

"Well Ricky, what will it be?"

"Give us a half one and a pint please Jack."

"Off duty tonight Sarge," says Scar Face,

"I am surely, well Mr Goggins, do you ever go home?" asks Ricky.

No comment from Scar Face, as he turns to ignore that remark.

"All ready for the Christmas Ricky?" says Jack leaving the half one on the counter in front of Ricky.

"All ya, just a few days to go now, we won't feel it, my God wasn't it a fast year," says Ricky.

"That's a mighty fine tree you have there Jack," says Scar Face, trying to get Ricky going.

"It is indeed, I got it from the boys yesterday. They must have about sixty of them in a car trailer and they flogged ten or twelve in about twenty minutes, just outside the door there while they were parked up bringing in mine," says Jack.

Ricky looks at the trees. He gets a flashback to the trees in the van at the back of the Garda Station. Scar Face is in a mood to wind up Ricky about the Christmas trees.

"I heard, Sarge, the trees disappeared a while ago, from the back of the Station. Is there any truth to that I wonder?"

No answer from Ricky.

"And the van disappeared as well Jack," says Scar Face, looking at Jack with a wink in one eye.

"I tell ye one thing, that Station must be haunted," Scar Face says.

"What kind of vehicle were they using to tow the trailer Jack?" asks Ricky.

He ignores Scar Face, and takes a drink from his glass of whiskey.

"I think it was a Ford Transit, let me think, ya, it was a Blue Ford Transit van all right," says Jack.

"I can see how they took the trees, but how the van disappeared is a mystery to us, not even a witness in sight and only God knows where the van is by now," says Ricky.

"Ah probably ghosts Ricky, sure isn't that barracks haunted for years, sure if you go down in the cellar at about midnight you can hear voices of the prisoners sometimes. You can hear screams all right, sure they used to torture prisoners there, one time, there was a gang of hard cases living in this town long ago, they created hell for the local inhabitants," says Old Man Walter.

"And how would you know Walter, I'd say you spent many the night locked up in there yourself Walter, for poaching salmon, I'd say," says Jack.

He takes a pint of stout to Old Man Walter. They all laugh.

"Have you any clue at all Ricky, how they took the van?"

"No Jack, it was pinned in with other vehicles right up against the back wall it was, you couldn't even open the doors not to mind drive it away," says Ricky.

"Any chance of selling a few of them auld vehicles you are storing there Sarge?" asks Scar Face.

"I tell you one thing, a mockeen, you never miss a thing do ya, in the new year now I'd say, if they are not claimed in the next few weeks we will auction the lot off," replies Ricky.

"Sure what would they be worth anyway?" asks Walter.

"Not much Walter, but they would be fine for the likes of Scar Face here," replies Ricky.

Scar Face gives a sour look to Ricky, getting up off his stool to sit down to join Walter at his table for a drink. Ricky stands up, finishes his pint.

"Well, I'm off and happy Christmas to you all." He leaves.

The others stay drinking till closing time.

The travellers are having a drink in a pub in Mullingar. Dagger, Willie and a few more are there.

"Is it true, Dagger, that you stole the trees back from the Police Station?" says Hattie the swan.

"Shut up will ya, there is open ears around here there is, a lot of queer hawks hanging around here now sure there is, you would want to watch who ye are talking to."

He looks around at the other people in the bar.

"There are a few Police informers hanging around this place you know, they listen into other people's conversations, to see are they up to no good and notify the Police for a pay off. I'm well aware of this."

"Bloody hell Dagger I never knew that," says Malachy Barry.

"Come on, to hell with them lads, tell us how you got the van back," says Hattie. He looks at Dagger and Willie for response.

Dagger starts to tell the story to the other travellers about how he got the van back and they are visualising it as he is telling the story.

Dagger and Willie drive along the road with a load of scrap metal on the back of a flat body truck. They drive into a local scrap yard to deliver the load of scrap, they unload the truck. The scrap yard owner comes over to the two lads.

"Right Boss what will ya give us for that lot?" asks Dagger.

"I tell what I'll do, I will give ya £10 for the lot, how's that lads?" says the scrap yard owner.

"Ah, come on Boss, it's worth about at least £15, you're fleecing us now sure you are," says Willie.

"Right, we'll split the difference, £12.50," says the scrap yard owner.

"It's a deal Boss," says Dagger, spitting on the palm of his hand, and they agree on the £12.50.

"By the way Boss, can I borrow that machine you have there?" asks Dagger, looking at a truck with a magnet grab used to pick up scrap cars.

"What do you want that for?"

"It would be very handy for loading some auld cars we have, I want to load them on the truck and that motor over there would be very handy," says Dagger.

"Ok, take it with ya and mind yourself, there's no insurance on it."

"Sound you are Boss. We don't need insurance," says Willie.

Dagger hops into the truck and drives it away. They drive to Ballinasloe; Willie is driving the truck behind Dagger in the machine. They go into the car park behind the Garda Station. Garda Mick Malloy is on duty at the Station watching TV; he cannot hear the noise of the truck. Dagger pull the machine close to the wall and works the grab with the magnet. He picks up the van from inside the wall and leaves it down on the back of their own truck.

Willie gets into the truck and drives away in one direction

while Dagger drives off in another direction, so it won't look suspicious. Willie drives the truck back to the halting site and unloads the van. He hides the van behind some trailers and covers it so it can't be seen from the road. Dagger heads back with the machine to the scrap yard, where Willie picks him up later.

"Well now lads, that's how we got our van back," says Willie.

"Well, ye sneaky bastards," says one of the other travellers. He raises his pint to the two lads to cheers to the occasion.

Christmas Day Dinner Party

All the travellers and Dagger's family go to the community hall for their annual Christmas dinner; there is a party with a disco. About one hundred travellers, women and children attend the annual Christmas dinner.

The hall is fully decorated with Christmas decorations and a massive Christmas tree, that Willie supplied. There are tables laid out along the hall. They all sit and eat.

"That's a grand Christmas tree Willie, where did ya come across that one?" asks an old traveller woman.

"£4 he bought that one for from a farmer down the country, ha, isn't it some tree? You wouldn't get a tree as big as that one around here," says Roger Barry, throwing a side eye at Dagger.

"Tis a fine stump of a Christmas tree sure it is and that's for sure," says another traveller.

They eat and pull crackers and have a brilliant time. They drink beer. The children run around pulling crackers and blowing whistles. They open presents, as the disco starts. The D J plays a Joe Dolan song,

"Love of the Common People" as the lights are dimmed.

They dance with each other. Dagger goes over to ask Fay to dance, where she is sitting with a few other woman, where their husbands are gathered around the bar drinking bottles of Guinness. Fay is in love with Dagger, so she wouldn't refuse dancing with him, she hopes some day herself and Dagger will marry. Fay is over the moon dancing with him, she has her arms around him for a slow dance.

"You know something Máirtín, I wouldn't mind having you all to myself," says Fay.

Outside the hall Mary is parking her car. Her flat is across the street from the community hall, she notices all the vans, she gets out of her car and goes to the front door of her flat, puts the key in the door. She can hear the music from across the street, stops and thinks for a moment putting her keys into her handbag, goes across the road and into the hall. When she goes inside she notices all the travellers having a ball, she is amazed with the layout. She notices Dagger dancing closely to Fay, with their arms around each other.

She goes to leave, when Bridie calls her.

"Hallo Mary, well God love ya, fancy seeing ya in here."

Mary looks over at Bridie, with sadness in her eyes.

"Why don't you join us Mary, come on come over here, we won't bite ya."

Mary goes and sits with Bridie and her family, her grandchildren and a few other women.

"Bridie, how are you keeping, you're having a great spread here sure ye have altogether."

"I love this Mary, you know, I look forward to this every year, we do have these Christmas parties for years, they're great," says Bridie.

"She is talking about this for months sure she is, that's all we listen to, is Grandma talking about the Christmas party," says Fay's young daughter Lizzy .

"After the Galway Races she starts talking about the Christmas party, and tomorrow she starts talking about how she is looking forward to St Patrick's Day," says Katie, as she gets up to join her friends across the hall. They all have a laugh.

"Ever since my husband died, Mary, this is all I have to look forward to. God rest his soul," says Bridie.

Mary is keeping a close eye on Dagger and Fay.

The Big Tom song "Four Country Roads" comes on the sound system. Most of the travellers get up out of their seats and dance to this song.

"Who did you have Christmas dinner with yourself Mary?"

"I went home Bridie, for a few days to my parents. I tell you one thing, I had to get away today. My father drives me crazy and oh God, he never stops," says Mary.

Meantime, Helen is on her own drinking in her house. She has the results of her pregnancy test. The results are positive. She is devastated, pacing up and down the sitting room. She picks up the phone a few times to phone Mary but doesn't have the courage to tell her that she is pregnant.

The Christmas party is in full swing. While Dagger is dancing with Fay, he notices Mary sitting with his Mum.

"Fay, you won't mind if we dance later on, I see someone I want to talk to." he says.

"'Tis her again, isn't it?"

She notices Mary with Bridie and the other women.

"Look Máirtín, nothing will be come of that, you know the way her father is. He'd rather shoot his daughter or you, than see you two together and that's the gospel truth," says Fay, with a jealous look on her face.

"I'll take my chances," replies Dagger.

"Anyway, what about us?" asks Fay.

"I'm sorry Fay, I want to talk to Mary. There are a few things I want to talk to her about," he says.

"You promised me that we would be together some day," Fay cries.

He leaves the dance floor and goes over to Mary.

"Well, look who's here, 'tis yourself Mary Buckley. What brings a girl like you into a place like this I wonder?"

He looks happy to see Mary. Fay looks over at them. Disappointed and hurt, she sits down beside Katie.

"What's up with ya, you look like you seen a ghost or something?"

"Ary, shut you Katie will ya, you know nothing," says Fay, getting upset.

"Well, I beg your pardon, excuse me for asking," says Katie.

"Well, mind your own business. On my dead husband's grave I promise ya I bust ya, you never had a man anyway sure what would you know?" says Fay.

Katie walks off. Fay cannot take her eyes off Máirtín and Mary.

"How are you? I see you were fairly enjoying yourself out there on the dance floor," says Mary.

"Ah ya, you cannot beat a good dance."

He notices young Seánine, Willie's oldest son, standing close to him.

"Hi Seánine, come here a minute, I want ya," says Máirtín. The young boy goes over to him.

"What's on ya Uncle?"

"Look, will ya ask that man up there to put on Joe, look see that man playing records," he points up at the stage.

"Ya," says Seánine.

"Ask the man to put on Joe Dolan will ya?"

Young Seánine goes up to the D J. to tell him to put on Joe Dolan for Dagger.

"Right, this is a special request for Martin Dagger Ward and his new girlfriend Mary Buckley, a policeman's daughter I might add." He plays the song "The House With The White Washed Gable."

They go out on the dance floor.

All the travellers start to clap and join Dagger and Mary on the floor, they all clap and cheer. Fay is not too happy, she sits on her own. Dagger takes notice of Fay but ignores her.

"See that woman you were dancing with, she was giving me sour looks the other day when I called to your place, she seems to fancy you," says Mary.

"Look, take no notice of her, she's just a friend, you know she is very angry 'cause her husband and his brother died within a couple of months of each other, anyway this is my favourite song," says Dagger.

"Oh my God that's awful, what did they die from," replies Mary.

"Sorry Mary, I'd rather not talk about it."

They all dance and have a good time.

Helen is on her own in her house, with no Christmas decorations, she is sprawled out on her bed drunk, with the whiskey bottle on the floor and the pregnancy test on the bed. She is depressed and unhappy. She feels she has made a mess of her life, she doesn't know how she is going to handle it when the news spreads that she is pregnant by a traveller.

It's about two am. Dagger and Mary are making love in the

back of his van for the first time in a remote place out in the country side. There is nice soft music on the van stereo.

"Tonight's the Night," a Rod Stewart song.

"Máirtín I love you so much, I never stop thinking about you, you are on my mind all the time." She hugs and kisses him.

"I feel the same about you Mary, but we can't be together, you know that." He puts on his trousers.

"Why do you say that, does this mean nothing to you?" cries Mary. She is getting upset.

"It does, but what will people say about us, how can we be together? Your father is a cop and you know how they feel about the travellers," he says.

"I don't care, I want us to be together that's all I want, I don't care about the feckin Guards."

"Well, I do want to be with you, but you know, Mary, that travellers and the settled people should never marry, it's like the Protestants and Catholics, they should never marry either. It causes too much hassle and I don't think I can handle that shit now to be honest with ya," says Dagger.

"I know all that, you said that before, I don't care about what people say, I want to be with you. I love you Máirtín, and that's all that matters to me," says Mary.

"It's not my people that matter Mary, it's yours. The settled people don't like travellers not to mind marrying one of us, and everyone knows that."

"Who said anything about marriage?" asks Mary.

"Well, you know what I mean now Mary don't ya." He's getting embarrassed.

"I think you are thinking ahead there now, Máirtín. Hold on a minute."

"I don't know Mary, maybe we will give it a go and we'll see what happens," he says.

They put their arms around each other and give each other a hug.

"Oh, I love you so much Máirtín. Anyways my arse is freezing, take me home before I catch pneumonia!"

They drive back to Dagger's trailer for a late night drink, where

Mary ends up spending the night.

It's St. Stevens morning, they are in bed together, both of them are asleep. Fay's two young children, young Johnny and Lizzy are standing staring at them asleep. They have sad faces. Johnny wakes up Dagger.

"Hey uncle wake up, it's eleven o'clock, come on, wake up, you promised us you'd take us to the fun fair today? Come on, wake up will ya?" tugging at Dagger to wake him up.

"What time is it, where am I?" asks Dagger.

"It's eleven thirty, it's St Stephen's day, the fun fair is on. Come on, you promised to take us," says Lizzy.

"All right, all right, keep your hair on," says Dagger.

Mary wakes up.

"What's all the commotion?"

"I promised the children I would take them to the fun fair in Mullingar today," he replies.

"That's fantastic, can I come to the fun fair with you as well?" asks Mary.

"Will we take her?" he asks the children.

The two children just lift their shoulders.

"Ara, why not?" says Dagger.

"Come on, lets get out of bed and head off," he adds.

At The Fun Fair

The children are happy that they are going to the fun fair. Dagger and Mary get ready to travel to Mullingar. They all hop into the van. Mary turns on the radio, the song on the radio is "Rock Around the Clock." Bridie and Fay's two children are in the front of the van. Mary, Fay and Katie and a few other children are in the back, sitting on car seats. They get to the fun fair. They are all very exited. They go on all the attractions; the bumper cars, darts, play cards. Dagger wins a teddy bear and sweets for the children.

"I haven't had so much fun in years Máirtín, could you believe that?" says Mary.

She holds his hand as they walk around eating ice cream cones.

"Do ya, know, I feel guilty for enjoying myself, anyways I have to work here tonight," says Dagger.

"Oh really, so that's why we got everything free. Listen, don't feel guilty for being happy, this is the way things are supposed to be," says Mary.

"Yes, 'tis easy to say that anyway. Forget that, 'tis my cousins that own the fun fair. That's him over there with the black beard, he's Beardie Ward, that's what we call him," he says.

Beardie is working on one of the machines with a few other men.

"Good, so lets try the bumper cars again," says Mary.

They go into the bumper cars and drive very fast. The whole place is thronged with people, there are a lot of children there with their parents. Bridie and Fay and other traveller women are watching Máirtín and Mary. Fay looks jealous and sad.

"Look at Máirtín, I haven't see him so happy in years," says Bridie. Her eyes fill up.

"Julie would turn in her grave if she seen what's going on here today, it's not right."

"Now Fay, don't be jealous at all you," says Nina Barry, who has just joined them.

"How's Nina, how are you?"

"Fine now Bridie, how ye all keeping?"

"Never mind her Nina, she's only jealous because she is in love with Dagger," says Katie.

"Shut up you Katie, I am not jealous at all. I wouldn't go around him anyway, you're only a big buffer fool Katie Ward, that's all you are and everybody around here knows that," says Fay. getting annoyed.

"Well, excuse me for asking," says Nina.

"You are jealous Fay, he told me himself that you thought that you and him would marry one day, and don't ya deny it, 'cause tis the truth," says Katie.

"Mind your own business you Katie, your nose is too big for your face sure it is," shouts Fay.

She walks off in a huff, gets her two children. The children don't want to leave. She hits them across the back of their legs. The children kick up a racket, they tell her they don't want to leave.

"Well excuse me, you have a big ugly gob yourself Fay Barry, anyway everyone knows you killed your husband, and over my dead father's grave I'll swear by that," says Katie.

"Stop that now you Katie and behave yourself," says Bridie, walking over to one of the stalls.

"Look you little whore, what are you saying about my husband, watch your big mouth or I will close it for ya. My husband died of a heart attack and everybody knows that," yells Fay.

"Oh ya, he died of a heart attack all right, and you caused it with giving him rat poison," says Katie.

Fay goes over to Katie to stop her saying anymore, hitting her across the face. The two start fighting, pulling each others hair. They fall to the ground. Everybody gathers around to make a circle to watch the two women fight. Fay sticks Katie's face in the mud, they roll around in the mud punching each other.

Máirtín and Mary don't see the fight, they are having too much fun to notice anything. When the fight is over everybody claps their hands and has a good laugh.

Fay, covered in mud with a nose bleed, gets her children to leave.

"Come on ye two," says Fay, getting furious and shouting at the children.

"Come on will ye I said!"

She grabs her two children by the hands to leave the fun fair. She goes over to one of her cousins for a lift back home. Katie is covered in mud also, and has a split lip. Bridie comes back, when she sees Katie covered in mud and bleeding from the mouth, when she learns what has happened, she tells Katie twas good enough for her, that she might keep her big mouth shut from now on.

Mary's Parents House

Sheila and Tim are home. Tim is reading the Connacht Tribune. A knock comes on the door. It's their son Timmy and his girlfriend Ann. They go into the sitting room, which is decorated for Christmas.

"You're welcome, and happy Christmas to you both, I was just putting on the kettle, you timed it well. Ann, will you have a hot toddy?"

"Ah no Sheila, I'll just have a coffee, Timmy doesn't like me to take a drink, he says it doesn't suit me, says I talk shit when I have drink taken, isn't that right Timmy?"

"You do more than talk shit, now Ann sure you do."

Tim looks out over his glasses at that comment.

"Go on will ya, have a hot toddy," Sheila says.

"All right so, just give her one and make it a small one," says Timmy.

He picks up a copy of Ireland's Own to read, and puts his foot on his knee.

"For shit sake Timmy you're worse than your father, let her have a drink will ya, what kind of a dry bollox at all are you," says Sheila, getting annoyed. She goes to the kitchen to make the hot toddies.

Tim looks out over the paper at Sheila, and puts his eyes up to heaven.

"Will I tell her, or will you?" Ann whispers to Timmy.

"Tell them what?" asks Timmy.

He looks confused as to what Ann is on about.

"You know," says Ann, turning her eyes down to her tummy.

"What's up, is it good news or bad?" asked Sheila, pouring out the hot toddys in the kitchen.

"Sheila, I'm pregnant!"

"What, I don't believe this, you're pregnant, what will people think? We'll be the laughing stock around here," Tim says, with a frown, leaving down the paper.

"Shut up you Tim, look I'm glad for ye both, it will be my first grandchild! I tell you what you should do now is get married and say nothing to anybody, and nobody will know the difference, we will keep this to ourselves."

"Mum, no way, we're not getting married!"

"What did you say Timmy? Ye will get married, what will people say around here, it's bad enough having a daughter chasing around after a tinker, and now this, what kind of family did I rear at all? We will be the laughing stock of Ballycrackn," Tim says, angry and annoyed.

"Look Dad, we decided not to get married for a while now, and that's it. It's not up to you, and we don't care what people think around here anyways."

"What's a while?" Tim asks.

"A few years at least," Timmy says, looking to Ann for support. Ann is disappointed with the reaction from Timmy's parents.

"I don't know what the world is coming to at all, the whole world is upside down if you ask me, and I tell you something else, worse it's getting," says Tim.

The phone rings. Sheila picks it up.

"Hallo?"

"Hello Mum, I'm phoning you from Limerick."

"Limerick?" Sheila says, they all look at each other.

"Mary, what are you doing in Limerick?"

"I'm with my boyfriend."

"With who, I didn't know you even had a boyfriend."

Tim looks at Sheila with a frown.

"I'm with my boyfriend Máirtín Ward."

"Máirtín Ward?" Sheila says.

Sheila faints and falls to the ground.

"What, I don't believe it! My daughter is with that tinker again, well over my dead body, this will finish before it goes any further. I will see to that, there is no way any member of my family is going to marry any tinker and that's one thing for certain!" shouts Tim

Timmy attends to his mother; he puts a cushion under her head, while Ann gets a cold glass of water from the kitchen. Sheila comes around; Tim and Timmy get her up on her feet and lay her down on the couch to give her a chance to come around and take it all in.

In Limerick, Máirtín asks Mary what did her Mum say.

"She is very happy for us and she gives you her regards."

He smiles, and hugs Mary, she looks unhappy.

Chapter Nine

Helen Breaks The News To Mary

A couple of weeks later Mary's at home in her flat, looking at old photos, and reminiscing on her past, listening to soft music on the radio.

After a while, the phone rings. She picks it up.

"Hello?"

"Mary, it's Helen, you won't believe this, I'm pregnant."

"What, you can't be serious, who's the lucky father, is he someone I know?" asks Mary jokingly.

"Mary, stop pissing around, this is serious, remember that day I went to Dublin?"

"Ya."

"Well, remember the tinker, Cathal something or other."

"Oh—-my—-God, you don't say, oh Helen, what are you going to do?"

"I have my mind made up; I'm going on my own to London tomorrow."

"Janey-Mack Helen, have you thought about this, that's a big decision to make!"

"I have and I do not care, I am going in the morning and that is it, I can't live with this any longer.

"Oh my God, look, I will come with ya; I couldn't let you go there on your own."

"Oh thanks Mary, will I see you at the C I E Station in the morning, and we will get the eight o'clock train to Dublin. Is that ok?"

"Right, I will be there, look after yourself Helen and I'll see you in the morning."

"Thanks Mary, I love you, bye."

C I E Railway Station

The next morning eight a.m. Helen is waiting at the platform on her own, not another person in sight. The train pulls in, nobody is getting on only Helen, no sign of Mary. The Train Conductor says "All Aboard!"

She gets on, the train goes to pulls off. She asks the Conductor could he stall the train for one minute, that she was waiting for a friend, who has not arrived yet.

"No, we're on a tight schedule, we have to go," replies the Conductor.

Helen is devastated when the train begins to move off, she starts to cry.

"Look Sir, can you not stop the train for just one more minute, my friend said she would definitely be here."

"No miss, I am sorry, we are already on our way," he replies.

She is on her own crying, sad, angry and lonely. She looks out at the platform to see is Mary anywhere. There is no sign of her. She's in a mess, thinking of London and the ordeal she will have to undertake on her own.

After a minute or two, Mary arrives and touches Helen on the shoulder.

"Mary, oh God, I thought you were not going to come!"

Mary sits down.

"Look Helen, it's com-ing that got you into this mess in the first place. Anyways, I was on the wrong side of the platform, the train was just moving and I hopped on as fast as I could. I had to squeeze in the door, look at the state of my coat, it's all black from the door."

"Anyways, how are you?"

"Oh brilliant Mary, how do you think I am?" Helen says, sarcastically.

"I'm sorry, anyways have you really thought about this. Are you really sure you don't want to keep it, after all it's a big decision you know," Mary says with concern.

"No, I made my mind up, I'm going ahead with it," Helen says, she stares out the window.

"Ok, lets do it so; you know somehow, I think you are doing the right thing."

"I know I am Mary, there is no doubt about it."

They both chat for a while. Helen goes to the buffet bar for some drinks to settle her nerves, they both chat as the train makes it's way to Dublin.

The train arrives at Heuston Station at approximately eleven o'clock. They get on the bus going to the airport, sitting on the left hand side of the bus. When the bus pulls up at another bus stop on the way, Helen notices 'Cathal the Stud' Holms at the bus stop with a young woman. Helen covers her face so he will not recognise her. When they enter the bus, Helen gets nervous, Mary notices this.

"Are you ok, you are freaking out there! What's wrong with ya?" asks Mary.

"I am all right; I just feel a bit sick because of this journey."

Cathal and the woman make their way to the back of the bus, passing Mary and Helen going to their seats. Helen keeps her head down when they pass by.

When they arrive at the airport, Helen is terrified, and afraid as she feels there's no going back.

Ballycrackn Dump Site

Tim and Sheila are in the car going to dump the Christmas tree at the local dump site. They have the Christmas tree and other rubbish bags on the car trailer that Tim just purchased a few weeks before.

"I can't believe I have reared a daughter to do this to me, Janey Mack, does she know the worry she is causing us?"

"Let's pray Tim, it's only a phase she is going through," Sheila says.

"Oh, I don't know," says Tim.

They arrive at the dump. Tim reverses his car and trailer beside a pile of rubbish bags. He gets out and off loads the rubbish. While he is doing so, a man approaches him.

"Good morning Sir, you don't mind if I ask you where you got this trailer from?"

"Why? who wants to know?"

"That's my trailer," the man says.

"Well is it now, and how do you make that out, look, I bought this trailer from a man in Castlebar in good faith, just a few weeks ago." Tim says.

"It is my trailer all right, I had it made especially, look at those twin wheels, you won't get a trailer like that this side of the Shannon," says the Man.

"Is that so, if this is your car trailer you might come down to the Station first thing in the morning, and we will sort this mess out."

"I will indeed Sir, and I want this trailer back, look, I have a great mind to call the Police."

"Don't bother, anyways where do you live?" Tim asks.

"Just outside Roscommon, I am here helping my daughter clearing out rubbish out of her out houses, herself and her husband run a small farm just outside Newport," says the man.

Tim empties the trailer, he gets into the car and drives off.

"You won't believe this," says Tim.

He bangs the steering wheel.

"What's wrong now with ya?" asks Sheila.

"Do you know what, this trailer was stolen. I paid a lot of money for this trailer. I would not mind, I only bought it a few weeks ago."

Sheila smiles and turns her head away.

Dublin Airport

The two girls check in at the departures desk, with only one weekend case apiece. The departure attendant ask Helen how long are they staying.

"Three days probably."

"That's ok, did you pack this bag yourself?" The Attendant asks.

"Yes, I did," Helen replies, looking at Mary annoyed.

"Don't look at me Helen like that, it's you that got yourself into this mess."

The attendant gives the eye to Helen.

"I will have to check your passports, because of the troubles in London."

"Ok, that's fine."

She checks their passports.

"You can put your bags through," the attendant says.

They browse around Duty Free while they are waiting to board the plane. Helen is uneasy, with not much to say, the passengers are called over the intercom to board the plane.

The plane lifts off.

"Oh my God, this is scary," says Helen, looking out the window to watch the ground disappear from beneath them.

London England

The plane comes down at London Airport. The two girls collect their bags off the conveyer belt and go to the airport taxi rank. They get into a black Taxi. The driver gets out of the car and puts their bags into the boot. They're driving to London.

"Well, what part of Ireland are you from darling?" says the driver, looking at Mary in his rear view mirror.

"Westport, driver."

"Is that in Southern Ireland?" he asks,

"Yes, it's in Mayo," Mary answers.

"O ya Mayo, do you know Ballina?"

"We do," says Mary.

Helen is very quiet and stone faced. Mary notices this and gives her a little pat on her knee, to reassure her that she will be all right.

"My wife's family is from Ballina you know."

"Oh is that right," Mary says.

"I haven't been there yet, this summer we are planning to go there, what's the weather like in Ireland during summer time?"

"Ok, sunny, I suppose," says Mary.

"What brings you to London, business or pleasure?"

"Just visiting some friends for a few days," says Mary.

She looks at Helen sensitively.

"What part of London?" asks the Taxi driver.

"I don't know, city centre I suppose, we have the address in our luggage."

"Ok darling, I will have ye there in no time at all," says the taxi driver.

Back Home With Tim And Sheila

They are at home, it's Tim's day off, there are having their tea. The house is quiet, the clock ticks slowly. Tim is stressed out over the car trailer.

"Look Tim will you calm down, you are making me nervous."

"£450 I paid for that trailer Sheila, it's the first time in my life anything like that has happened to me. I'm dealing with this kind of crime all the time, I never thought it would happen to me, I just can't believe it."

"By the way Tim, Mary phoned. She and Helen are gone to London for a few days."

"You're not serious, I hope they will look after themselves over there, London is a queer place nowadays with all the I R A bombings."

"Do you know something, you always think the worst, how's that?" says Sheila.

"You cannot be too careful these days, what's bringing them over to London?"

"Well, she told me she was going to visit a friend of Helen's, that's all I know."

"Did that tinker go with them I wonder,"

"I'm not sure, probably not. Do you know something, I had a stressfull few days, I think I will go to the doctor in the morning for something to calm my nerves," says Sheila, as she wipes her brow.

Taxi Driver Brings Up A Sensitive Issue

"Is your friend all right darling, she seems upset, is it anything I said?" asks the Taxi driver.

Helen starts to cry.

"She is ok, don't worry yourself about her."

"Are you sure? You can talk to me you know, I'm not just a driver, I'm a good listener too, I heard it all, I listen to everybody's problems, the taxi driver is a good man to talk to!" he says.

"You're so kind," says Mary, sarcastically.

"It's all part of the job, do you know we get a lot of Irish Catholic girls coming over here for abortions, you don't believe in abortions in Ireland do you?"

"No, it is against our religion," says Mary.

She is annoyed with the taxi driver, as she comforts Helen.

"Is it true that if you get pregnant in Ireland, the Bishops, or your parents, put you into care or a home for unmarried mothers, is that true?"

"Yes, in some cases," says Mary.

"I heard that all right," he says.

Helen looks at Mary in sadness and annoyance with the driver.

"That's true in some cases, it doesn't happen as often as it used to in the past," replies Mary.

"My wife was telling me that there is a town over there in Ireland, oh, what's it called, is it Galway or something like that?" he asks

"Yes, Galway, what about it?"

"There is a home there for young girls that get themselves into trouble, they are put in there I believe for the rest of their lives, is that the case?" he asks.

"It's called the Magdalene Laundry; the bishop arranged that, there are a lot of them sort of places all over Ireland. Look, you might watch where you are going, you almost crashed into that truck that just overtook us," says Mary.

She gets a fright because she thought they were going to crash.

"You're all right, thank God I'm not a woman, it must be hard to be a woman in Ireland."

The two girls cannot wait to get out of the taxi. He drives into Central London where he drops them off. They pay him; he thanks them, and drives off.

"The bastard, I'm a good listener he said, he never shut his big mouth, he was the only one that was talking, good listener in my hole. Look Mary, I don't feel well, can we have a drink or something, I just want to unwind," says Helen, sitting on her suitcase on the side walk at Piccadilly circus.

"Ok, look at this place, bloody hell it's massive," says Mary.

They look around at all the massive buildings.

"How in the name of feck could you drive over here with all them double decker buses, they must be hundreds of them, they would drive over ya, sure they would," says Helen.

They go into a pub nearby to have a drink; when Helen gets her drink, she gulps it down as fast as she can.

"Feck it, Helen, take it easy will you for feck sake. You'll be drunk again in no time, you didn't eat a thing all day. The last thing I need now is you getting pissed on me again."

"Look Mary, I don't care, do you know something, I just want to die, this whole charade is driving me insane."

"I'm sorry, Helen." She puts her arms around her.

"If it is any consolation to you, this time tomorrow it will be all over." Mary says.

"For you maybe but not for me, this will haunt me for the rest of my life. I'd rather be dead than carry this guilt around with me for the rest of my life, do you know that Mary?"

"Helen, just look at the bright side, this time tomorrow it will be all over. Just imagine being nine months pregnant, and having to raise that child for the next eighteen years; do you really think you could cope with rearing a child on your own, not to mind what people would be saying?" says Mary.

"Couldn't you imagine the gossip, ya, I see it now, a tinker child, Helen Conway is rearing a tinkers child, my God I can hear them now." Helen says.

"Anyways, I think you are thinking too much about this, lets not say anymore about it for a while," Mary says.

They leave the pub to book into a small hotel. It is sleazy and dirty. The hotel owner is behind the reception desk. He is smoking a cigar and is unshaven.

"Hello," says Helen, approaching the man behind the counter.

"Yes, what can I do for you darling?" says the man.

"We are looking for a room for the night."

"For one or two?" asks the man.

"How do you mean, one or two?" asks Helen.

"One or two people?"

"Oh ya, I lost you there for a minute, two people of course," says Helen fatiguedly.

He looks through the hotel guest book.

"Right ladies, I have a double room on the top floor, that will be £6 each for just the room, breakfast is extra," he says.

"That's all right Sir, we will have the room only, isn't that all right Helen?"

"That will be fine," says Helen.

"How many nights?" asks the man.

"Just the one for now, we will see tomorrow if we are staying an extra night."

They both take their bags up the stairs to the top floor. Going into the room they notice it's dirty and untidy. The wallpaper is old and damp and falling off the wall, the toilets are filthy.

"Jesus Mary and Saint Joseph, look at the state of this place, it's filthy. Look at the state of the bed, it's rotten; it must be at least fifty years old," Helen says, with a disgusted look on her face.

"Oh God this is scary, how did I get myself into this mess," Helen says.

It's late and they get into bed. They both cannot sleep, they are scratching, twisting and turning all night. They are very uncomfortable, the springs are broke in the mattress. Helen is getting more fatigued and depressed as time goes by, thinking to herself that the man that helped get her into this situation is probably off somewhere on holiday with his girlfriend.

After having a restless night, they get out of bed at nine am, where they go to a nearby cafe to get breakfast. Helen is unwell, and is unable to eat breakfast, she only has a fag and a mug of coffee.

At A Secret Hospital In London

They make their way to the Hospital, where they go to reception. Helen is feeling distraught and uncomfortable.

"Hello, what can I do for you?" asks the receptionist.

"I'm Helen Conway, I have an appointment here at ten thirty with Dr Harnet."

"Do you have an appointment card?"

"No, he told me to be here at this time, I talked to him on the phone."

"All right, wait till I check."

"Oh Mary I'm scared, this is terrible, how did all this happen, I feel sick?"

"I don't know, anyway Helen, you can still back out you know, you don't have to carry this through."

"No I'm going ahead no matter what happens. I don't want anybody knowing about this, things are bad enough. I would die if anybody back home knew about this."

The receptionist comes back.

"Right, if you go through them doors at the end of the corridor, just take a seat. Dr Harnet will be there in a moment. And don't worry, you will be fine."

They go into the waiting room where Dr Harnet joins them after a short time.

"Good morning, I'm Dr Harnet, which of you is Helen Conway?" He looks at the chart he has in his hand.

"I'm Helen Conway."

"Come with me to my office. Are the both of you together?" he asks.

"We are," Helen says.

"Well then, the both of you come along," he says.

Helen is tense, the Doctor shakes her hand.

"Right, I will talk you through the procedure. First thing first, I want to know have you thought about this operation seriously and what it contains. Now it's a very simple procedure, it will only take a few minutes, ten minutes at the most, you will lose a little blood, but I would not worry about that. You have eight pints in your body anyways, I'm sure you are well aware of."

"Oh, right?" says Helen.

"We will keep you in over-night and all going well we will let you go home in the morning."

"Now I have to tell you, that if you are going to try to have a baby in the future there might be complications for you."

"What kind of complications Doctor?" asks Mary.

"Well, there will be a certain amount of damage done to your uterus. Probably that will heal up completely. There is no way of knowing what will go wrong in the future, I'm only warning you that there may be complications and maybe not."

"So what you are saying is, I might not be able to have a baby in the future, is that what you mean?"

"I'm not saying that exactly, but it's a possibility."

"Ok," says Helen.

"Right, any questions?" asked the Doctor.

"Have you carried out many of this type of operation in the past Doctor?"

"Yes, but I can't disclose specific information, everything in this clinic is confidential."

"Right, thanks," says Mary.

"Now Helen," says the Doctor, holding her hand.

"Do you have any second thoughts?"

"No, I'm fine, I just want this over with,"she says with a sigh of relief that in a short time the operation will be over with so she can go home.

Sheila Is Concerned About The Girls

Sheila goes to Helen's mothers house to see does she know why the girls went to London. They are having tea.

"And you have no idea what brought the girls to London, at all have you?" asks Sheila.

"Not one idea, sure Helen doesn't tell me anything anymore. If you ask me, all she does with her spare time is drink. I don't know how she is holding down her job in the bank at all," says Nellie.

"I wouldn't mind Tim is so worried, two little girls in a big city like that, on their own in London," Sheila says.

"Well, now Sheila, I wouldn't go as far as to call them little girls, women more like it. They are well able to look after themselves, they're not like we were. I was afraid to cross the road when I was their age, the thoughts of a big city would frighten me."

"I know Nellie, I'm just concerned, we didn't go far in our time, anyways we will find out soon enough when they get back. I suppose all we can do now is pray to the Blessed Virgin to bring them home safely."

The Termination

Helen is anxious to get the operation over with, on the other hand the doctor needs to be convinced.

"Before we go any further Helen, can you see yourself having this baby?" asks the Doctor.

"I don't know," Helen says.

She puts her head down, and weeps.

"Well, let me help you; do you want to have this baby? Do you want to bring this unwanted foetus into the world?" he asks.

"I don't know Doctor. When you put it that way I suppose it is unwanted."

"And I must stress it is a foetus, like you told me you got pregnant over eight weeks ago, look, its like this Helen, can you see yourself rearing a baby on your own, I take it that you don't have a regular boyfriend?"

"Doctor, I came here for a reason and that was to terminate this pregnancy, I don't want it, it all happened when I was drunk, I want to go ahead Doctor. I can't have this child, that's it."

"Are you really sure?" asks Mary.

"Mary I am, I'm sure, does anybody believe me?"

Her hands are sweaty and shaking.

"100% sure?" asks the Doctor.

"Yes Doctor 100%, I'm sure, I have no doubt in my mind,

please believe me, I have my mind made up and there is no going back."

"Well, that will be all, you can sit in the waiting room, and a Nurse will call you as soon as possible," says Doctor Harnet.

They both take a seat in the waiting room. Helen is feeling low. They both sit with nothing further to say. Nurse comes in to take Helen to the operating theatre, she is terrified, she holds Mary's hand for a moment and then lets go. She makes her way with the Nurse to the theatre. The termination is over in a matter of minutes.

After the operation Helen is in the recovery room. Mary is by her side holding her hand, she wakes up, and starts to cry when she sees Mary.

"Oh Mary, it's all over is it?"

"Yes it's all over Helen, how do you feel?"

"I don't know, Mary have I done the right thing?"

"I think so, Helen. I feel inside it was the right thing for you to do." She puts her hand on her heart. Doctor Harnet enters the room.

"Well Helen," he says.

"We have some good news for you, the operation went very well. You lost very little blood, which is a good sign. I don't think there will be any complications in the near future. As far as I'm concerned everything is fine."

"Thank you very much Doctor, and when can I go home, I want to go home!"

She starts to cry again.

"I will keep you in overnight, just to be sure, you will be right as rain in the morning. I'm giving you a leaflet about the after effects, emotional, that is, now I recommend that you go to your own doctor when you go home so he can set up counselling for you straight away."

"Counselling, what's that for Doctor?"

"You might get depressed. Now Helen you're not unique, most patients who go through trauma like this do experience some kind of setback, let it be depression or otherwise. Now, on the other hand you could be fine, but to be on the safe side, I would seek help if I were you."

"Oh that's all I need now is depression, I can't believe it."

She folds her arms to face the wall.

"Look, I will leave it with you both and I will call to see you later on." The Doctor leaves the room, while Mary comforts Helen.

"Thank you Mary for standing by me through all of this, I don't know what I would have done without you."

"If it was me that was in your situation, I would like to think Helen you would do the same for me."

Helen is kept in over night. Mary sleeps on a chair, at her bedside all night. The next day Helen is released from the hospital. They come out from the hospital. They both walk along the sidewalk to get a taxi to go straight to the Airport, to get back to Ireland.

"Depression, that's all I need now, look Mary if I get depressed I'm going to kill myself and that's for sure. I don't think I could handle depression, things are bad enough," says Helen.

They both walk along Trafalgar Square to flag a taxi to take them to the airport.

"Shut up you will ya, and don't be talking like that. You will be fine," Mary says, with concern for Helen.

"Anyways I could murder a bottle of vodka right now, sure I could."

"Look, if anything is going to make you depressed it's that drink, look, you drink to much alcohol, anyways sure you do," Mary says.

"I have nothing else, alcohol is my friend, it keeps me sane."

"That's what all alcoholics say, alcohol is my friend, I would die without it, that's what they always say."

"Well excuse me now Mary Buckley, I'm not an alcoholic, look here comes a taxi now."

Helen puts her hand out to stop the taxi. The taxi stops, and the driver gets out to put their luggage in the boot. They get into the taxi.

"Where to ladies?" asks the driver.

"Heathrow Airport," says Mary.

"Ok sweetheart."

The two girls look at each other and smile, they both get a flashback to the other taxi driver who had taken them to London in the first place.

"Not another one," says Mary, with a sigh.

"What's that darling?" says the Driver, looking in his rear view mirror at Mary.

"Oh my God, not another one is right," says Helen.

They arrive at Heathrow Airport, where they board a flight to get back to Ireland. The two girls are glad they're are on their way home.

Gossip Spreads Around The Town

There is a lot of gossip around the town about Mary having to go to England to have an abortion, there is a lot of talk that Máirtín Dagger Ward has got her pregnant. A couple of women who are in Kelly's Supermarket shopping and gossiping to Mr Kelly about Mary Buckley.

"Well, Mr Kelly, I suppose you heard the rumours that's flying around the town, the latest gossip I believe," says Mrs Finell, the policeman's wife.

"And what gossip might that be?"

"She is pregnant and gone to England I believe for one of them operations, what do we call them?" says one of the women.

"An abortion that's what it's called," says Mrs Finell.

"Who are ye talking about?" asks Mr Kelly.

"Don't tell me you didn't hear, it's that Nurseen, you know the one, Mary Buckley."

"For God's sake woman, where in the hell did you hear that, do ya know, Sergeant Ricky Molloy is very good friend with her father, Timothy Buckley, in Mayo somewhere, sure didn't they train together in Templemore sure they did. If he heard ye spreading them rumours he would lock the both of you up. You should be ashamed of yourself," he says, pointing at Mrs Finell.

"With your husband being a member of the force and all," says Mr Kelly with annoyance.

"Ary, shut up you, I tell ya, he won't be too pleased when he finds out what his little girl has gone and done and that's for sure," says the other woman.

"And to top it all off, the lad that got her into trouble is a tinker, living on the side of the road up the road there someplace," Mrs Finell says.

"Oh for feck sake ye two, will ye ever keep your big mouths shut, do ye know what ye are saying at all do ye, ha! Anyways, ye have no proof, unless you Mrs Finell, you are listening to telephone conversations down the post office."

"Excuse me Sir?" she says, shocked with that remark.

"Look." Mr Kelly puts his hand up.

"I will have no more of that kind of talk in my shop, now clear out the both of ye." He walks off annoyed.

At the travellers' trailer site, all the Ward family are there! Bridie, Fay, cousins, and a lot of children, dogs, horses, ponies. Dagger is breaking in a young mare, for the pony and trap races at Carlow town, which is an annual event and gathers a large crowd from miles around. He is trying to put her under a pony trap. Willie comes driving into the site very fast in a Hi Ace van. He hops out of the van and runs over to Dagger. All the rest of the travellers are looking at Willie. Bridie and Fay look out the window of their trailers. His cousins (two women) start talking to Willie.

"Hi, Willie what's wrong with ya?" says one woman.

He keeps running towards Dagger.

"Willie, a mockeen, what's up with ya, is there somebody dead?" says another woman.

"Hi, Dagger wait till I tell ya."

"Not now Willie, I'm busy can't you see, look, give us a hand here, till I put the strap on this bitch."

"Look it's important, ya better listen to me now," says Willie, getting very excited.

"Ok what's up Willie? This better be good, or I'll shit on ya, can't you see I'm busy?" he says, holding the pony by the halter and feeding her with sugar balls.

"There is a lot of talk around the town, about you and the Sergeant's daughter; you know, a lot of tongues wagging you see."

"What do you mean tongues wagging?"

"It's about you and her, I'm telling ya."

"All right, what about me and her?"

"They're all talking about the Nurse that works in St. Brendan's Ward, you know beyond at the hospital?" Willie says.

"Ya what about her?"

"She is gone over to England, 'cause she is up the stick, they say."

"What? Who's up the stick?"

"Who do ya think Dagger?"

"Who in the hell told you that?"

"I was in O'Reilly's bar and I heard that Scar Face talking at the bar about you, and her, the Sergeant's daughter in Westport, they were talking about ye, I tell ya."

"Jeaney Mac, will ya hold onto this one for me," says Dagger, giving the reins of the pony to Willie.

He goes to leave; his mother and Fay come running out of one of the trailers.

"What's wrong Máirtín, is there something up?" Bridie says.

"What ever it is it must be very important, I suppose it must have something to do with that Nurse bitch," says Fay, with a sly sarcastic look.

"It's all right Mum, don't worry yourself, I'll be back later." He gets into his van and drives off. Bridie and Fay are left bewildered.

Dagger is driving along the road looking very stressed out. The Joe Dolan Song, "The House With The White Washed Gable" is playing on the van stereo, he hits the radio with his fist to turn off the song. He drives at high speed to Mary's flat. Jumping out of his van he goes knocking at the door. There is no answer. He shouts her name in the letter box, he looks in the window, no sign of Mary to be seen.

A women comes out next door, it's one of the woman that was talking in the shop earlier.

"You won't find anybody there, she is gone over to England, up to no good I believe, I hear she is up the stick," she says, with her arms folded, wearing a blue flowery apron and smoking a cigarette.

"What do you mean Mrs, when did she go to England?"

"I heard one of ye tinker people put her up the stick, 'tis yourself I suppose, you know, I have seen you around here before. Do you know that Nurse's father is a Sergeant down in Mayo somewhere, I tell you, when he lay his hands on you, he will strangle ya, ha!" she says, with a sly smirk on her face.

"Look Mrs, have you seen her anywhere at all, have ya, look, stop talking shit and tell me the truth," he shouts.

"No, I haven't, I'm saying no more now, I don't want to be accused around here of spreading rumours, now piss off and leave me alone!"

"Anyways Mrs, it's none of your business, you shouldn't be spreading gossip about things you don't know anything about, now keep your big mouth shut, or I will close it for ya," he says.

He is in a temper, getting stressed out.

"Hmmm, you can put a note in the letter box if you wish," she says.

"Can't write," he says.

"Ah, well, serves you right, now go away before I call the Police on ya. My friend's husband is a policeman, he wouldn't be too pleased to see the likes of you around here, now clear off."

She puts her head in the air, goes inside and puts the bolt on her door. Dagger gets into his van, frustrated and annoyed, and drives off.

Mary And Helen On There Way Home

They are in the airplane, unaware of the gossip that's on the streets of Ballinasloe town.

The airhostess is going around with food and drinks; she come to the two girls. Helen looks very sick and unwell.

"Well ladies, what would you like to drink?"

"Have you vodka?" Helen asks.

"Yes I do, how many do you want?" asks the airhostess.

"I will have the largest bottle you have."

The airhostess gives the bottle to Helen, it's a very small bottle of vodka.

"Look at the sizeene of it, Jesus will ya give us a few more of them will ya, they wouldn't get a birdie drunk."

"Helen look, two will do, you look like hell as you are," says Mary, getting annoyed because of Helen's drinking.

"Are you ok, you don't look well?" asks the airhostess.

She looks at Helen with concern.

"I'll be fine when I drink a few of those," says Helen, holding up the vodka bottles.

"We are fine now Miss, thank you very much," Mary says.

The airhostess pushes on.

"I can't wait to get home to see Máirtín, I wonder what he is up to now?"

"It's all right for you Mary, you have him to go home to, I have nobody, nobody cares about me."

"Look Helen, stop that talk, someday you will have a man of your own, so don't be feeling sorry for yourself, you will be fine."

Helen looks at Mary with hurt in her eyes.

They arrive back home and are getting off the bus in the centre of the town. Helen is a bit tipsy again, Mary is pissed off with her. Scar Face is in a shop across the road purchasing twenty Carrolls, he notice them getting off the bus. Little Seánine is watching them also.

"Let's go into O'Reilly's for one."

"Ok Helen, but just the one, I just want to lie down I'm so tired. Really all I want to do is go home."

They walk across the road to O'Reilly's Bar, there are about ten people inside including Scar Face, who is telling the men at the bar, that the two girls are back from England.

When the two girls go to the counter, everybody inside has their heads together talking about them, they are all looking at Mary.

"Is everything all right around here? I get a weird vibe in here, what are they all looking at?" Mary says to Jack O' Reilly.

"Everything is fine in here," Jack says.

"I don't know, ye all seem a bit freaky."

She takes a glance around.

"Ah, never you mind them, gives us two pints of Smithwick's Jack, before I collapse," Helen says.

Helen whispers to Mary.

"Mary I want this to be our secret, lets keep this to ourselves, lets not tell a soul,"

Scar Face comes up to Mary and Helen and speaks in an English accent.

"All right mate, everything ok, have a good trip," he says.

"Where did you get your accent from?" asks Mary, looking at Helen in suspicion as Scar Face walks off.

"Now, that's weird," Mary says, getting uncomfortable.

"Mary, will you just leave it, don't mind that asshole, twas his ex-wife that gave him that scar he has across his face. He almost killed her in a jealous rage 'cause he thought she was having an affair with a younger man I was told. Never mind that bastard, he's only a bollix, come on let's sit over here to rest our weary bones." Helen says.

Máirtín's in his trailer stressed out, pacing up and down. His phone rings, he answers it. Seánine is in the town phoning from a kiosk to tell him Mary has arrived back in town.

"Ya" he says, when he picks up the phone.

"Hi Dagger, that lady you told me to keep an eye out for, you know the one you had at the trailer a few weeks ago, she works in the hospital?"

"What about her, Seánine?"

"She is gone into O'Reilly's with some other girl, you owe me €1 for that now Dagger, I was here all feckin' day, I'm famished with the cold."

"Good lad Seánine, I'll talk to ya later."

He puts down the phone, rushes out the door, into his van and drives straight to O'Reilly's. He runs into the pub, looks around for Mary, when he spots her sitting with Helen he dashes straight over to her.

"Mary come outside awhile, I want to talk to you."

He pulls Mary by the arm towards the door, as everybody in the pub looks on.

"Up out of that you boy ya, there will be crack in the camp tonight, and that's for sure. Jack fill us up another pint there will ya, the crack is good."

"Take it easy there will ya, twasn't long since you were in the same situation yourself, Scar Face," Jack says.

"Let go of my arm, you're hurting me, what's up with you at all?"

"Look Mary, I'm sorry, come outside will ya, I have to talk to ya, I can't talk in here."

Everybody is looking, they all know what's going on except Mary.

"What's his problem I wonder, he has it bad whatever it is," says Helen, drinking her pint.

"What's wrong ? You are hurting my arm, let me go now?"

Dagger pulls Mary by the hand, to go outside.

"Stop will you now, and tell me what's wrong."

"Tell you what? Look Mary, it's more like, you tell me what's going on with yourself."

"Tell you what Máirtín?" asks Mary.

"All right, what brought you over to England, now tell me?"

"How do you mean England, I wasn't in England, who told you that?"

"Tell me the truth or I'll pin ya to the wall," he says, holding up his fist.

"All right, calm down now a minute Máirtín Ward. Look, I went with Helen to see her aunt that's all."

"That's not the truth, you had an abortion, or whatever you call it, isn't that true?"

"Máirtín, who told you that?"

"It's all over the town, is that true or not."

"What are you talking about?"

"Look, it's against the travellers' religion to do anything like that, I can't believe this," Máirtín says.

"I didn't do anything in England."

"You must have done something, now tell me what brought you over to England!"

"All right Máirtín if I tell you, you promise me not to tell a sinner, and I mean don't tell anybody."

"I promise Mary from the bottom of my heart, now out with it, tell me now, I want to know the truth."

He blesses himself with the crucifix he has around his neck and kisses it, they both walk down the street so they can't be overheard.

"It was Helen."

"What about Helen?" he asks.

"Shut up till I tell you, it was Helen, she had an abortion, now I promised her that I wouldn't tell anyone about this, so promise me you will keep this to yourself."

"O feck Mary, everybody thinks it's you that had to go to England."

"Oh my God, what will I do? If my parents find out, my father will kill me." She sits on a window sill. Dagger starts to laugh.

"What are you laughing at?"

"The people around here are stupid, they couldn't even get that right," he says.

"Thanks be to God for that, ah well, in a few days this will be old news, it's me that knows the truth and that's enough, let them say whatever they want," says Mary.

"And what about your father?"

"Ah feck him, I'll take care of him, anyways Máirtín, how's your family?"

"Ary, they're fine, I tell ya Mary, I miss Johnny's singing, sure he hasn't come back from Manchester since he went to visit Etna."

"Come on Máirtín, we'll go to my place for a cup of tea, how's that, wait till I get my bag and tell Helen I will see her later."

Tim Buckley Confronts Máirtín Dagger

They are in bed making love, when there is a hard knock on the door. Mary hops out of bed in a panic, looks out the window to notice her father in a temper outside, accompanied by her Mum. They both get dressed in a hurry, she goes to let them in. Her father is annoyed and enraged.

Scar Face is observing again from across the street, he goes back into O'Reilly's pub to spread the gossip again.

"Is it true?" Tim yells.

He makes his way inside Mary's flat.

"Is what true, Dad?" says Mary, looking at him in confusion. Tim sees Máirtín; he goes for in him in a rage.

"You're the tinker bastard that caused all this, I'll kill you with my bare hands, sure I will!"

"Dad, calm down, what's wrong with you, are you crazy or something?"

"Timothy keep the head will you now, we will get to the bottom of this somehow without arguing," Sheila says.

Tim is out of control, he grabs Máirtín by the throat, putting him up against the wall, knocking over a coffee table.

"Dad what's come over you, will you let him go?"

"What the hell is up with you Sir, calm down now Boss, you have the wrong man now sure you have, let me go."

"Wrong man? I'll kill ya," says Tim.

Mary and Sheila are trying to pull Tim off Máirtín.

"If you don't let me go, I'll harm you Sir."

"Oh will ya now, you're good at that, you have already harmed my daughter, you feckin Knacker," Tim yells.

Dagger reaches down into his boot and pulls out a nine inch dagger knife.

"I'll stick this in ya, if you don't let me go right now." He points the knife at Tim's throat.

"Calm down the both of you, please," screams Mary.

"Calm down Tim, let Mary speak," Sheila screams.

"Ok, you tell me what's going on around here, come on out with it," Tim says, letting Dagger's throat go.

"Look Dad, sit down, there is nothing to worry about, I'm all right."

Tim lets go of Máirtín, and sits down, he is exhausted and confused.

"Well, what brought you over to England, look no lies now, I want the truth," he says.

"I just went with Helen that's all, what's the big panic about, there is nothing wrong?"

"For what, to have an abortion was it," Tim says.

"Jesus Dad no, where did you hear that?" says Mary, pretending she doesn't know about the gossip.

"It's true she…"

"Shut up Máirtín, will ya, you're in enough trouble as it is."

"What trouble are you on about Mary?"

"Look Dad, Helen asked me to travel with her to London, I just accompanied her, now that's all and nothing else, ok now that's it."

"What brought ye to England Mary, I want to know the truth." Tim shouts.

Sheila sits down, Dagger turns his back to Tim, he goes to the window to look outside, and ignores what's going on.

"Look Mam, it's Helen's own business not ours, now let it go, now that's it."

"Mary, I will ask you for the last time. Mary, look just tell me now."

"No Dad, I didn't have an abortion, right, is that enough for you, what more can I say?"

"Well, who did then, was it Helen?"

"Dad it's none of your business what Helen Conway does with her life, or anybody's else either, now mind your own business. Just because you are a Police Officer you think you should know everybody's business, and no, she didn't have an abortion, ok?"

"OK, that's all right Mary, but there is one thing for sure, I want that tinker out of your life forever."

Mary and Dagger look at Tim with concern. Sheila has a throbbing headache from all the commotion. Tim storms out the door in a rage.

Back in O'Reilly's Bar, Scar Face tells the lads inside about the commotion between Mary and her father.

"Lads, I just seen that cop from Westport go into a house down the road, by heck he was in a foul mood, I thought he'd break down the bloody door with his fist, ha."

"That would be Mary's father, fliping hell he will kill her when he gets his hands on her," says Jack, drying the pint glasses.

"I'd say there would be skin and bones flying over there I'd say ha, I wouldn't mind the tinker is in there as well," Scar Face says.

"Well, leave it to themselves, I'm sure they will be able to take care of their own problems, anyways Mr Goggins you know everything that goes on around here, how's that?"

"Well 'tis like this Jack, he is only trying to drag people down to his own level. Scar Face, you were very lucky your own Mrs didn't chop your own head off," says Brendan the bar man, playing a game of cards with a few others.

"Look, I was only defending myself." he says.

He walks out the door.

"He is a terrible fool that Scar Face is, see the ways he takes off the minute you ask about how he got the scar," Jack says.

"He is one hell of a sly fox, and that's for sure," says another man playing cards.

Chapter Ten

Knock Shrine, Co Mayo

Sunday morning the nineteenth of February 1979 a cold windy day. The Ward Family are on a one day pilgrimage to Knock shrine, they pray the stations of the cross. They stroll around Knock observing all the stalls. They buy holy figurines of Jesus and the Blessed Virgin.

"Well isn't this a lovely place, the first time I came here I was only a child, me and your father, God rest his soul. We never missed a year without coming to Knock."

"You know Mum, the auld man enjoyed coming here, sure it was the journey that made it, 'twas great coming here in the bus, remember that Máirtín?"

"You're dead right there Willie."

They look around. Fay's little boy Johnny picks up a figurine of Our Lady.

"Granny will you buy this for me," he asks.

"No Johnny, we don't have enough money to buy any more figurines, now leave it back where you got it," Bridie says.

Young Johnny puts the figurine into his pocket, Fay has seen Johnny steal the figurine of Our Lady.

"I've seen that, Johnny don't take anymore. We have enough of them back in the trailer."

Seánine takes some figurines behind his father Willie's back, and the other children stuff their pockets as well, when Fay turns her back.

"Right, are we finished here?" Máirtín asks.

"I am anyways, what about the rest of the clan? lets have something to eat," Fay says.

"Well do ya know something Fay, I'm famished with the

hunger as well, lets go up the road here, there is a lovely lounge bar there, I think they do sandwiches," says Willie.

Paddy Walls Lounge Bar

They all head up the road in their vans. They head into the lounge bar. Inside, the pub owner Paddy Wall sees the travellers across the road heading his way. He goes to the window to see are they going to enter. There are a few other men and women and a few children inside the lounge bar. A man at the bar makes a comment about the travellers. His name is Laddine McAlester, a bachelor, joker and a messer, he winds people up and he is a lorry driver.

"Hi Paddy, you want to put the clasp on the door fast and keep that lot out."

He starts to laugh with the others.

"Shut up Laddine, and let me think."

Paddy is worried.

"Well you better think fast, they'll be in here in a jiffy."

He looks out the window to see the travellers coming into his pub.

"I'll give you a ya jiffy, sure I will Laddine, if you don't shut up. They're coming in lads, what will I say to them? Sure if we let them in, they might wreck the place." Paddy says.

The rest of the people in the pub look worried, some of them get up and leave.

"Look Paddy, if you serve them lot here now, they will be like flies around a shit, do you see this entire place?" Laddine says.

He looks around at empty seats.

"It will be wedged with that clan in no time, I don't know how they do it, how do they pass the word around the country so fast when another Knacker dies, within hours they all gather from all over the country, I don't know how they contact each other so fast, sure they have no phones or feck all."

"Shut up Laddine, here they are, keep your big mouth shut now and don't be upsetting them," says Paddy.

Dagger and his family enter the pub. Paddy is very tense.

"Look now, stop, go no further, I can't serve ye here," he says.
"What's that?"

"It's all right now Máirtín, we know where we are not wanted," Bridie says.

"Sure ye only stink the place out," Laddine says, holding his nose.

Dagger gives him a dirty look for that comment, he is getting annoyed.

"Sorry about that, I'm only messing, 'tis the drink, you know it would make a man say terrible things," says Laddine, turning his back to the travellers.

"Well shut your mouth now or I'll shut it for ya."

"Don't mind them Máirtín, it's not worth it, come on we will leave now."

"No, Mother, I want to know why aren't we served here."

"Go now and don't come back," Laddine says. speaking with his back turned to the travellers.

Timmy's New Ford Cortina

Tim and his son Timmy are out test-driving a brand new Ford Cortina, for Timmy. Tim has just purchased a good second hand one for himself, he says they're the best car to buy. Timmy is test-driving the new car.

"Ha, this is the way to go, well Dad what do you think?" Timmy is proud to be driving the new Cortina.

"How does she handle?" says Tim opening the glove box to look inside.

"She's mighty, sure she is, hold on till I turn on the radio, well isn't that great dad, do you hear the sound of that."

"Timmy, never mind the radio, it's the car that's most important, you cannot beat the Ford Cortina, they're the best car ever, and never forget that, now turn that radio off so you won't be distracted," Tim says.

They are driving through Knock when Tim notices the Hi Ace vans parked on the street outside Paddy Wall's lounge bar.

"Will you look who's here will ya, ha."

"What's that dad?"

"Máirtín Dagger Ward, well I cannot believe this, they pray as well do they, well that's hypocrisy for ya, one minute they're robbing other people's property, and the next they're down at Knock praying."

"Is that the lad that fancies Mary?"

Tim looks at Timmy with a frown and doesn't comment.

"Look, pull over here, I put a pound to a penny that they're in the pub. I better check, in case Paddy is in trouble."

"Look Dad, it's your day off, now leave them alone."

"Well, I tell you something, if that Máirtín Dagger Ward causes trouble around here, I will make sure he never will see the light of day ever again."

"Dad, take it easy, what are they doing to you, sure they don't even live around here. Come on, lets go back with the car before the garage reports it stolen, anyways this is not even your area."

"Listen to me one minute and get this straight, I'm a member of the Garda Síochána wherever I go in this country, and never forget that my son."

Laddine goes out next door to the shop for cigarettes, he spots the two men park the brand new Cortina across the road. He says nothing, he looks at the car and goes into the shop.

"Can I have twenty Major please, they don't have any next door." Laddine says.

"25p please?" asks the young shop attendant, behind the counter.

Laddine makes a joke to the young attendant about the travellers next door.

"Listen to this Hoggy."

He opens the fags and puts one in his mouth and lights up.

"Two Knackers go into the pub."

As he is just about to tell the joke, Johnny and Lizzy come into the shop unknown to the attendant and Laddine.

"The pub owner says to the Knackers, I can't serve ye, one of the Knackers asks the pub owner, why not. 'Cause ye're smelly, said the pub owner. What said the Knacker, or tinkers, or whatever you want to call them nowadays, we are not smelly you stupid ass, replies the traveller." "Anyway, Hoggy what do ya think of that, look I better be off, see ya," Laddine says. He notices the young travellers behind him.

Hoggy is a ten year old boy serving behind the counter. He looks at Laddine confused.

"What was that guy on about?" he says to himself.

Young Johnny and Lizzy are filling their pockets with food and sweets, they leave the shop. Nobody notices them in the shop, they go outside quickly.

"Ha, that was very easy, we must come down here more often."

"I think Johnny, it's Our Lady, she wanted us to have the food."

"You know something Lizzy, I felt that myself."

Back in the pub, the bar owner Paddy is still arguing with Dagger and his family.

"Look now lads, I can't serve ye, and that's it, now I'm saying no more, off with ye now."

"Why not, are we not good enough, all we want is a few sandwiches for the children, they had nothing to eat all day," Dagger says.

Young Johnny and Lizzy go back into the pub. Johnny pulls Dagger's jacket to get his attention.

"Dagger it's alright now, I have some food." Dagger ignores Johnny.

"Look, off with ye now, clear off the whole damn feckin lot of ye, we don't want your kind around here," says Paddy.

"Well isn't this some place, I thought Knock was a holy place, and where good people lived, sure isn't that Catholics for ya. I suppose you will be across the road later on kissing the statues' feet, do you know something, you're nothing but a shower of hypocrites."

"Never mind them Máirtín, may God's curse be upon them, come on children they will never have a day's luck for this. Don't worry, Our Lady is across the road, she will deal with ye don't ye worry," Bridie says, gathering the children to leave.

Tim and Timmy enter the pub; they see what's going on. Tim pretends he doesn't know Dagger.

"Well, well, look at what's here, what brings ye lot around here?" Tim says.

"We were only visiting Our Lady's shrine Sir, what's it to you anyways?" says Fay.

Dagger turns his back to Tim. Laddine walks back into the pub.

"Is that right, ha, you can visit Our Lady across the road, you won't find her in here," Tim says.

"Our Lady don't go into pubs you know," says Laddine.

Tim gives Laddine a sour look.

"Sorry, I'm only having you on, sorry about that Sir."

Laddine goes up to the counter. He passes a comment to another man, about the smell in the pub.

"A while ago I could smell smoke, now I can smell pigs."

They both laugh; they get a grim look from Tim.

"I tell ya what I'll do with ya, go outside and I will bring ham and cheese sandwiches out to ye, now that's the best I can do and no alcohol mind," Paddy says.

"That will do Boss," says Dagger.

Mary Is Anxious To Get In Contact With Máirtín

She is in great need to talk to Máirtín, there is no answer on the phone.

She is trying to get in touch with him all day.

"Oh come on, please pick up the phone, Máirtín where are you all day?"

She then calls Helen. Helen is in her flat lying on the couch drunk. She is too drunk to answer the phone, she opens her eyes when she hears the phone ringing.

"Oh go away whoever you are," she mutters.

Mary leaves the phone down and goes to work. Dressed in her Nurse's uniform, she leaves the flat.

The travellers are outside the pub sitting on the wall, others are sitting on some Guinness barrels. It's cold and it's beginning to rain.

Paddy comes out with a large tray of ham and cheese sandwiches and a couple of bottles of soft drinks.

"Now there you go, sorry about this, I cannot serve you people because ye break the place up on me when ye get a few drinks inside ye."

"Not us Boss, we never cause trouble anywhere," replies Dagger.

"Look, I let a family just like ye in here last year, and they wrecked the whole place, and during the October fair in Ballinasloe I heard they wrecked a lounge bar there as well, where are ye from?" Paddy asks.

"Athenry," replies Fay.

All the travellers look at each other.

"Right, well, enjoy your sandwiches, I'll be off now."

Dagger goes to pay for the food and drinks; he puts his hand in his pocket for the money.

"No, you're all right Sir, now that's on the house."

Fay grabs the money and gives it to Paddy.

"We don't want any of your charity Sir, we pay our own way."

They take the tray of sandwiches, walk away towards their vans.

"By heck Willie you had nothing to say ha, that's not like you, what happened, did the cat take your tongue."

"Look Dagger, I let you do the talking. I'm sick of it, this shit, them shower sickens me."

"Me too, I'm pissed off with them all. I was afraid to get excited in case I'd have the baby, now don't make me angry I had enough, lets eat those sandwiches and get back home," Margaret says.

Inside in the bar, Laddine is winding up Tim.

"Who ever owns the new Ford Cortina that is across the road, ha, he won't be too happy when he sees the state of it," he says with a grin from ear to ear.

"Why's that?" says another man, sitting at the counter eating chicken sandwiches, as Tim and Timmy look concerned.

"An articulated truck with a huge trailer tore the back wing straight off a while ago," says Laddine, giving a wink to Paddy and the other man at the bar.

"What, that's my car Daddy!"

Tim gives Timmy an unpleasant look for calling him Daddy in front of the men. They run out to check the car. Laddine finishes his pint and goes out to the back door.

The travellers are in their vans eating sandwiches, the windows are all fogged up as its raining down heavily. They notice Tim and Timmy come out of the lounge bar and checking the Ford Cortina behind them.

Laddine waits for Tim to pull off, he goes to get into his truck.

Dagger lets down the window and calls him over.

"Hey Boss, come over a minute here, I want ya."

Laddine goes over.

"What can I do for ya Sir?"

"Is that your own truck?"

"No, I was only stealing it, no, not at all, I'm only messing with ye, it is mine, why?"

"Look Boss, will you do a small run for me sometime during the week, will ya Sir?" asks Dagger.

While the rest of the travellers eat their sandwiches, Laddine takes note the way all the travellers are in the back of the van sitting on car seats.

"And what might that be?"

"I'm Dagger Ward, what's your name?"

"Laddine McAlester, I live just up the road there, pleased to meet ye, sorry about that messing inside there," he says.

He puts his hand out to shake hands with Dagger.

"You're all right Boss, don't worry about it," Dagger says. He shakes hands with Laddine and winks one eye at Willie.

Mary is at work at reception, phoning Dagger's trailer, still no answer. All the dogs start barking when they hear the phone ringing.

A local farmer hears the dogs; he is talking to another man that was out walking his dog, in a nearby field.

"Well, do you hear that racket, it's like that all day, they're isn't a soul there all day long, and them dogs are barking like that since this morning," says the farmer.

"Maybe we should call the I S P C A, they will take care of the dogs, and that's for sure. I wouldn't mind, a young woman from the pools was telling me the other day that them boys won £20,000, ha, now could you beat that?" says the man with the dog.

"Do you know something, that doesn't surprise me at all, sure if you ask me I'd say they have more money than anybody," says the farmer.

Laddine Is Driving His Truck To West Clare

He is picking up some pony traps for Dagger, about four in total, he's driving his truck along the road; he stops and looks at the directions Dagger mapped out on the back of a cigarette packet.

He finds it hard to read the directions, there is no writing, just a diagram to navigate where he should go. Turning the paper upside down and sideways he cannot make it out. He stops his truck to ask a man for directions that comes along in a red Hi Ace behind him.

"Hi, excuse me Sir, would you tell me where I would find Willie the Horse Ward?"

"The tinker Ward, you mean?" says the man, speaking in a Cork accent.

"Ya, he is around here somewhere?" asks Laddine.

"Right boy, just go right there, and take the first right, after the fork on the road. Go over the hill, you will come to a cross road, there is a pub, a mighty fine one indeed it is boy, sure it is, turn left and go down there for about three miles and your man you want is on the right hand side, you can't miss him, by the way boy, what are you after?"

"Pony traps," Laddine says.

"Ah, well you're in the right place all right." replies the man.

Laddine takes off, he drives along the road, turns right, driving for about five minutes. When the road comes to an end, the road turns into a cow track through a hazel wood. He keeps on going for about a few hundred yards, the hazel trees are growing over the road, they're a lot lower than the truck, he keeps driving to discover he has gone too far to turn back, the hazel trees are scraping along the top of the truck making a terrible squeaky noise, Laddine is worried.

"Ha, I must have taken a wrong turn, take the next right turn after the fork on the road, isn't that what I have done," he says to himself.

He keeps on driving for about one mile, through the hazel wood; the trees are scraping along the top of the truck. He is very worried about the truck, he doesn't want to damage it. He comes to the end of the cow track, and he notices the pub across the road and another road on his left hand side.

"I bet that's the shittin' road I was supposed to take, frig it, how did I make a mistake like that?"

The man that gave the directions to Laddine is also a traveller and a friend of Dagger's. He is in a telephone box phoning Dagger.

"I did exactly as you said Dagger."

"Good Man."

"He took the bait all right, I'd say he is a bit of a fool is he?" said the man.

"He's that all right, he's a bit of a gob shite if you ask me, sure what other way would he be coming from Mayo, anyway and did you follow him?" asks Dagger, as he starts to laugh.

"No, I was afraid he would see me, I let him find his own way. I tell ya one thing he would find it hard to steer that size of a truck through that hazel wood, ha, 'tis no joke making his way through the woods with that truck," the man says.

"I'd say that all right, I tell ya it's the last time he will make fun of us, he's a right smart ass, I'm sorry I didn't send him to Cork." They both have a good laugh.

Laddine drives along the road, he sees the travellers site on the left hand side. Pulling over he gets out of his truck to approach them.

The man that gave him the directions is there with Willie the Horse that has the pony traps for Dagger, it's a typical traveller site with caravan, dogs, vans and children and women, they are parked on a lay by on the side of the road near Kilkee. The two men find it hard to keep a straight face, when they notice Laddine approach them.

"Well here he comes now Willie, he is a right looking idiot all right isn't he?" says the other man.

"Look at the state of that Lad," says Willie the Horse.

They start laughing at Laddine.

"Well men, God bless the work," says Laddine.

"You too, you too."

"Aren't you the man that gave me directions a while ago?"

"You're dead right there, what kept ya?" the man asks.

"Nothing, I took my time, sure I'm in no hurry."

"How come I didn't pass you on my way here so?"

"Ara sure I pulled over to take a leak," says Laddine.

"Did ya now?" says the man, as he smiles at Willie the Horse. "Did Máirtín Dagger send you?"

"He did indeed, so you're Willie the Horse are you?"

"I am, right we're losing daylight, lets load them up," says Willie the Horse.

They walk towards the pony trap, with Laddine walking behind them. They load up the pony traps, they invite Laddine in for a drink and something to eat.

It's about three in the morning. Laddine is on his way back from Clare. He's driving along the road towards Dagger's site.

"Ok, here I am, I hope this crowd are not in bed," he thinks to himself.

Dagger and his mother and Willie and the children are in their mum's trailer waiting for Laddine. There are children outside playing, and cycling around the site, like it's three o clock in the afternoon.

"The fool must be lost, he should have been here hours ago," Dagger says, drinking almost the last drop of Poítin out of the bottle.

"Give us a drop of that will ya?"

He passes the bottle to Willie.

"That's the last of it so make the most of it."

"We have to go to Connamara during the week Máirtín, for another few more bottles," Willie says.

He takes a drink out of the bottle.

"By heck that's strong, oh heck, what in the hell is in that?"

Willie has a sour face on him after drinking the Poítin.

"Look, I see truck lights, it must be him," Bridie says.

Young Seánine runs into the trailer to tell the lads that the truck has arrived. There is excitement in the air.

"Hi lads, the truck is here," he says.

They all rush out to welcome Laddine. While he drives into the site, he is greeted by about fifteen to twenty traveller women and children, there are children cycling around and others playing football.

"Ha, it's like three o'clock in the middle of the day here sure it is, feckin hell ha," he says to himself.

He parks his truck and gets out.

"You took your time, what happened did you get lost or something?" Dagger says, giving the eye to Willie.

"No, Mr Ward, but you live in the middle of nowhere, it's nearly impossible to find this place, come on lets unload. I have to drive back to Mayo yet tonight."

They take the pony traps off the truck. Laddine is invited in for a drink. They drink till six in the morning, Laddine is too drunk to drive to Mayo, he sleeps in a spare bed in Dagger's trailer.

Chapter Eleven

Máirtín And Mary Get Engaged

He surprises Mary by buying her an engagement ring, walking along a busy shopping street. Mary is suspicious why he has taken her to Mullingar, he has already told her he has a surprise in store. Mary is impatient.

"Look Máirtín, I can't wait any longer, why don't you tell me why you brought me here?"

"Ok, here we are."

They come to a jewellery shop. Mary doesn't notice the shop.

"What?" she says, excited and bewildered.

"Right, cover your eyes now Mary, we are here."

Mary covers her eyes with her hands so she cannot see.

"Why, what's this?"

"Ok, follow me."

He leads her into the jewellery shop by the hand.

"What's happening, where are we?" she says, with excitement.

"Right Mary, open your eyes now."

The woman behind the counter is looking at them in suspicion.

"What's this?" asks Mary

"Well, what do you think, it's not Tesco, I can say that for sure."

Mary is all excited when she opens her eyes to see all the sparkling jewellery.

"Right, there you go, pick one."

"Máirtín what do you mean, pick what?"

"What do you think?"

He is looking at the engagement rings.

"Oh my God I can't believe it, are you serious?"

"I sure am," he says with a gloat.

They both look at the rings; the woman behind the counter is looking at them a little bit funny, because of a traveller getting engaged to a settled person.

Mary is excited and over the moon that she is getting engaged to Máirtín.

They both come out from the jewellers very happy, they are very excited, they hug each other and dance on the street. A young traveller boy is watching them.

"Máirtín, you know, I love you so much, you are the best thing that has happened to me, I'm so happy."

"Mary, you are the best thing that has happened to me in a long time, I love you too." They hug and kiss each other.

"Do you know what would be nice now, a good drink, to celebrate," Máirtín says.

"Right, oh I'm so happy I can't believe this is true!"

They walk towards a pub nearby, the young boy dashes inside to inform the others that they are on their way, there are about two hundred travellers inside, they're having a surprise engagement party. Everybody is there, all the travellers including Laddine, the travellers from Co. Clare, Bridie, Fay, all the children. They walk in the door, the pub is in darkness. The lights are turned on, Mary cannot believe it when she sees the crowd, and everybody shouts—

"Surprise!"

"Oh my God!" Mary says.

She puts her hands up to her face, and starts to cry. Johnny the Singer is home with Etna for the occasion. He sings Máirtín Dagger's favourite song, "The Girl with the White washed Gable." Everyone is in silence as Johnny sings.

Helen Is Drowning Her Sorrows

She is in Jack O'Reilly's Pub, drinking on her own, she is sitting at the counter drinking vodka. Jack is behind the counter. Scar Face is gossiping about Mary and Helen.

"Look at her now, well I tell ya something Jack, keeping secrets is a bad thing. They could be the cause of killing you, do you know that," says Scar Face.

"Give me a double this time, Jack, and don't mind that loud mouth. Don't worry Scar Face I heard you, I tell ya one thing, you cannot talk yourself, everybody knows around here how you got that scar on your face, and it wasn't from a pint glass either."

"That's the last one now Helen, I'm not serving you anymore drink, you had enough."

"Jack will you ever piss off, and stick it up your arse, and you too Scar Face, you have nothing else to do all day but sit here and bad mouth people, I'm sick listening to you."

She gets up off her seat and staggers towards the door. She falls to the ground, she gets up on her feet again and staggers out the door.

"I can't believe that one, she would want to get a grip on herself," Jack says, shaking his head with disgust for Helen.

"Well if she didn't get—-" Jack stops him from saying anything further about Helen.

"Now stop that kind of talk Scar Face, she did what she did, and I won't have any more of that gossiping around here, no more of that talk now I am sick of it, you cannot piss in this town but everyone talks about it," says Jack. He gets annoyed.

"There is a price on everything, sure isn't her best friend living up the road with the tinkers," Scar Face says.

"Now, say nothing else now you, I've heard enough, the best thing you can do is finish your drink and off with ya." There is tension between Scar Face and Jack.

Back in Mullingar the travellers and Mary are having a ball, dancing to a live band. There is plenty of drink, food, party hats, everything is laid on. Mary and Máirtín are out on the floor dancing with the rest of the people in a circle, clapping their hands. Laddine turns to Willie with a comment about Dagger and Mary.

"I'd say she will get it up the arse tonight, ha, what do you think Willie?"

He looks at Mary, with the sweat running down his face from drinking whiskey and dancing.

Willie gives him a nasty look.

"I'm only messing Willie don't mind me, I'm only having the

crack." As he starts laughing, Willie walks off.

Helen Collapses On The Footpath

She is on her back on the footpath, getting sick, she turns her head to the side and throws up, with her face on the pavement.

Scar Face comes out of the pub, he steps over Helen and walks down the street singing a verse of David Bowie's song. "Sorrow."

"With your long blond hair and your eyes so blue, the only thing I get from you is sorrow." He walks down the street with his head held high.

Helen is still on the footpath, a car is passing by, it stops. It's Jim O'Sullivan and his wife Annie, from Ballycrackn, they are coming from Dublin, he slows down to have a look at Helen, letting his window down.

"Isn't that Helen Conway, isn't it?" Annie looks to see can she recognise Helen.

"It is her Jim, slut that's what she is, a slut, oh my God look at the state of her, she used to be such a beautiful person, oh I don't know what has happened at all to her, her mother would die if she knew Helen was drunk on the streets like that, she is a disgrace to her family, not alone herself, her mother must be disgusted with that one. Drive on Jim, will ya, and stop looking at her," says Annie.

"I think we should help her Annie."

"Let up your window and drive off, she did it to herself, never mind her," Annie says.

Back at the party, there are having a sing-song, some of the travellers are leaving and saying goodbye to Mary and Máirtín, everybody is happy for the newly engaged couple except two old women, they don't like to see Máirtín with another woman.

"Look at him, has he no shame, his poor wife Julia would turn in her grave if she knew what is happening here today. God Bless her poor soul and her poor children, may God have mercy on them," says one old woman.

"Ah, times are changing, when ya become a widow or widower I tell ya, they wouldn't be anymore messing around with anyone else, it's respect it is, that's what it is, I tell ya he has no respect for Julia."

"Ah shut up ye old hags, ye are only jealous, who would be bothering with ye two anyways?" say Fay.

She was listening to the two old women. She is sad and gloomy herself because Máirtín is engaged now and that could be the end of her chance to be with him.

"You're only jealous yourself Fay sure you are, 'cause you fancy Máirtín yourself," says one of the women.

"Mind your own business you, sure what is it to you?" The woman turns her head away from Fay.

The singsong continues. Johnny the Singer is pissed and is singing his head off. It's getting late and the party is over. Out in the street they are all saying goodbye to the happy couple, there is about twenty travellers, Laddine, Willie, Johnny and Bridie. Fay is unhappy.

"Do ye know what we all should do now, lets go to our halting site, and we'll finish off the night ha," says Hattie the swan.

"Why not?" says Mary.

"Yippee," says Willie, "lets go, Laddine you can travel with us, come on lets get out of here!"

They all get in their vans and drive off. Fay doesn't go with them, she starts to cry, and walks down the street on her own with her head down, feeling lost, and broken hearted.

Helen Gets Depressed And Is Suicidal

Helen is being taken to hospital by ambulance, she is in casualty department, she is strapped to a bed, the ambulance driver is checking her in at reception.

"Well, what has happened to her, she looks terrible," the receptionist says to the ambulance driver about Helen.

"Drank too much I'm afraid, she has been drinking heavily for the last few months, I believe, I'd say her liver is damaged at this stage," says the ambulance driver.

"I hear ye, and shut up, look I want to go home, let me off this shittin thing and take me home!" says Helen.

She tries to get off the trolley, the ambulance man talks to her.

"Look be quiet, you're not going anywhere," says the driver.

"Just bring her in, and I will prepare her file, sorry driver, what's her name?" asks the receptionist.

"Helen Conway," he answers.

"Ok, just bring her in and I will send down her file right away," she says.

The driver pushes Helen into the casualty ward, while Fay is being taken into reception by an old man with her wrists all bandaged up.

"What happened to her?" asks the receptionist.

"I think she slashed her wrists, I found her sitting on a park bench, only for I came on her she would have bled to death," says the old man.

"Who put on those bandages?" asks the receptionist.

"I did, I'm a retired Doctor," he answers.

"She is a very lucky woman, she could have bled to death," he adds. Fay is very weak and distraught.

The travellers are back at the trailer site in Mullingar, they are dancing, singing, and having fun, it's dark and the place is lit up with flood lights, they are all dancing to a full Ceili band of travellers, they play the accordion, tin whistles, guitars and banjos, nobody misses Fay.

"I didn't have fun like this in years," Mary says.

She is dancing with Katie that was fighting with Fay at the fun fair in Mulingar.

"Are you really happy Mary?"

"Oh ya Katie I am, I really love your brother, you know he is the best thing that has happened to me in years."

"You know Mary, Fay thought it would be her that would marry Máirtín, she has fancied him this long time now."

"I know Katie, he told me."

They stop dancing and sit down.

"He told me a few other things about her as well you know."

"And what would that be now Mary?"

"To tell you the truth now, Fay was always in his heart, and he said that she was too much like Julia, that's why he couldn't marry her, because of Julia, every time he looks at Fay he sees his wife Julia, same face and brown eyes, he told me."

"Well is that right Mary, I was always wondering why he's running away from her all right. After Julia and the children died, I seen him crying on Fay's shoulder, and called Fay Julia, I will never forget that. It didn't bother Fay one little bit, that's because she fancied him I suppose."

"I know Katie, I suppose you can understand that."

"I can Mary." Mary starts to cry.

"Anyways you're his woman now, and don't mind Fay, she will get over him alright."

"Thanks Katie you're so kind."

"I'm really glad Mary you told me that, because it was bothering me that Fay was in love with Máirtín, I was afraid she would attack you like she attacked me at the fun fair." Mary puts her arms around Katie and they both cry.

"You know, he is very lucky to have a sister like you."

"Thanks Mary, you are so kind ya know."

Máirtín comes up to Mary, he goes down on one knee to ask Mary to dance.

"Oh, what are you doing now, you're not going to ask me to marry you in here are you?"

She looks around at everybody as they are all looking at Máirtín.

"Will you get up, you are making a fool of yourself in front of everybody," Katie says with embarrassment.

"What's on ya, I'm only asking my fiancée to dance."

"Oh, sorry, well excuse me, off ye go so and don't mind me," says Katie.

At Helen's mum's house, her parents are getting ready for bed, the "Late Late Show" has just ended on TV, the Late News comes on. They both are watching TV, there is a warm coal fire on in the open hearth. The news reader reads the news. "Good Evening, and this is the news headlines:

There has been an explosion in Belfast. At about eight o'clock this evening, two people were killed and four taken to hospital with minor injuries. The IRA claimed responsibility. Jack Lynch announced that he will be running for election next month, and the weather forecast. Tomorrow there will be sunny spells in the morning and showers later in the afternoon. That's all the news for now till seven thirty, tomorrow morning. Good night from all here at the news room."

"Right, that's it Jack," Nellie says. She gets up and turns off the TV.

"Right, it's time for blanket street," Jack says, getting up out of his armchair.

The phone rings.

"Oh my God Jack, who's phoning us at this time of night?"

She picks up the phone.

"Hello?"

A Nurse at the hospital is on the phone. She tells Nellie about Helen.

"Hello, are you Mrs Nellie Conway?"

"That's right." Nellie looks at her husband Jack in worry.

"I'm calling from the General Hospital, it's about your daughter Helen."

"Ya?"

"Ok,"

"And how is she now?" Jack looks worried.

"Ok, right, ok right, well when she wakes up, will you tell her we will be there first thing in the morning."

"Ok, thank you very much."

"That's good, good night now". She puts down the phone.

"What's wrong Nellie, is there something up with Helen?"

"She had too much to drink and she is in hospital, there is nothing to worry about, she will be fine, the Nurse said."

"Oh thank God, I'm really worried about her, the last time she was home she looked a holy show, anyway it's that demon drink," says Jack, blessing himself.

"I know, ever since she came back from England she hasn't been herself, maybe we shouldn't have told her, we had right to leave well enough alone," Nellie says.

"Maybe, maybe, we should, anyway she knows the truth now, it's up to her, lets go to bed, we can say the rosary, maybe that might help put things right," Nellie says anxiously.

They switch off the TV, rake the fire and retire to bed.

Next morning, Helen is in a hospital ward, on her own, looking depressed, her mother and father arrive. Helen is worried she will get a telling off from her parents.

"Mammy, don't be cross with me now."

Her mum and dad come into the room.

"Not at all love why would we, as long as you're all right," Nellie says.

She gives Helen a hug, her dad gives her a kiss on the check.

"Well tell us, how did you land yourself in here?" He looks around.

"Ara it's nothing dad, I just had one too many last night."

"They told me at reception they picked you up off the street, did you hurt yourself?"

"Not at all Mam, I tripped and fell, sure when the old biddy across the road seen me on the footpath, she called the ambulance. Sure there's nothing wrong with me at all, I will be out of here in an hour or two, you didn't need to drive all this way to see me, I'm fine." Helen is putting on a brave face for her parents.

"Anyway you are not looking good, you better look after yourself."

"I know Mam, I'm fine, I am dying for a cup of tea."

"Well do you know something, now Jack what did I tell ya," Nellie says.

"We brought you a flask of tea and some corn beef sandwiches, your favourite." Jack says.

"Well do you know something Dad, I'm glad ye did, because the food in here is like shit."

Helen sits up in the bed to have her tea and sandwiches. A Nurse comes in to tell Helen that she will be assessed by a psychiatric doctor in the morning. They all look corcerned.

"Look there is nothing to worry about, it's only procedure," says the Nurse.

Chapter Twelve

St Anita's Psychiatric Hospital Dublin

Helen is taken to a psychiatric hospital in Dublin a few days later. She is sitting in the day ward in her nightgown. There are a few other patients there, they are sitting in a row by the wall in silence. Helen is sitting there spaced out with the medication, she is in a bad state, rocking back and fourth on the chair. The rest of the patients are very sad and depressed.

Máirtín Dagger and Willie, Willie's wife Margaret, Katie and a few children are in the hospital visiting Fay, while Fay lies in bed.

She is kept in for observation for a few days.

"Well, ye took your time, I could be dead for all ye care."

She sits up in the bed annoyed.

"What did you do Fay?" asks Katie.

"Nothing, what brings you in here you nosey bitch?"

"Look Fay, there will be none of that shit talk, and if you must know Katie was sick with worry about you, isn't that right Willie?"

"You're right there Dagger, sure you two used to be the best of friends, anyway what did you do that to yourself for?"

"No why, look I was pissed off that's why, now piss of the lot of ye, and leave me."

"Right Fay, have it your own way. Don't mind her Willie, look Fay we are going to Connamara for a couple of bottles of Poítin, will we get a bottle or two for ya?" Dagger asks.

No response from Fay. She covers her head with the blankets and ignores everybody. They leave Fay to her own devices and head off.

Travellers Driving To Connamara To Purchase Poítin

It's Thursday mid-day, they are on their way in high spirits. They are in an old battered white Hi Ace van, Dagger is driving. Willie and Katie are in the front, Margaret who is going to give birth any day now, is in the back with the children and another woman. They come to a cross road, there is a sign post reading Galway five miles. Driving on they come to the outskirts of the town, they see two Gardaí, and one of them is a Ban Garda.

"Hi, look at the two cops, I wonder do they want a lift, hey Dagger slow down a bit. Hi Boss, do ye want a lift?" Willie says to the two Guards.

The Guard gives an unpleasant look at the travellers, taking note of the state of the van.

"Hey come on Dagger, put down the boot before they check us for tax," Willie says, they drive off fast to avoid being caught with no tax.

"What in the hell are you playing at Willie, you will get us arrested for that crack."

"Ara, for feck sake Margaret, it's only a bit of fun, isn't that right Seánine."

"That's right Dad."

"Look Margaret be careful you now, ya don't want to have the baby in the back of the van now would ya."

The children are having a good laugh at Willie.

"I wonder did Etna and Johnny get back to England all right after the party?"

"Well Willie, 'twas a hell of a surprise when I seen him there, I never knew he was coming home at all you know," says Dagger.

"Remember lads when Johnny wanted to join the Irish Republic Army, that was the funniest thing ever, sure they told him they didn't take travellers or Spanish."

"Do you know something Willie, I can't understand what they meant by that with the Spanish?" Margaret says.

They all look at each other, lifting their shoulders.

"Now that you said that Margaret, I couldn't understand what they meant by that either. Don't ya think that Johnny thinks he's some kind of rebel or something," Dagger says.

"Rebel without a cause if you ask me," Willie says.

They all have a laugh.

"I thought Margaret and Etna would have the babies together, with the size of the both of ye at the party."

"You never know, Katie, that could happen yet," Margaret says.

"Why, what are ye saying, that Johnny and Etna and Margaret had sex the same night, is that what you're saying Katie?"

"Shut up you Willie, and don't be talking shit in front of everyone in the van, that's private, now shut up now you fool ya."

"All right, all right, keep your hair on Margaret," Willie says.

Margaret sits in a huff, there is a silence between them.

"Hey Seánine, why didn't ye lot get up for school, ye shower of shits. Hi Margaret, why aren't they at school today?"

"Willie, you're such a bollix, do you not remember, you told them last night you would take them with ya today, or were you too drunk to remember that as well?"

"Oh ya, I forgot," replies Willie.

"Do you know something Katie, he's drunk since the engagement party, he hasn't sobered up since."

"Ah shut up you Margaret, what do you know?"

"He came in two nights ago Katie, and had a piss in the baby's new cot, now what do ye think of that kind of behaviour?"

"Shut up you Margaret, and don't be telling lies."

"Ah, now dad that's true, you always does things like that when you're drunk," Seánine says.

"Is that right Willie, do you piss in the child's cot when you're drunk?" asks Dagger.

They all have a laugh.

"Shut your mouths now, this is the last time I bring you Seánine with me anywhere if ya don't stop telling lies." Willie says.

"Máirtín wait till ya hear this one, when he came over from Uncle Michael's last night, Michael had given him whiskey or something you know."

"Look Margaret, shut up will ya, there isn't anyone interested in that shit talk."

"No, Willie this is funny, listen to this will ya."

She starts to laugh.

"Wait till ya hear this, didn't he go into Bridie's trailer, his own mother 'twas, do you know what she was telling me this morning?" says Margaret, bursting out laughing, and gets a stitch in her side.

"Will ya tell the story or shut up your hole!"

"Stop Willie, will ya, and listen to her," Dagger says as he drives the van.

"He went into his mum's trailer, and got into the bed beside her. Three o'clock in the morning it was, and do ya know what, he said to Bridie?"

"What?" asks Dagger. He bursts out laughing.

"Do ya know what he said, shove over there Margaret, I'm feeling very horny tonight, tonight is your lucky night love!"

They all have a good laugh at Willie.

"Well when Bridie was telling me that this morning, I almost pissed on myself laughing, that was so funny."

"I didn't do that, did I?"

"You did"

"When I came home last night?"

"Ya, last night!" says Margaret.

"Anyways you're a awful ass when you have drink taken, do ya know that Willie," Máirtín Dagger says.

The children and women are bursting out laughing.

They drive out through Salthill and onto the road to Connamara.

Mary Breaking The News Of Her Engagement

Mary is at her parents' home. They are in the sitting room: Mary, her mother, and brother and his girlfriend Ann, and uncle Bill, a small farmer who lives in the neighbouring village to Ballycrackn, and his wife Peg. They are having a drink, her father Tim is at work, and is due home at any moment. Mary is nauseous with worry as to how they might react.

They are watching "School Around the Corner" on TV.

"I'm sick watching that fella on the television," Sheila says.

"Mam, I have something to tell ya."

"You're not getting married Mary are ya?"

"Not at all Peg, she doesn't even have a boyfriend."

"Well not quite Mam, but near enough."

"What do you mean?" asks Sheila.

"I got engaged a couple of days ago."

"What, to who?"

"Who do you think, Mam?"

"Ah no, look Peg, she's only having us on." says Sheila, getting embarrassed in front of Peg her sister and her husband Bill.

"No Mam it's true, I got engaged last week."

Sheila attempts to quieten Mary.

"Shush Mary, the whiskey is going to you're head, now be quiet."

She reaches over to take the whiskey off Mary, and puts it under her own chair. They are all looking at each other, confused.

"No Mam, be quiet you, I got engaged to Máirtín I'm telling you now."

"Who's Máirtín, do we know this lucky fella?"

"No one Bill, she is only having us on," says Sheila, dying with embarrassment.

"I can't believe this Mary! You didn't did ya, ah well, he was in Knock a few Sundays ago, praying with the whole family, for God sake there was about ten of them there."

"Shut up you Timmy, at least I'm not pregnant."

When Timmy's girlfriend hears that comment she gets embarrassed and blushes.

On The Road To Connamara

It's about four o'clock in the afternoon, Dagger and his family are still on the road, they are almost there, they come to a sign post that states Rosmuck one mile, the smoking in the van has them stifled.

"We are not far now," Dagger says.

"Are we nearly there Uncle Willie, and for shit sake will ya open a window so I can breathe?"

"Not far now Johnny, relax will ya, we will be soon there," says Willie, letting down the window to let out the smoke.

They drive along the road, a Police car speeds past them.

"Pooh, frig it that smoke is choking me," Young Johnny says. He starts to cough.

"Lads, where are the cops off to I wonder?"

"Slow down Dagger, let them off, they didn't take any notice of us, let them off now, we mind our business and let them mind theirs."

"Well, you're dead right there Willie."

He slows down the van to let the Garda car off.

"Look now Dagger, the last thing we need now is bothering with those guys, just let them off and say nothing," says Willie.

Back At Mary's Parents House

Tim comes in from work, he is in his Garda uniform, he goes into the kitchen. He can hear the commotion going on in the sitting room next door, where they are smoking and drinking.

"I wonder what's going on in there, this hour of the evening," he says to himself.

He goes into the sitting room to investigate.

"God bless the work Tim," says Bill, as Tim enters the sitting room and is stifled with the smoke.

"You too, you too, well are we having a party or something, what are we celebrating? Ha, is it someone's birthday or what."

"Nothing Tim, Peg and Bill called unexpectedly and we are only having a drink," says Sheila.

"Well somebody open a window, or we will all smother in here with the smoke, it's cat in here," Tim says.

Sheila gets up off her chair to opens the window, as she gives a frown to Mary.

"Don't look at me like that Mum, I was just going to open the window before you stood up, now."

"I tell ya one thing, them God damn fags are no good for

anyone, people are dying by the minute with cancer from them rotten fags, I don't know how ye are still smoking them rotting things," Tim says.

Mary slips off the ring and puts it in her pocket, she is too afraid to say anymore about the engagement.

"Shut up you dad, just because you're off the fags for a few weeks, you think nobody should smoke."

Tim gives a side eye to Mary for that comment, as Bill gives a wink to Mary.

"Isn't that what happens to smokers when they quit, they become anti smokers."

"And not alone that Peg, they become antichrists as well," Sheila says.

"Well Bill, any lambs yet?" Tim says, ignoring the comments about the smoking.

"No, not yet, but soon now I'd say, I wouldn't mind the fox is around as well you know, they're very plentiful this year you know Tim," Bill says.

"Speaking of foxes Tim, do you know what I heard the other day, remember about fourteen or fifteen years ago when Jim O'Sullivan shot the fox that was at his chickens, well at least he thought it was a fox." Bill says.

"Oh ya, I remember that, you remember that Mam, don't ya, Jim O'Sullivan was up at our house telling us the story next day, remember that Mam," Timmy says.

Mary starts to smile, she covers her face, she was told the full story herself by Máirtín.

"Well apparently it wasn't a fox at all, it was one of them tinkers, remember them Tim?" Tim looks at Sheila.

"Oh, faith I do Bill."

Sheila looks at Mary and snubs her as Mary sniggers to herself, she is red in the face and is trying to keep in the laughter.

"What's wrong with your face Mary?" Peg says.

Mary's face is purple-red, she bursts out laughing and runs out of the room and goes in the kitchen and leaves the door open to listen.

"What's happening to Mary's face, is she getting a heart attack or something?"

"Never mind her Peg, 'tis all that drink she's taking," Sheila says.

"Anyway wasn't it one of them little feckers he shot in the arse, that was robbing the eggs."

"Bill, will you mind your language," Peg says, looking at Sheila and Tim embarrassed.

"Stop will ya until you hear this, apparently it was one of them young tinkers, now I don't know which of them was it, but I believe which ever one it was he had a sore ass for a while, stealing chickens they were, and I wouldn't mind poor old Jim O'Sullivan thought it was foxes, ha, could you beat that now Tim?"

Mary is having a good laugh at Bill, telling her father the story.

"Dad won't be too pleased when he finds out that Máirtín and I are engaged."

She talks to herself in kitchen, pouring herself a whiskey.

"Whatever happened to them lads anyways Tim?"

Mary comes back into the sitting room to join them.

"What lads Bill?" asks Tim.

"You know, them tinkers that I was talking about, where did they ever go to at all I wonder, they didn't stay very long in Ballycrackn now did they?"

"Oh I don't know Bill, I think they cleared off to England or somewhere like that," says Tim looking at Mary and Sheila. Timmy and his girlfriend start to smile.

"What tinkers do you mean Dad?"

"Now look, a girline, nobody is talking to you at all and mind your own business."

It's getting dark and the travellers are looking for Pat Walsh that sells the Poítin. They come to a small village with only a school and a grocery shop that sells supplies to the locals, they all get out of the van and run into the shop, where the shopkeeper is behind the counter looking at all the travellers run into the shop. Some of the women running across the road to have a pee behind a hedge.

"If ye want to have a piss now is the time lads, 'cause I'm not stopping again," says Dagger.

He goes into the shop to asks the shopkeeper for directions.

"How's it going there Boss, will ya tell me how to get to Pat Walsh's place?"

"Right, you're not far away at all, just up the road, it's about one mile I'd say, about the third house on the left, you can't miss it, ya can't miss it unless you're blind, now the bog is on the right and the house is on the left."

Máirtín looks at the shopkeeper funny.

"I'd say ye are buying the strong stuff off him, I'd say are ye," says the shopkeeper.

He watches the youngsters go behind the biscuits counter.

"Sound, did you get that Margaret?"

"I did, Máirtín, just down the road, third house on the right."

"You got it wrong now Miss, third house on the left I said, well, where did ye come from lads?"

"Just outside Ballinasloe Sir," Willie says, as he enters the shop.

"Do ye know Jack O'Reilly's Pub?"

"Why would we Boss, sure it's the only pub in the whole town that will serve the travellers." Willie says.

"Well young man, when ye see Jack again, will ye tell him that Tae-Pot was asking for him?"

The travellers look at each other, they leave the shop to go to the van.

"Who the hell is Tae-Pot?" asks Willie as he gives a wink to Máirtín.

A short time later they are driving down the road; they have two ice cream cones each they got from the shop keeper.

"He's one decent man that fella is, isn't he, ha ha, he must have given us about £3 worth of stuff there now for nothing, what do ye think lads. He must have given the youngsters there about thirty pennies bars at least, sure that's thirty pennies, before you say anything, not to mind the ice cream," says Máirtín.

He is driving along the road, eating an ice cream cone, looking out for Pat Walsh's house.

"Oh shit I have an itch and I can't scratch it."

"Where are you itchy Willie, I'll scratch it for ya."

"Here Katie, scratch it fast before I throw these cones out the window."

He starts to move around the seat with the itch.

"Where are you itchy, on your back is?"

"No, my bollix, oh hurry up Katie, will ya scratch it fast, the itch is killing me, please."

"Go away you will ya, ya feckin tit, what do you think I am, did you hear that Margaret he wants me to scratch his bollix for him, sure isn't that your job Margaret?"

"What's that Katie, what did he say?" Margaret asks.

She comes from the back of the van between the seats.

"Well did you ever hear the likes of that, he wants me to scratch his bollix!"

Margaret has a good laugh at Willie, she reaches between the seats to scratch Willie. The children in the van thinks it's very funny, and burst their sides with laughter.

"Did ya hear that fella in the shop, tell Jack Tae-Pot was asking for him," says Willie.

Dagger is just taking a lick of his ice cream, when he bursts out laughing at Tae-Pot, and splatters the ice cream all over the windscreen.

They notice the Garda car that passed them earlier parked on the side of the road where two members of the Gardaí are coming out of the bog with large bottles of Poítin in hand. They also have a man in custody.

"Shit look at that, damn it I bet that's Pat Walsh now, that has the Poítin for us, well bugger on them pigs anyway! Wouldn't you think they would mind their own business."

They drive slowly towards the Gardaí car to see what's happening.

"Never mind them lads Dagger, keep going and say nothing," Willie says.

Just as they drive past the Gardaí, Dagger lets down the window and asks one of the Gardaí where is Pat Walsh's house. He tells him that it is about the third house on the left. Dagger thanks the Garda and drives on. Willie is annoyed because he is afraid the Gardaí might pull them over for no tax, and wonder why they are looking for Pat Walsh.

On the way home with the bumping of the van, Margaret goes into labour, she is rushed into one of the houses, where the local doctor is called. Margaret gives birth to a bouncing baby boy. Willie is excited, opening one of the bottles of Poítin to celebrate.

St Anita's Hospital

Helen is still in the day ward while the nurses go around with the patients' medication. They give the medication to an old lady. Helen looks on. A male nurse attend to Helen.

"Now Helen how are you today?"

Helen just nods her head.

"I see here in your chart, you're down for more electric shock treatment this evening, right here's your medication and I'll come back for you later, I'll take you down to the E S T room myself later on, Helen is that ok?"

There is no response from Helen, she puts the tablets into her pocket when no one is looking, her hair and eyebrows are shaved off. Her head is covered in red marks from previous electric shock treatment, she is in a state. She looks terrible, still dressed in her nightgown since early morning.

On The Train To Visit Helen

Helen's mother and father, Mary and her father and mother, Bill and his wife Peg, are going to Dublin to visit Helen. The atmosphere is cold between Mary and her father, Tim found out Mary got engaged.

"I cannot get over that, I never thought my only daughter would do something as stupid as this."

"Look Dad, if you don't shut up I'll never speak to you ever again."

She turns away from her father to ignore him.

"Can you not see what you are doing to your mother and I, can you?"

"No Dad, I don't care, and don't ever attack me again the way you did last night, never do that to me again. If you can't accept it, tough on you, that's your problem not mine, go throw yourself in the river for all I care."

"Look, just quieten it now the both of you, I cannot take anymore of this agro between you two, now stop it for once and for all, there happens to be other people on the train you know," Sheila says.

She looks around embarrassed, as Peg and Bill give a smile and turn their heads away.

Helen's mum and dad look at each other in amazement.

"Right, shut up all of you, I'm sure nobody else around here is interested in my love life, hallo. Look I'm sure Jack and Nellie have enough on their plate to worry about, with Helen in hospital."

"I'm sure Mary, they are certainly not interested in listening to you two arguing all the time now shee the both of you," Sheila says, annoyed with Tim and Mary.

Tim turns his head away with disgust.

At St Anita's Hospital

They arrive at the hospital, they are brought to the day ward by a Nurse, pointing down at Helen. They don't recognise her. Mary goes into a state of shock when she sees her best friend in that state, she cannot believe it, she goes over to Helen.

"Oh my God, what have they done to you, oh my God Helen, what's happening to you, what has happened, where's your beautiful blond hair?"

As she rubs Helen's head, she starts to cry. The rest of them are speechless and in shock.

"Talk to me Helen. Please talk to me, say something what have they done to you."

There is no talk out of Helen, she sits with her head down. Mary gets hysterical; she cannot believe the state Helen is in sitting there like a zombie.

"I can't believe this, oh you poor thing, please talk to me, what has happened, who did this to you?" she cries.

"I'm sure now Mary, she will be all right, I'm sure the doctors know what they are doing. This is the best hospital in the country you know."

"What are you saying Nellie, this is a loony bin; everybody here is crazy including the nurses and doctors. Helen shouldn't be in here, I'm taking Helen home with me today. She is not staying in here with these lunatic doctors one more night, she's coming home with us right now."

Mary tries to put Helen standing up on her feet. There is no response from the others, they are alarmed with what they see, as they weren't prepared for this.

"Will one of you please help me get Helen up on her feet please?" says Mary, trying to lift Helen off the chair.

"Stop that nonsense now Mary, leave Helen where she is, I'm sure she will be all right, I'm sure she is like this for a reason."

"All right, all right, is that all you can say mum, look at the state of her will you for God's sake, just two weeks ago I was talking to her and there were nothing wrong with her then, how did she get so bad looking so fast? Bill, Nellie, will you do something, this is your only daughter."

"Mary, what can we do, we weren't expecting this," Bill says.

Nellie sits beside Helen to comfort her, she rubs her head and weeps. A doctor arrives.

"Mr and Mrs Conway, are they here?" asks the Doctor.

"Yes, that's us," Bill replies, with a tear in his eye.

"Are you Helen's Doctor?"

"Yes I am, Mrs Conway, and can I talk to you in private please?"

They go into the Doctor's office. Mary sits down beside Helen and holds her hand, she is in tears. Sheila and Tim sit beside her, with nothing to say, while the doctor is discussing Helen's treatment.

"Do you know why your daughter is in here?"

"We are not really sure Doctor, they told us at the other hospital, that they recommended she come in here for a short rest," Nellie says.

"Well that's right, but your daughter is not well, she took an overdose the night she was discharged from her own hospital, she drank on top of the pills."

"What kind of pills Doctor?"

"Well I'm afraid to say Mrs Conway, she took sleeping tablets."

"How many?" asks Bill.

"At least a hundred?"

"Oh my God," says Nellie, putting her hand over her mouth in disbelief.

"Where do we go from here, Doctor, what do we do now?"

"Well we started E S T on her yesterday."

"Sorry Doctor what's E S T?" asks Bill

"Electric Shock Treatment, it's just to help her with her depression."

"Oh ya, does she need that, is that necessary?"

"We think she does Mr Conway, she is seriously depressed and psychotic, she is suicidal, she told the doctors at the hospital, that she would rather be dead, and only for she got sick after taking the overdose, she wouldn't be with us now. She threw up most of the pills, actually only for she panicked and dialled 999, she would be dead now, she is a lucky young woman I tell the both of you now."

"Oh my God, I cannot believe this Bill, what will we do now where do we go from here?"

"I think we should leave her to the hospital's care. I'm sure they know what they are doing?"

"You're right Mr Conway, just leave her with us, we will take good care of her, she will be as right as rain in no time," says the Doctor.

Bill and Nellie goes out to join the others, and their daughter in the day room.

Pit Bull Fight At Travellers Halting Site

At the travellers' site in Mullingar, they are having a pit bull fight with two bit bull terriers; there are about fifty traveller people in all, women and children. Dagger and Willie are there also, they're betting on the dogs. Willie puts on a bet with Luke the bookie.

"I put £20 to win on the black and white one, Luke."

He gives the money to Luke the bookie.

"Right Willie, that's £20 on Psycho."

There is a lot of shouting and barking of the dogs.

"Who's Psycho?"

"The dog you're betting on, you fool."

"Oh right Luke, I picked the right one didn't I, Psycho, that's a good name for a dog, do ya think so?"

"You certainly did pick the right one Willie, sure you're a bit psycho yourself aren't ya?" Luke has a laugh at that.

"Ah fuck off Luke, that's not nice."

"Ary, I'm only having the crack, how's your mother keeping those days."

"Not bad at all, not bad at all, Luke."

Dagger comes up to put on a bet, he has Fay's two children with him, he picks up young Johnny.

"How ya Luke?"

"Well how's the man, how in the hell are ya."

"I'm all right now Luke, I tell ya one thing I could do with a bit of good luck, any tips for me?"

"Na, there's no tips in dogs fighting, 'tis the strongest and more aggressive dog that will win you know, you will find out that next year yourself, when you will fight for the title, king of the travellers."

"Never mind the title Luke. I will put £40 on that brown one there, with the piece of his ear missing, you never know, he might be out for revenge tonight," Dagger says.

He points at a brown dog, while he is holding up young Johnny, that has the money for the bet in his hand. He gives the money to Luke.

"I'll take that young man, what's your name?" he says, taking the money from young Johnny. Dagger lets young Johnny down on the ground.

"Now Johnny, I hope this brown bull dog is the lucky one."

Young Johnny runs off.

"Luke, that's your grandson you know, 'tis a wonder yourself and Fay don't make it up."

"Look 'tis her that caused the death of my son, and I'll never forgive her for that, now say no more about that, anyways, how's your Mother?"

"Why do you ask that, you asks me that before? Do you have an eye for my Mum or what?"

"Just wondering, I haven't seen her for this long time."

Dagger walks away with Willie.

"Hi Willie, he's always interested in our mother do ya know that, every time I am talking to him, he asks me how's Mum."

"I wouldn't be too worried about poor Luke, he is a harmless auld soul," Willie says.

Luke The Bookie Gives Bridie A Visit

He calls to Bridie's trailer, he is dressed in a white bellbottom suit with a red shirt and a white tie with a white matching hat. He also has a bunch of flowers accompanied by a large bottle of Guinness in his hand, knocking at the door to surprise Bridie. A young boy answers the door, the boy gets a fright when he sees what's at the door.

Bridie is inside with Fay and her two children, and two other women engaged in conversation about when Fay went into hospital.

The children eat cake.

"Gran, Joe Dolan is outside," shouts the young boy in a loud voice, Bridie looks surprised.

"Joe Dolan, sure what would Joe Dolan want of me."

"Is herself in?" asks Luke.

"Gran, he is looking for you and he has flowers."

Fay pulls opens the blinds to looks outside.

"Oh shit will ya look who's in it?"

"Who's in it, Fay?"

"Oh, look who's outside, the rotten bastard. Look, I'm out of here," Fay says.

She grabs her children by the hands and leaves, ignoring Luke as she passes him by.

Bridie takes no notice of Fay, she gets up and fixes herself, she takes the dishes off the table to put on a clean tablecloth.

"Where is your manners, will ya tell him to come in, come on ye lot go outside, there's nothing in here to see, come on clear off the lot of ye," says Bridie, to the other women and children.

Making Plans To Rob A Post Office

Máirtín Dagger, Willie and the Barry brothers meet up at Dagger's trailer to plan the robbery. They have knives and balaclavas left up on the table, they drink whiskey and beer. Máirtín Dagger is head of the post office robbery and he expects the others to follow his orders.

"Now lads this one is easy, the couple that own the shop and post office, are in their seventies, now look lads no one gets hurt, we will bring our weapons just in case, all we are after is the cash nothing else, do ye hear that now you two?" He refers to the Barry brothers, who are known trouble makers.

"At six thirty the shop closes, the post office closes at five o'clock, now we will wait until about three in the morning, till everyone is gone home from the pub across the road," Willie says, drinking some whiskey from the bottle.

"Lads, I believe they don't even have a safe now, they put the money in a hole in the ground behind the counter," Máirtín says.

He points at one of the Barry brothers, Malachy.

"Look now, I want you two to go to Dublin and picks us up a van with a Dub Reg, that will put the cops off."

"Don't you think mate, that if we have a van, that might look suspicious, don't you think." Malachy speaks in an English accent.

Roger starts to laugh at Malachy.

"All right mate, that's a big word for you Roger, su-suspicious."

He opens a bottle of beer and has a cock shot with the lid to put it in the bin.

"Right, this is not England, nobody comes to any harm, I don't give a fuck how ye were doing it in England, ye are in Ireland now, so you both do things my way, is that understood now lads?" Dagger says, pointing the finger at the two Barry brothers, who were reared in England, and had to come back to Ireland when their father died in a car accident.

Bridie Has An Confession To Make

She is on her own with Luke, they are having a drink and Bridie shares an old secret with Luke. He drinks the bottle of Guinness he brought for himself.

"You know Bridie I always took a liking to you, have you ever known that?"

"I know that Luke, the boys tell me you ask for me all the time, we are not stupid around here you know."

She puts the flowers into a vase, leaving them on the table.

"Sure anyway, you told me that many a time yourself."

She sits down.

"I tell you now Bridie, ever since my Maggie died I've been on my own, you know that yourself don't ya?"

"Say no more Luke, look, I know what you went through when Maggie passed over, may God rest her soul, and there's no doubt that her soul is in heaven. I've been alone too, and I certainly could do with a man around here".

Luke looks surprised.

"And would you have somebody in mind now Bridie would ya?"

"I might, you never know now, if he is kind to me I might take him in." She gives him the side eye.

"You know I'm worried about Máirtín, you know about the Garda Officer's daughter, don't ya?"

"In fate I do Bridie, sure he confides in me all the time, every chance he has he talks to me about her, Mary Buckley I believe her name is. You know it might be a bit chancy getting involved with that sort, sure if it's what the lad wants, fair play to him, all I can say, I hope he is doing the right thing."

Bridie is apprehensive.

"I have something to tell ya now, look I'm terrible sorry I haven't told you this before."

She puts her head down with shame.

"What's that Bridie is there something wrong?"

He gets up off his chair to get closer to her.

"Sit yourself down will ya, twas the time we were together shortly after my husband died God rest his soul."

She blesses herself. Luke has a worried look on his face.

"You can remember that can't you?" she says.

"Now look Bridie, 'twas the drink you know, sure the both of us was flat on the ground with whiskey, sure whatever happened it was a long time ago."

"I know that bloody well fine, well I have to tell ya this now, and may God forgive the both of us."

Luke is perspiring because of what she might say.

"'Twas your child I was carrying at the time."

"What Bridie, are you sure about that?" he asks, nervously.

"I'm certain about that, you know he only lived a few minutes after he was born."

"I'm terribly sorry Bridie, why didn't you tell me this before?"

He takes a swig out of the bottle of stout.

"I could not, because of Martin, he thought he was the father of the child, may they both rest in peace, God bless them." she says.

"Does Fay ever mention how my son died at all to ya?"

"No Luke, not a word about him at all, she is a heartless little woman she is."

"Well Bridie they say she poisoned him with rat poison you know, in his porridge she was putting it we believe."

"Ary, who said that, I wouldn't believe that kind of thing at all, sure people say the queerest of things."

"Now, there's no smoke without fire, sure didn't we find a half empty box of rat poison in the drawer, with a spoon, after he was found dead?"

"And why didn't ya give it to the Police?"

"Na, stop, we never get them mixed up in our affairs at all, what they won't know won't bother them. Sure that's why I don't talk to Fay, I never seen my grandchildren or nothing."

"Look Luke, get that out of your head, 'twas probably mice in the cupboards or something she was killing, now let me never hear you say that again. She has her problems, but Fay is no man killer."

Garda Jim Gets Acquainted With Gypsy Woman

Garda Jim is in the Police cell with the Gypsy traveller woman, while Anthony is at the reception desk, working on Garda files.

"Hurry up there Jim, Sergeant Molloy is due back soon."

"I'm coming," Jim replies.

Anthony puts his eyes up to heaven as he goes back to his duties.

"Well, hurry up then."

Garda Jim comes into the counter area to join Anthony.

"Well that was quick Jim."

"Ah well, sure under the circumstances, what could you do," replies Jim. They both laugh.

An old lady comes into the Station. Her handbag was robbed.

"Well, then, what can I do for you?" says Jim tucking his shirt into his pants, the old lady notices this.

"Look Garda, my handbag was robbed, just five minutes ago."

"And where did this happen?"

He is pulling himself together.

"Just down the road as I made my way from twelve o'clock Mass."

"Well, I see, and can you describe the person who stole your handbag?"

The prostitute comes out smoking a fag, and asks is she released, or are they pressing charges.

"I know you, you're the Gypsy woman that's prostituting yourself across from my house," says the old lady.

"Oh, and you are the auld hag that reported me to the Police aren't you?"

"'Tis no wonder the country is the way it is, with scum like you polluting our streets." the lady says.

Jim gets embarrassed, as Anthony smiles to himself as the Gypsy woman leaves.

"Right Mam," Jim says, with a little cough.

"Perhaps you might describe the person who stole your handbag?"

"It was one of them Barry Gypsies, or tinkers whatever you call them now days. They live out the road, you know, the one with the weird mother called Fay."

"Oh, right Mam, we think we know who you are talking about. I will give his mother a call right away."

Robbing The Post Office

It's three a.m., the four lads are sitting outside the post office in a black B M W car.

"Get down lads," says Willie, "the fuzz is coming, Roger, get to feck down now, will ya, before we're seen," he adds.

"I am down, get down yourself Willie, they can see your big thick head sticking out there over the door window."

They hide in the car, the cop car passes by slowly, looking at the black B M W and drive off.

"By golly, that was close, right lads there is no one else about, let's go Malachy, Willie, Roger are ye ready to do this?" Dagger says.

"Ready as we'll ever be, come on let's go," says Willie. They make a fast exit from the car, to run around the back of the Post Office.

Next day at Police Station the Garda are having a meeting about the robbery in Tullamore Post office.

"Right, I have a report here from the Garda Station at Tullamore, now, the post office over there has been raided last night, fortunately enough, nobody was hurt, the raiders or raider, went in through a back window, some time between two in the morning and five a.m."

"Well Sarge, I don't know what this place is coming to, yesterday we had an old lady's hand bag stolen, with her pension money inside," Garda Jim says.

"Right, from now we are to keep our eyes and ears open, I want to know every movement around this town. They might strike again. Also a black B M W was spotted not far from the crime scene, whether that car was involved or not, we don't know as of yet," says Sergeant

Ricky.

"Do we have any other leads other than that Sarge?"

"No Anthony, just a Dublin Registration number of the Black B M W, the Officers are speaking to the elderly couple as we speak, when they have any more information they will notify us right away."

Chapter Thirteen

St Patrick's Day Parade

It's the 17th of March and all the travellers are at the St Patrick's Day parade in Galway town, there is a massive crowd about. They are watching the parade, the children are eating ice cream cones, the parade is passing and Mary and Máirtín are holding hands.

"Hi Dagger give us a fiver will ya, I've only got a twenty, I don't want to break that."

"For what do you want a fiver for Johnny? And where did you get the £20?"

"Look Máirtín, I found the £20 all right, now will you give us a fiver for fags?" young Johnny says.

"Feck off or I will give you a punch in the face, the size of ya smoking fags, shut up and watch the parade will ya?"

The children run down the street. Mary notices the way he is taking care of Fay's two children all the time.

"You treat Fay's two children like they're your own."

"I know I do Mary, sure they're the ages my two would be now if they were still alive."

His eyes fills up with tears as he looks at the children run down the street.

"You're a good man, and maybe that's why I love you."

"Maybe, maybe," he replies, wiping the tears off his eyes with the sleeve of his jumper.

"You know we come here every year to watch the parade. Julia loved this town, she always planned to settle down here some day," Máirtín says.

The Parade passes by, it's made up of about twenty floats, with school bands marching. There is a flat spring cart made up as a float of tinkers, with an old canvas camp and a tin smith repairing an old bucket, followed by two barrel top wagons while some other young tinkers dance around a makeshift campfire. There is a lot of excitement, Willie has young Seánine up on his shoulders.

Helen's Last Electric Shock Treatment

Still in hospital, she is sitting on her own in the dining room, staring out the window, with her head shaved. She puts her hand in her nightgown pocket to check the tablets she has saved.

The Doctor and two male nurses are looking out the one way window from the doctors office.

"Look at her. She hasn't improved one bit since she came here, I don't know, anyway nurse, how many E.S.T. treatments has she had?" the Doctor says, with a sigh.

"I think Doctor, this will be her fourth."

He checks his charts.

"Well we better get it over with, if she doesn't respond after this one, I don't know what we should do."

"What about her medication, maybe if we change her tablets she might respond better?" says the other male nurse.

"We will see, just bring her down, we better get this over with," says the Doctor.

The two nurses go to Helen, to take her to the electric shock treatment room. She refuses to go for treatments. They grab each arm to walk her down the long dark corridor.

"Wait one minute, I want to go to the toilet," Helen mutters.

"Ok, we might as well otherwise while you are receiving treatment you will wet yourself, we don't want that to happen now do we, remember the last time Helen, you shit all over yourself," says one of the male nurses, opening the door for her to go onto the toilet.

Helen goes into the toilet, she takes all the tablets out of her pocket and takes them, swallowing them down with tap water she drinks with the palm of her hand.

Mary and Máirtín are in love

Mary is walking along the river bank with Máirtín, they are on their own, holding hands as they are very much in love.

A couple that knows Mary stares at them as they pass by; the couple put their heads together as they pass a smart comment, about Mary with a traveller. Máirtín stops.

"Mary, I have something to give you," he says.

"Is it a surprise?" asks Mary.

"Maybe, close your eyes now till I take it out?" he says.

"You're not going to do something naughty now are ya?"

"No Mary. Just keep your eyes closed."

He takes out a jewellery box and gives it to Mary.

"Now open your eyes."

"Oh my God, what's this?"

She opens the box to see a beautiful Claddagh Ring.

"Oh my God, I can't believe it, is this for real?"

She is so surprised.

"No, you are only dreaming," says Máirtín.

"Am I?"

"Na, it's for real all right, it's yours, try it on."

"Thank you very much, it's gorgeous."

She takes the ring out of the box and gives it to Máirtín to put it on her finger.

"I cannot believe this, I always wanted a Claddagh Ring, now I have one." She cries.

She puts her arms around him to hug and kiss him.

"I love you so much…"

"I love you too Mary, you are so special to me."

"Ok, from now on nobody comes between us, not my parents, from now on we both will just take care of each other, nobody, just you and I from now on," Mary says passionately.

They walk along the river bank. She starts to get sad.

"I have something to tell you."

"What's that love?"

"It's about my friend Helen, she is in hospital in Dublin you know, I feel so sad for her."

"What kind of hospital?"

"A psychiatric hospital."

"A loony bin, you mean, you know Mary, that's for crazy people."

"I know that Máirtín."

"Why, is your friend crazy or something? I had an Aunt Phyllis, Phyllis the pill we called her, she died in a crazy hospital, cracked up after her husband drowned after swimming in the sea, somewhere in England."

"Oh, that's awful, look I want to tell you this, and promise me you won't tell a soul."

"I promise Mary, sure why should I?"

He puts his hand on his heart.

"Well, you see Helen thought that you and I were having sex, now that was in the beginning of course, didn't she take herself off to Dublin, where she thought nobody would know her, and she found one of your people and slept with him."

"You mean a traveller and that's who got her pregnant."

"Ya, now she only did it for the experience."

"I'll kill the bastard when I catch him, what's his name, I'll kill him!"

He is raging with anger.

"Calm down a minute will ya, it's wasn't his fault. Helen thought that sex was brilliant with travellers, you know just like a black man, once you have black you never go back, well that's what she thought."

"And wasn't she right, don't ya think?"

"Right Máirtín, don't flatter yourself."

"So she got herself up the stick for that, well, oh my God, the poor little stupid bitch, mind you we are good at it, aren't we? Do you know his name Mary?"

"I do, but promise me you won't fight with him, his name was Cathal Holms."

"What, I don't believe this, him, he is such a freak, I can't believe him, oh my God, how did she get involved with that buffer?"

"It's obvious you know him."

"I do Mary, and do you know something, he is no good, that's all he does is pick up women and use them."

"Stop now Máirtín, I don't need to know anymore, lets go back to the pub to meet the others."

Sheila Calls To Visit Nellie

She is concerned about Helen, she calls to see is there any other developments.

"Any word from the hospital on Helen?"

"No, Sheila." Nellie stares in wonder.

"Na, nothing yet, still the same, she hasn't snapped out of it yet." she adds.

"Well, the doctors should know what they're doing I hope."

"I wonder? I wonder do they, it was only a few weeks ago she was full of life, now she's only a zombie locked up in that crazy house."

"I wonder Nellie have you made the right decision, sending her to St. Anita's at all."

"Oh don't say that Sheila, look, trust in God, do you know what we will do, lets get down on our knees and say the rosary and ask God to help us."

"Well now, I'm sure you should have said the rosary before you let her go to Dublin, if I was you now Nellie I would call the hospital first thing in the morning and have her taken home."

"I think you're right Sheila, you know Jack said that. He said Mary was right, maybe we should take her home. I'll do that first thing in the morning, we must have been crazy to allow her to go to St Anita's in the first place."

"Now come on, don't be too hard on yourself, the best thing to do is take Helen home."

St Patrick's Day Celebrations Continue

Máirtín and Mary go into a pub to join the rest of his family for St. Patrick's Day celebrations. The pub is full of people, there is a ceili band in the corner, there are Tayto bags everywhere, and a big tray of sandwiches and drinks on the table in front of his family. They come in holding hands and looking very happy.

"Well, what's with ye two fools?" says Fay, with an envious look.

"Shut up you Fay, leave them alone, they're in love," Bridie says.

The rest of the women have a laugh, as Fay looks sad.

They both go dancing, the rest of the family clap their hands as they dance a quick step. Later on Mary shows off the engagement ring to some of the traveller women that haven't yet seen it. Fay has a sad face, she cannot help being hurt, because it's not herself that got engaged to Máirtín. She still has the bandages on her wrist since she was discharged from hospital.

The band is singing, "She Moves Through the Fair." Everybody is happy, dancing up on the tables and singing. It's a very exciting time for the travellers, there is a big celebration going on. They are still celebrating the engagement and also St. Patrick, who put the snakes out of Ireland.

Helen is strapped to a chair by the two nurses. They put on the head piece that gives the E.S.T. One of the male nurses turns on the radio. The song "Nights in White Satin" comes on.

The nurse leaves the room for a minute, while the other nurse turns on the switch to give Helen the E.S.T. He turns his back to check notes on a table behind Helen's chair. She has a black rubber mouth piece, so she won't bite her tongue while she is receiving the electric shock. She starts to have a reaction straight away to the treatment, frothing from the mouth.

He turns up the radio, so he can listen to the song which consequently happens to be Helen's favourite song. He gives a little dance to the music. Helen is trying to call for help, strapped to the chair by her head, hands and feet, starting to trembling and shake, she cannot get the Nurse's attention, he cannot hear her because he is too much engrossed with the song on the radio.

Helen is frothing heavily from the mouth, and is also having a serious convulsion, she is going to die if she doesn't get help fast.

Her face turns purple, trying to scream out but cannot, she is getting flashbacks of her childhood, times like when she fell off the wall outside Ballycrackn shop, burning her feet and hands with nettles, also having fun on the beach with her mother and father, as she faintly hears her favourite song in the background.

Mary is in the pub enjoying the fun, she gets a sudden pain in her chest; she gets weak and falls to the floor, everybody gets a fright. They give her a glass of water, that Bridie fetches from the bar. Fay looks on with a sarcastic smile.

At the same time Sheila is still with Nellie, they are just after saying the rosary, when a picture of the sacred heart falls off the wall, they both get a fright.

"Somebody must be dead, any time that happens you will hear of a death."

"Ary, will you stop with your pirogues surely to God Sheila, you don't believe in that."

Helen is on the E.S.T chair turned purple and cannot breath, the other Nurse returns with an attendant, to find Helen frothing from the mouth. He gets a fright.

"Jesus, oh my God, what in the hell have you done, what has happened to you?"

He is in shock as he notices Helen frothing from the mouth.

"What up?" says the other Nurse, as he turns around.

"What's happening, what is that stuff coming out of her mouth?" he asks.

"She is having a convulsion of some kind, she must be having a negative reaction to the treatment, look, you go and call a doctor," the nurse says to the attendant.

They take Helen from the chair and lay her down on a trolley nearby, they clean her mouth and gives her mouth to mouth resuscitation, checking her pulse; they do this for a minute or two, they try and resuscitate her.

"It's no good she's dead, she's gone, there's nothing we can do, she is dead." one of the nurses says.

"No, she is not, Helen wake up, wake up Helen," says the other.

He smacks her across the face.

"It's no good she is dead, there is nothing we can do now."

Helen is dead, the two nurses are devastated. They check to see what the froth is from her mouth.

"Look what's this?"

"Show me, that looks like tablets, I can't believe this, don't tell me she OD'd again, how will we explain this to her parents I wonder?"

Mary Being Informed About The Bad News

That evening Mary is walking around the town park on her own, grieving and confused over the death of her best friend, sitting on a park bench with her head down, stroking her engagement ring and crying, reminiscing about the good times she had spent with Helen. She also feels guilty because she spent most of her time with Máirtín.

"Oh God, why did you let this happen, why God, what did Helen do to deserve this, oh God I loved Helen so much, why did she die?" She screams and is frustrated with God.

Back at the Police Station, Garda Anthony gives a report he was working on to Sergeant Ricky Molloy. He reads it and nods his head as he reads the report.

"Well now, that's interesting," he says.

Mary's sitting on the park bench, a man called Sylvester with long grey hair, a beard and a long trench coat, approaches her, he has a Bible under his arm.

"Well my child, what's the matter with you?"

As she looks up at him, she notices how he is dressed and that he is holding a Bible.

"Piss off you, you have no business here, now off with you!"

"Oh my child I can see you're troubled, my name is Sylvester, what's yours?"

"Never you mind, I don't want to talk to you, I couldn't care less what your name is, now piss off."

"Well, I can see you are bothered my child, what weighs down your shoulder, what is the matter?"

He sits besides her, he opens the Bible and starts to read a passage from it. "And the Lord said, a burden shared is a burden halved,

as he shall remove our burdens as Jesus died on the cross for Us,"
Sylvester reads.

Sergeant Molloy phones Sergeant Tim Buckley to tell him
about the black B M W.

"Yes Tim, they were seen driving a black beamer, through the
town earlier on, that very evening."

"Are you sure about that Ricky, how reliable is this witness?"

"Very reliable, Tim."

"Yes we got him this time, when I'm finished with him he
won't see the light of day for a long time, and I'll make God damn sure
of that," Tim says.

Hair Salon In Westport

Three local women from Ballycrackn are at the hairdressers, getting
their hair done for Helen's funeral, one of them is under the dryers,
while Molly Walsh is waiting to get her hair washed. Miss Waters is
getting her hair cut by the hairdressers.

"That's terrible Molly, isn't it, about poor Helen Conway?"
says Miss Waters.

"Wasn't that awful, I cannot get over that, she shouldn't have
left Westport at all, sure we have lived here all our lives and we're all
very happy," says Miss Waters.

"Suicide, I believe it was ladies, what did ye hear," says another
woman.

"Now ladies you cannot be going around saying things like
that, wasn't it a brain haemorrhage she had, who said suicide," says the
hairdresser, annoyed with the woman.

"Well, that's what I heard now, ye can think what ye like and
another thing I can see that Mary one, you know Sheila's daughter that's
messing around with them gypsy tinkers, ever since they both moved
up there, they both went a bit funny."

"Do ya know Molly, I believe Helen was drinking heavily, so
her mother told me. She said her heart was broken with Helen's
drinking when she lived at home, she thought when she moved away
she would pull herself together," says Miss Waters.

"Sure they're all a bit funny up there anyways if you ask me," says Miss Waters, reading a magazine.

The hairdresser puts her eyes up to heaven, and makes a gesture with the Scissors over Miss Waters head as she cuts her hair.

"I'm sorry now, Mary and Helen were my two best friends at school, now watch what you are saying, Lord God I hate gossiping." She cuts a chunk out of Miss Waters' hair.

Helen Is Laid To Rest

The funeral Mass is at eleven thirty at Ballycrackn church and afterwards Helen is laid to rest at the graveyard nearby. Her coffin is put into the ground, the whole family are there. Mary's family, friends, Garda and the Ward family, with a few other travellers.

Mary is hysterical, her mother and school friends try to comfort her. Nellie and Jack Conway are numb, they are both in disbelief, it hasn't hit them yet that their only child is dead.

Father O'Breen says prayers and two men put the coffin in the ground. Everybody starts to cry, the travellers get an unpleasant look from Sergeant Tim and a few old women.

Cathal the Stud Homes, that got Helen pregnant is standing on his own away from all the others. Máirtín doesn't notice him.

When Helen is laid to rest, the travellers are the first to leave. Máirtín Dagger spots Cathal Homes waking towards the gate of the cemetery, he catches up with him. Cathal turns around to see who is coming behind him.

When he sees Máirtín he is surprised and puts his hand out to shake on the fight they had at the horse fair.

"'Tis not your hand I will be shaking, but blood from your stinking body I will draw."

"Come on now Máirtín, 'twasn't the first time you were scrapping in a lounge bar, nor will it be the last," Cathal said, speaking in a Dublin accent.

"What did you do to Helen Conway will ya tell me now, before I ring your neck off."

"What's on ya, I did nothing to her, I only spent the night with her, that's all what are you on about."

"Look you little shit you got her up the stick sure you did and I tell you one thing for certain over my dead brothers grave I will make you pay for this."

Some of the travellers and a few other people that were at the funeral heard what Máirtín said as they passed by.

"Keep your loud mouth down will ya or I close it for you right now, you have no right to talk to me with that tone."

"You're the loud mouth Cathal."

Máirtín strikes him a blow in the face, the two lads start punching each other.

The women start to scream, the others that are around Helen's grave hear the commotion at the cemetery gate. Tim goes out to investigate, Mary follows, with a few others. When Tim gets to the gates there is a crowd gathered, the two lads are belting each other in the fashion of a fist fight. Mary starts to scream at Máirtín.

"Get back here you young woman, it has nothing to do with us."

Mary hears her father, but ignores him, and keeps on going to stop the two lads from fighting.

Tim is embarrassed, Mary starts screaming at the two lads to stop, she is knocked to the ground. Tim goes over to her to take her away, she screams at him to tell him to mind his own business and it has nothing to do with him.

The people around start to mumble about what's happening. They talk about Mary and Máirtín and the people that heard what Máirtín said to Cathal about getting Helen into trouble gossip to each other. Tim overhears the conversations. He grabs Mary by the hand and put her in the car to take her home.

"There won't be another word out of you missy, get into the car and be quiet, I don't want to make a scene here."

They get into the car and drive away. Máirtín and Cathal come to their senses and stop fighting. Cathal gets into his car and drives back to Dublin.

Helen's Parents House

They have a full house: Mary's family neighbours, Molly, Miss Waters, Jim and Annie, and friends, also three or four widows and the priest. The women are drinking tea and eating sandwiches, the men are drinking bottles of stout, there are a few children sitting on the ground. The travellers are kept outside in the back yard, they are drinking bottles of Guinness. Johnny the Singer is home from England, with Etna sitting in the front seat of their Hi Ace, with new born baby Joseph, he sings a Scan-nós song. Máirtín is still bleeding from the mouth.

"Well, Mrs Conway that's a fine spread you have laid on. Tell me this Tim, who was doing all the shouting outside the cemetery gates, did any of ye hear the commotion?" says Father O'Breen, as he looks around at the others.

"Ah, it was nothing Father, only a few young lads messing about."

Tim gives a nasty look at Mary.

"All right so, I must be off and once again, Nellie and Jack, I can't stress how sorry I am about your poor daughter Helen, she was such an innocent child, I can recall the day she made her Holy Communion with great happiness and it brings great sadness over our lives today," he says, holding Nellie's hand.

"I know Father, you're so good." She weeps.

"Well, before I go lets join hands and offer up our prayers for Helen's family in their hour of grief, in the name of the father, son and holy spirit, May God bring peace and glory back to Nellie and Jack, and may Helen your daughter be at peace forever more, Amen, in the name of the father, son and holy spirit. Now I must be off, and once again thank you for the lovely meal, it was wonderful."

Looking around at all the others, they look at him and smile.

"You're welcome father, I'll see you out."

"That's ok Nellie, I'll see my own way out, don't stir."

He leaves by the back door, when he goes outside he notices the travellers. A young traveller woman asks the priest to bless them.

The priest blesses all the travellers and says farewell.

Inside, a young neighbour's child pulls at Mary's clothes to get her attention.

"Is it true you're going to marry a tinker?"

Mary is embarrassed, a few heads turn together gossiping about Mary again.

Tim gives the eye across the room to Sheila, as she sips from a glass of red wine.

Everybody gets up to leave, they shake Jack and Nellie's hand and sympathise with them again for the loss of their daughter. Jack takes a walk in the fields on his own to come to terms with what has happened.

Nellie, Sheila and Mary sit and talk.

"Sheila I have a confession to make, I've never told a soul about this, maybe I should have done this a long time ago."

She stands up and picks up a school photo of Helen from the mantelpiece, sitting back down grasping the photo close to her heart. Sheila and Mary look on wondering what Nellie is going to confess.

"You know Sheila, we adopted Helen."

Sheila and Mary look at each other, amazed.

"Nellie I never knew."

"I know, we decided not to tell anybody, not even Helen, you know my sister Maeve that worked in the government buildings, you know she worked in Jack Lynch's office in Dublin?"

Sheila looks at Mary, putting her eyes up to heaven.

"She knew an adoption agency in Dublin, that take unwanted children from nursing homes, and get good homes for them down the country. I believe Helen's real mum was Swedish, fifteen is all she was when she gave birth to Helen."

"So that explains the foreign complexion she had, you know something Nellie I always knew she looked different, she was so pretty."

"I know Sheila, I think Helen's problems started last year, when I told her the truth."

"And why did you tell her, what she didn't know wouldn't bother her."

"Now Mum don't you think now that she was entitled to know the truth?"

"Look Mary it's too late now arguing about it, it was my idea to tell her, Jack wouldn't have any part of it, he always said leave well enough alone. I should have listened to him, she went to Dublin last year to check out the adoption agency, but they closed down ten years ago due to lack of funding. When she went to London with you Mary I think she had some connection to her real mother there, I don't know maybe she had, did she say anything to you, Mary about it?"

"No nothing, we only went for a weekend break that's all," says Mary, with a guilty look on her face.

"Look Nellie you're not to blame, now don't be too hard on yourself, it's God's will what has happened, no one could have prevented it happening."

"I know Mary, you're such a good person. Helen talked about you all the time."

Nellie and Mary start to cry while Sheila takes the photo off Nellie and puts it back on the mantelpiece.

"You know I couldn't ever have children of my own, we tried for years, it was the doctor that recommended adopting."

She bursts into tears.

"Oh, Nellie, I'm so sorry, If I could take your pain way I would, it's closer to God we all should be at a moment like this."

They all sit in silence as the clock ticks, strikes at eight o clock, and rings out.

Mary Has An Intimate Conversation With Her Mum

She is listening to music, she is broken hearted over her friend Helen, she cries on her bed for a while, her mother comes into her room.

"Please, Mum I just want to be on my own."

"I can understand, look I thought we might have a chance to talk, we haven't talked much lately, because of all that was going on," Sheila says.

She is feeling guilty she hasn't spent time with Mary and for not giving her support.

"I'm sorry mum, but I'm busy at work and I don't have the chance anymore to come home as often as I would like too, and the way dad is, it's not easy."

"Alright, I'll leave it with ya." Sheila goes to leave.

"Don't, don't go mum, please stay, I would like to talk." Sheila sits on the bed beside Mary.

"You know Mum, I really miss this room, I see you painted over the stars I stuck to the ceiling." Looking up at the ceiling, her eyes fill up.

"I know, I covered them stars, it wasn't my idea to paint them over, it was your father, you know the way he is, anything that is different or out of the ordinary he cannot stand it."

"Ha, I know all about that mum don't you worry." She sits up on the bed.

"You know Mum, I feel so sorry for poor Nellie and Jack, you know Jack finds it hard to come to terms with it, he's carrying on as if nothing has happened."

"I know Mary some day he will, give him time, he will be fine, he'll work through it, men are strong, they don't want to show their true feelings."

"I suppose you're right mum."

"What's the story with what's his face? Oh ya, Máirtín, are you as serious about him as you say?"

"Ya Mam, I am."

Mary looks at the ring.

"It's a lovely ring you know, did he pick it himself?"

"We picked it together."

"I didn't think Mary, those people were romantically inclined at all."

"Ah Mam, what do you mean by those people, you make out they're some kind of tribe or something."

"I'm sorry but you know what I mean, you know travellers are different."

"I know that Mam, but they are still human, it's only because of the way they live, anyways I like the travellers' way of life, I love the freedom they have, the simplicity of their lives."

"Well, they seem to have that all right, their lives seem to be basic, I suppose there is nothing wrong with simplicity."

"You know mum I never really told you how I felt about Máirtín I always loved him, ever since the first time I met him, all these years ago, I really love him you know."

"You were too young to love anyone, you were only a kid."

"I was twelve years old Mum, and I did have feelings you know."

"I know Mary, but back then you were too young to decide for yourself."

"How do you mean decide, I'm wasn't deciding anything, all I'm saying is, I always fancied Máirtín, and when we met up last year I knew he was the one for me, that's all I'm saying mum."

"Ok love, whatever you decide, I'm with you, no matter whatever your father says, I'm on your side from now on. You know poor Helen's parents would do anything to have their daughter back home with them, always remember, this room is always here for you, no matter what happens, you can come home here anytime you want."

"Thanks mum, I appreciate that, I thought there for a long time nobody was on my side, even at work they gossip, snigger and look down at me, to tell the truth mum I haven't gone to work much at all in the past couple of months, I cannot stand the staring, and gossiping."

"Well, whatever you do, don't give up your job, you always need to work."

"I don't care, Máirtín says if we get wed, he will support me, and I don't need to work, I know dad won't hear of that, but it's my life and I'm old enough to make my own decisions."

"I'm sure you are old enough, but if it's what you want?" Sheila says. She stares out the window, with worry and concern.

"Yes Mum, with no doubt in my mind, I want to be with him."

"Ok Mary, if you feel you are doing the right thing, that's fine by me."

"Oh look I almost forgot, look what I found the other day."

She takes a photo of Mary and Helen, and another friend, out of her handbag that she has left on the floor.

"Oh my God where did you get this from, we are only about nine or ten, oh my God look at Helen."

"I know, wasn't she beautiful?"

"She sure was Mum. I remember it quite well when this photo was taken, we were only after climbing Croac Patrick, it was on a school trip, it was our teacher Mrs Doherty, that took the photo, remember her mum?"

She starts to cry.

"I sure do, indeed she was a good teacher, that other girl is a hairdresser now in Westport you know."

"Ya Mum, that's her, she was beside me at the graveside."

"She's such a lovely person. Look at poor Helen."

Mary cries, as her mum comforts her, she remembers all the good times she had with Helen and talks to her mum into the night about her fond times with Helen.

Chapter Fourteen

B M W Found At Travellers Halting Site

The Garda drive into the Halting site with high speed, in squad cars and Garda vans. They go into the travellers' trailer and arrest all the men, and put them into the vans, about six men in total - Dagger, Willie, the Barry brothers, Luke the bookie, and two other traveller men. There is a lot of screaming, the women fight with the Garda hitting them with their fists.

"Come on lads, quickly, load them up," demands Sergeant Ricky, pushing Máirtín Dagger into the van.

"Watch it Boss or you'll be sorry, what's all this for, we haven't done nothing."

"You'll find out soon enough my boy, come on, in you go and not a word out of you," says Officer Jim.

The women and children are screaming.

Officer Anthony goes behind the caravans; there is a large hole in the ground with a green canvas truck cover covering the hole, he goes over to call Sergeant Ricky.

"Sarge?"

"What now?"

"I think you should have a look back here."

Sergeant Ricky goes behind the caravans to find the black B.M.W. in the hole with the white Hi Ace van, also the Massy Ferguson Tractor under the green cover.

"I want this site closed down and that car, tractor and van taken back to the Station."

The Guards drive out onto the roadside where Sergeant Tim Buckley is parked across from the halting site, watching the travellers being taken away.

Ballycrackn Church

Mary, Sheila and Tim are going into church, there are a few old women looking at them and starting to gossip, the same ones that were gossiping fifteen years earlier, they are looking at Mary up and down. There are a lot of people about.

"I don't know how she can hold her head up, with the company she keeps," says Miss Waters.

Mary notices that Miss Waters and Molly Walsh are talking about her, as she walks towards the church.

"Never mind them Mary, they can't mind their own business not to mind ours. You know I'll never enter that shop again with the big mouth that Miss Waters has, she has everybody's business, I can't stand her," Sheila says.

Mary gets annoyed.

"Mam as far as I'm concerned she can drop dead."

"'Tis because of you they are gossiping sure it is, you and them feckin' tinkers."

"Shut up Timothy, will you please, for God sake, can you not keep your big mouth shut for once in your life can you, I'm fed up with ya!"

They approach the open door of the church, Father O' Breen is standing there welcoming the congregation as they enter the church.

"Well Timothy, I hear we are having a wedding celebration shortly."

"Over my dead body, Father, over my dead body," Tim says.

They enters the church, Tim is annoyed with Father O' Breen's comment.

"Did I say something wrong Sheila?"

"No Father, never mind him, he got out the wrong side of the bed this morning."

Next Day Mary Is Driving To Ballinasloe

She pulls over to buy groceries in Ballycrackn shop and have it out with

Miss Waters. She passes a remark to Mary, when she goes up to her to pay for the groceries.

"Well, Mary I heard you're getting married soon I believe," says Miss Waters, with a sarcastic smile.

"Well Miss Waters, have you a problem with that?"

"No, but is it true what they say about travellers?"

"And what might that be?"

"Oh well, they say Mary, there are like blacks, once you go black you never go back."

Another customer hears what Miss Waters said and gives her a nasty look.

"Look, mind your own business, anyways I heard you're queer, no wonder you never got married, anyway who would have you, you're stuck in this smelly old shop for the past thirty years, sure what would you know, you never went anywhere."

"How dare you say I'm queer!"

"Well I heard you are, now piss off and mind your own business from now on," Mary quarrels.

She takes her groceries without paying for them and leaves the shop.

The other customer is disgusted with Miss Waters' remarks.

"That's not fair, you know she is going through a hard time, after burying her best friend," the other customer says.

"Ary, shut up you and get out of my shop," says Miss Waters.

Scar Face Is Dead

Mary is driving back to Ballinasloe. She is listening to the radio, a news flash comes over the airways.

"There has been a fatal accident on the back road, between Ballinasloe Co Galway and Killmanally, between a heavy goods vehicle, and a pedestrian. It seems that the man was walking along the road when he accidentally fell in front of the passing truck, he is known locally as Finbar Coggins, better known to his friends as Scar Face.

"Oh, my God, I don't believe this, Scar Face is dead, oh my God," cries Mary.

She pulls over her car in dismay, to comes to terms with the bad news.

When she comes to terms with the awful news she drives on. Just as she is parking her car outside her flat, Katie, Nina Barry and two other women with three children run up to her all excited when they see her parking her car.

"Mary we're looking for you all over the place, we tried your flat, the hospital, everywhere, where were ya?"

"Calm down Katie, I was at home in Ballycrackn, I just heard on the radio about poor Scar Face," she cries.

"We know that, wasn't that terrible, the poor man, God have mercy on his soul, but that's not why we are looking for you," Nina says.

"Why, what else happened?"

"The lads were arrested yesterday, by the cops, for what, we don't know," Katie says, all excited.

"They came into our site yesterday like blaggards they were and arrested the men, and my two boys, sure my boys wouldn't hurt a fly sure they wouldn't," says Nina Barry.

"Oh look, I'm sorry, I just got back, I was at home; I just arrived back just now, anyway where are the lads now?"

"Down the Police Station."

"Right Katie, lets go there and find out."

They take off down the street; they walk very fast picking up other traveller women and children along the way. There are about twenty of them, arriving at the Station. Mary approaches the station. She notices her father's car outside.

"I don't believe this, I thought he was on duty at home, well, I don't care who he is, he will be sorry when I'm finished with him."

She goes inside with all the others. They cause mayhem inside, Mary goes to the counter. Garda Anthony is on duty.

"And what in the hell are you lot doing in here?"

"We are here to see our family," Katie says.

"Oh ya, they are locked up in the back for seventy two hours for questioning, they are not allowed any visitors as ye all were told last night, and if you all will be kind enough now to leave the way ye came in, I would appreciate that."

"No Sir, we will not leave, I want to see my father."

"And who might that be miss?" Anthony says, pretending not to know who Mary is.

"Timothy Buckley, that is Sergeant Timothy Buckley to you Sir, now get him out here straight away, come on move it."

"Right Miss, wait here."

Garda Anthony takes his time, he goes into the back office to fetch Sergeant Tim.

Tim comes out from the back, with Sergeant Ricky.

"What's all this racket about?" asks Sergeant Ricky.

"What's he doing here?"

"Look now Mary, it's about time all this farce was put to an end."

"Well Dad, what's that supposed to mean?"

"Look, I'm not going to discuss this any further in here, this is not the time or the place, and come on lets go."

"No, I'm not going anywhere till I find out what in the hell are you doing here?"

"Look now lass, your father is only looking out for your own good, you have no business hanging around with that kind of race," says Ricky.

"How do you mean race, who in the hell do you think you are, come out of my way. I want to see Máirtín, now can you please excuse me?"

She pushes the Garda out of her way. Tim gives the nod to Ricky to let her pass.

"All right but just a minute," Ricky says.

All the travellers cheer on Mary. She goes back to where Máirtín is held. Garda Anthony opens the cell door to let her in. She hugs Máirtín, they sit on a bed to talk.

"Máirtín what have you done?"

"Look Mary, I might as well tell ya, we held up a Post Office."

"Why did you do that, why, I can't believe this."

She holds her head to weep.

"I'm sorry Mary, I only did it for you, or for us I mean."

"How do you mean us?"

"For our wedding," he says.

"I thought you had money." She gets annoyed with him.

"I have, but it's all tied up in the vans and horses, look when I sell the horses I will pay back the money."

"I don't believe ya, why, have you done this kind of thing before?"

Máirtín turns his back on Mary and stares out the cell window, that is secured with security bars.

"Máirtín you don't have to rob to have money, you know that I cannot live like that."

"All right, all right, I'll pay back the money. Look at least, nobody got hurt, I didn't even go into the post office, 'twas the other lads did."

"How much did ye take?"

"£5000 Mary."

"Oh my God, ok, so when do you get out of here?"

"I don't know, they are talking about bail bond, maybe if we pay that we can go."

"And how much is the bail?"

"£500 for the whole lot of us, and don't worry about it, I have the money." He turns around to face her.

"Ya, the post office money I suppose."

"Ya, how else would I pay the bail bond?" They both burst out laughing.

"Máirtín Ward you're such a shit, but I love you anyway, now there will be no more robbing post offices!"

"I promise."

They both kiss. Máirtín gets down on one knee.

"Mary, will you marry me?"

"Oh, Máirtín, of course I will, and get up off the cold floor before you catch your death."

Mary starts to cry, she puts her arms around Máirtín to kiss him and give him a long hug.

"Lets get married as soon as we can, I've waited too long for this moment."

"Right Mary, lets show them, we will prove them wrong,

especially your old man"

"Mary Ward, I love you," he says.

"Hold on a minute will ya, we're not wed yet."

Mary leaves the Police Station, hurries on back to her flat, with all the travellers in tow. She gets the bail bond money, her savings she has stashed under the floor boards. She bails out all the travellers. Tim is fuming with rage with Mary.

Chapter Fifteen

The Wedding

A few months later, Mary is in her flat with her mum, brother and his girlfriend Ann and the baby. They are all dressed up for the wedding; Mary is wearing a pink wedding dress.

"I never heard the likes, who in their right mind would wear a pink wedding dress."

"Look Mum, this is what they wear all the time, they love this colour."

"Who picked this colour dress will you tell me?" Sheila says.

She is fixing Mary's headpiece. Ann and Timmy look on, sitting on the couch with amusement.

"His Mum picked this colour, I picked the dress."

"And how come I didn't have anything to do with picking the dress?"

"I'm sorry mum, but that's the travellers' way, 'tis usually the groom's mum that picks the dress."

"You know Mary, somehow I find it hard to believe that."

"You look like a pink flamingo," Timmy says. He has a laugh with Ann.

"Shut up you Timmy, what do you know," Sheila says.

"Never mind him Mary, he's only jealous," says Ann.

"You know Mary, you even have their lingo."

"Timmy, leave it now, and don't be like your father."

"Right mum, look I think it's funny to see Mary dressed up like this, that's all."

A knock comes to the door, it's the chauffeur of the horse drawn carriage that's taking Mary to the church.

Mary is on her way to the church, with two other brides-to-be who are getting married as well.

Timmy is driving behind the horse drawn carriage, with his Ford Cortina car.

"How come she didn't tell us it was a triple wedding, well, that's our Mary, she is something else."

"Mum, by the time we get to the church, we will have gathered a massive flock of flamingos."

"Well, do you hear that lad Sheila, Timmy will you stop that, you're terrible," says Ann, as she bursts out laughing.

"Behave yourselves ye two and have a bit of manners."

When they approach the church they notice the Hi Ace vans, horses, and ponies and traps all over the place. There is also a chip van parked in the car park across the road.

All the locals are out to watch the three brides arrive in their horse drawn carriages, there are at least two hundred travellers in all.

"Feck me ha, look at this," Timmy says, when he sees all the vans and horse drawn barrel top wagons and the three brides up on the open horse drawn carriages.

"Oh my God Timmy, there must be at least two thousand of them, and there are only a few of us, just as well your father isn't here, or he would die of a heart attack," Sheila says.

"If Dad was here he certainly would have a stroke."

"Shut up you Timmy, you have a big mouth, there is nothing wrong with this type of wedding, you should be proud of your sister," Ann says hitting him across the head.

"You know we should be proud of her in one way, she is doing things a bit different, you know that's what's exciting about the whole thing, it's different."

"Mam, I think you are getting carried away."

"Shut up you and park behind that trap and pony, you have to give Mary away you know," Sheila says.

Inside The Church

Johnny the Singer is singing a romantic song from the balcony while his wife Etna and Margaret are breast feeding their newborn baby boys at the back of the church.

The travellers are to one side of the church, there are at least two hundred of them.

Almost nobody is on the other side, only Ann, the baby, Sheila, Bill and Peg, Jack and Nellie Conway, Jim O'Sullivan and his wife Annie, Miss Waters and Molly Walsh, who are taking note of the way the church is decorated with beautiful flowers.

The three grooms are at the top of the church with best men Willie, Ollie and Jimmy who is home from England.

Bridie sits behind the bridesmaids with Luke the bookie. Sylvester come in and sits behind Ann.

Timmy leads Mary up the church, while the other two brides to be, wait outside to take their turn. When they get to the top of the church, Timmy hands over Mary to Máirtín. He joins his Mum and Ann, while the other two brides to be, enter one at a time.

Two traveller women look over and notice just a few invited guests on Mary's side. They whisper to each other.

"Look over there Brigit, only a few buffers on her side," says one of the women.

"Ah, never mind, they will probably come to the party afterwards," replied the other woman.

Father O'Breen and the local curate starts the ceremony.

"I gather you all here today on this wonderful occasion."

Father O'Breen continues on with the wedding ceremony.

"Do you Máirtín Thómas Ward, take this woman to be your lawful wedded wife?" Timmy sniggers at Máirtín's name.

Father O'Breen throws the eye at Timmy, and continues on.

"I do." Bridie cries out loud, while some of the young boys eat chips at the back of the church.

"Do you Mary Joanna Buckley take this man to be your lawful wedded husband?"

"I do."

"I now pronounce you man and wife, now Máirtín you can kiss the bride." Máirtín kisses his new bride. The local curate marries the two other couples, everybody throws flowers at the three couples. Mary's mum starts to weep.

Outside the church, when the three couples come out, everybody congratulates them, throwing confetti and rice at the married couples.

The children are running around. Young Johnny comes up to Mary eating a bag of chips.

"Does that mean you're my auntie Mary now?"

"That's right Johnny."

She picks him up and gives him a kiss on the cheek. He pushes her away.

"Yuck, let me down will ya?" He rubs his face to wipe off the lipstick.

She lets him down, he runs away, Sheila comes up and congratulates Mary and Máirtín, she cries and hugs Mary. The Gypsy prostitute congratulates the couple also.

Back At The Police Station

Sergeant Ricky, Garda Anthony, Mick and Jim, are discussing the wedding.

"Well now men, we have our hands full tonight with this wedding."

"Well Sarge, I hope it won't be like the last one we had in the town."

"I know Anthony, we won't forget what happened at that wedding in a hurry, and that's one thing for sure."

"What might that be?" asks Garda Jim.

"Well I tell ya something Jim, it cost £5000 to fix up the hotel after that particular wedding four years ago."

"Was it that bad Sarge?"

"You could say bad, they wrecked the place, I suppose they are the same way in Dublin are they Jim?"

"Well, they're not bad up there at all I must say," Jim replies.

"They must pay off Paddy Finnegan again for the field to set up the marquee," says Ricky.

Sergeant Tim Buckley comes in dressed in uniform with two Garda Officers from the Tullamore Garda Station, who are investigating the Post Office raid.

He is looking infuriated and means business, with a police file in his hand.

"Well Tim, what brings you here today? Aren't you supposed to be at the wedding? You look like you mean business."

"I do mean business Ricky."

Tim throws the file on the counter.

"Look men, I want these four good for nothings locked up, and locked up right now."

"Who are you talking about Tim?"

"Who do you think Ricky?"

"I lost you there now Tim, you might explain yourself, after all this is my jurisdiction?"

"The feckin travellers Ricky, that Dagger and his brother Willie, and the Barry brothers, your jurisdiction or not I want them arrested right now."

The two other Gardaí turn their heads away and snigger. Tim notices this.

"I want them put away right now!"

"Look Tim, you cannot come in here and demand we lock up four people just like that, what evidence do you have, what's the charge, what in the hell do we charge them with?"

"Look at that file, it's all in there, and see for yourself, I have two other Officers here with me from Tullamore Police Station, who are in charge of this inquiry."

Sergeant Ricky opens the file and reads it.

"I can understand the post office theft, and I'm glad the culprits were found out, but what's this about the car trailers?"

"Well," says Tim.

"That's only half, there are enough crimes in there to lock them up for a life time."

At Jack O'Reilly's pub, there is still great sadness over the death of Scar Face even thought a couple of months have passed. Jack is behind the bar as usual, with old man Walter, and a few other Customers having a couple of pints and playing poker.

"Isn't it quiet here today Jack, wouldn't you miss poor auld

Scar Face."

"You certainly would Walter, he is well missed around here.
You know I got the shock of my lifetime, when I heard the news.
Shocking, shocking thing altogether what happened to the poor devil,
I'll never get over it, and I wouldn't mind he was only after leaving
here an hour before that, and the funny thing about it, he only had one
pint," Jack says.

"Sure isn't that the way it goes, one minute you're there and the
next you're gone."

"You're dead right there Walter, you never said a truer word.
Here I will fill a fresh pint for ya, that one is there for the past hour, this
one's on the house. I wonder how the wedding is going.

"You will soon find out Jack, I'm sure they will arrive back
here afterwards," says Walter.

The Wedding Reception

The travellers are getting into their cars to drive to the reception. They
are cheering, laughing and having fun, bottles of champagne are passed
around outside the church. Mary and Máirtín get into the horse carriage,
while the other two couples get into two other carriages, and take off
down the country road to Paddy Finnegans's field, where the reception
is being held.

They arrive at a marquee that's pitched up in the middle of the
field. All the travellers arrive in vans, cars, horses, ponies and traps and
children on bicycles.

Young Johnny is on his bike smoking a Cuban cigar.

Mary and Máirtín go into the marquee, the Joe Dolan band
starts to play as they enter. Máirtín gets a surprise when he sees Joe
Dolan. He was expecting Brush Shiels, who wouldn't turn up after the
brawl at the October horse fair.

The three couples go out on the floor dancing to a slow set, all
the travellers come in and gather in a circle around them. Joe gives a
wink to Máirtín as he and Mary do a slow dance in front of the stage.
The tables go around the sides from wall to wall, they are full of food
and drink with a five tier wedding cake raised up on stilts to make it
impressionable. There are flowers everywhere.

The band plays on as they take a break from dancing to have some food. When they have eaten their food, they start to dance once again.

Sheila and Timmy and his girlfriend Ann are dancing with some of the travellers.

The Garda Officers are on their way in their squad cars, to arrest Máirtín and the three others.

Fay goes up to Máirtín to dance a slow waltz with him.

"Well Máirtín, I wish you two the very best of luck, you deserve her, you know like with all the misfortune you had in the past, I hope this is a turning point in your life for you now."

"I hope so Fay, I hope so."

"You know Máirtín, I thought it would be us that would marry." A tear falls from her eyes.

"Ah no Fay, you're too much of a friend to me, I couldn't never marry you, you will be always a friend to me, I hope now just because I am married that you will still be friends with me," he says.

"I'll try, it won't be easy, but I will try," Fay says.

"I'm sorry about your hand."

"Ah, never mind that Máirtín, it was a silly thing to do, anyway I didn't get much sympathy from you lot, sure I didn't, ye just came to the hospital stayed for ten minutes and then pissed off to Connamara for feckin Poítin."

"I'm sorry Fay, about that, but you were too cross, we couldn't talk to ya."

"I suppose I was a bit hostile towards ye all right, anyways it's water under the bridge now," she says.

"I tell ya something Fay, it has been one hell of a year and that's one thing for sure."

"You're dead right about that Máirtín Dagger." She puts her arms around him and dances close to him, as Mary looks on. Sheila notices this as well, Joe gives another wink to Máirtín as he dances with Fay.

Sheila looks over at Mary wondering what's going on between the two on the dance floor.

The Garda Officers are surrounding the marquee, there is about twenty in all. They park their cars and surround the marquee.

Mary and Máirtín are chatting to Sheila. Fay is having a slow dance with Sylvester. Bridie is happy. She has all her family around her, she is chatting to the members of her family that came from England especially for the wedding, she had not seen them since Uncle Martins funeral.

They all get a slice of the five tier wedding cake, young Johnny is still smoking a Cuban cigar sitting on a wall outside, he also is singing the rebel song "Kevin Barry" like his Uncle before him, the Garda Officers notice this on their way in. A few other children there are listening to young Johnny sing and they are eating a slice of wedding cake.

The Garda Officers burst into the marquee and demand the music to stop.

Mary screams. Joe Dolan gets a fright, he was singing Máirtín's favourite song.

"What's this, what's going on here on my wedding day?" Mary shouts. Everyone looks worried at what's happening.

Sergeant Ricky goes up to Máirtín.

"Máirtín Dagger Ward, I am arresting you on the charge——"

"For what, look Boss you have nothing on me, now piss off out of here."

Willie pushes the Sergeant, two other Garda grab Willie to restrain him.

"Now, we did not come here to cause trouble," says Sergeant Ricky.

"Trouble, trouble, this is our wedding day, who gave you the right to come in here like this, and arrest my husband, now get out of here now, who in the hell do you think you are?"

"Look Mrs, I'm only doing my duty."

"Duty, what duty, couldn't this wait till after our wedding day at least?"

"No, Mrs, it had to be done today," says Sergeant Ricky.

Everyone else stands around gobsmacked, Joe Dolan goes out the back through a back exit of the stage.

"No, I'm not going anywhere, I'm staying here with my wife and friends."

"Piss off out of here now ye smelly pigs, ye are not welcome here," Willie shouts.

Fay pushes her way in. The Joe Dolan band members start to put away their equipment in case their is trouble.

"Come back here now Fay, leave it to the men, they will take care of this."

"Bridie, I will not."

Garda Anthony stops Fay from going any further.

"Let me go!"

"It's all right Fay, let us handle this," says Máirtín. Fay settles down.

"I am arresting you and your brother William Jacky Ward for sixty counts of robbery of trailers, cars, vans and one Massy Ferguson Tractor including the robbery of a post office in Tullamore for which you are still out on bail. We know the names of the two other accomplices on the post office robbery, they are Malachy and Roger Barry, are they here?" asks Sergeant Ricky.

"No, there is nobody here by that name Boss."

Willie gives Máirtín a wink for not grassing on the Barry brothers, as the two lads boot it out the side door and hide in the back of one of the vans.

"Ok, they will be apprehended and you can rest assured, they will be brought to justice and face the full rigors of th Law."

"You can't pin anything on us Sir, we had nothing to do with anything and you know that yourself."

"Look Máirtín, I have a court warrant here for your arrest."

"Take them away lads," Sergeant Ricky says

"Now hold on a minute will ya," Máirtín shouts.

"Look now boys, we don't want trouble, we're only doing our duty." says Sergeant Ricky.

"On my wedding day."

"I'm sorry, I'm only carrying out my duty."

"I will put the widow's curse on the whole damn lot of ye, over my dead husband's grave may ye never have luck wherever you go, ever again, if their Father, or their Uncle Martin was alive, mark my words you would not get away with this, 'tis wrong what ye are doing here today, may God curse ye all," says Bridie.

She is in a rage with the Gardaí. The Garda Officers go to

handcuff the two lads to take them away. Before they do Máirtín takes out the crucifix.

"See that lads?" He stares the Garda Officers in the eye.

"This will save us, mark my words, God knows the truth."

"Right you said your piece, cuff them men and take them away."

Fay goes up to the Sergeant and spits in his face.

They go outside and the two lads are put into the back of the Garda van, everybody surrounds the vans as they drive away. They throw stones and hit the van with their fists, while the two Barry brothers look out the back window of the van. The others shout after the Garda Officers, calling them pigs, bastards and other names.

Mary notices her father sitting across the road in a squad car.

"You bastard. You will rot in hell for this," she cries.

Sheila, Timmy, and Ann see Tim also. They are disgusted with him.

"Well he's done it this time, tomorrow morning, I'm packing my bags and leaving him."

"Mum you're right, I hate him, he's nothing but a filthy pig, may God forgive me for saying that about my own father."

Timmy puts his arms around Mary and gives her a hug, Bridie and Luke the Bookie look on.

Sheila, Timmy and Ann join Nellie and Peg.

The travellers are still shouting as the squad cars drive away. The children cycle behind the squad cars. Joe and his band are packing their gear into a Ford Transit van. Luke the bookie goes up to Fay to shake her hand, she accepts, she is with Sylvester, they look at the two boys being driven away, they hug each other, as they hold hands. The other guests stand at the door of the marquee looking at each other, bewildered.

Mary stands on her own, in the middle of the road. Her father prepares to drive behind the Garda cars that Dagger and Willie are held in. She is left alone. She falls to her knees in the middle of the road as her father passes her by.

Luke turns to Bridie to say,

"This is certainly going to start a war between Them And Us."